Fantasy of Freedom

Fantasy of Freedom

FROM INTERNATIONALLY BESTSELLING AUTHOR
KELLY ST. CLARE

www.kellystclare.com

To my husband, Scott, who stops the ground from shaking.

When Kelly St Clare is not reading or writing, she is lost in her latest reverie. She can, quite literally, drift past a car accident while in the midst of her daydreams, despite the police sirens and chaos.

Books have always been magical and mysterious to her. One day she decided to start unraveling this mystery and began writing.

Fantasy of Frost, the first title in The Tainted Accords and her debut novel, was released in early 2015. She recently published the first book in her new series, The After Trilogy.

A New Zealander in origin and in heart, Kelly currently resides in Australia with her ginger-haired husband, a great group of friends, and some huntsman spiders who love to come inside when it rains. Their love is not returned.

Visit her online and subscribe at
www.kellystclare.com

Or find her on
Facebook, Twitter, and Instagram

SECTOR
SIX
SECTOR
FIVE
SECTOR
ONE
SECTOR
FOUR
OSCALA
SECTOR
TWO
SECTOR
THREE
GLACIUM

SECOND
ROTATION

THIRD
ROTATION

FIRST
ROTATION

FOURTH
ROTATION

SIXTH
ROTATION

FIFTH
ROTATION

OSOLIS

CHAPTER ONE

FOR THE FIRST time since I was stabbed in the back, I am washed and dressed, ready to step outside the stone walls of my castle room. The laughter and crashing of goblets from the food hall is just a faint strain from up here, but it speaks volumes about the number of people below. And I wonder if I am ready to look into the faces of those I saved from the Elite soldiers of my mother's army.

To see what expression those faces hold.

I wince as the wound in my back twinges.

The Elite soldier ran me through, from back to front, and I barely survived. It hurts to take a full breath—the angry red scars stretch and warp every time I do. Sadra says this will become easier in time.

Three weeks have passed since I helped my "enemy" defeat my mother's forces. We lost fifty-six Bruma men, and three women.

It is three weeks since I told Jovan that I love him.

And, as I've increasingly begun to dread, it is three weeks since I removed my veil in front of the women and children of the king's assembly.

Now Glacium knows my deepest, darkest secret: I am the Tatuma Olina. The next in line to rule Osolis. I have blue eyes. And I shouldn't.

I don't know how the Bruma have reacted. The scars of my past won't let me believe Jovan or Olandon; I have to see their reactions for myself. I could have left my room a week ago. I'd planned to. But each night I've backed out.

Will tonight be any different?

2 ➤ Kelly St. Clare

I've shown my friends and my brother, to mixed reactions. But I've never shown the truth to a whole race of people, or stood there as hundreds of people decide if they will accept or reject me.

It started when the peace delegation arrived from Glacium. I wore a veil back then—always had. It never came off unless I was washing. To remove it would be to bring suffering to any who glimpsed my face... including me.

Prince Kedrick was part of the delegation. It seems so long ago when I believed myself to be in love with Prince Kedrick. It was forbidden, of course. No one could ever find out that two members of royalty, who were supposed to be enemies, had overcome their mistrust and cared for each other.

The relationship was doomed from the start, and when Kedrick convinced me to remove my veil at long last, it ended in tragedy. The prince of Glacium took an arrow meant for me.

In the days after his death, the only thing that kept me going was the smolder of revenge. I vowed to find his killer, or die trying. The only clue I had was the arrow fletching I'd snapped off, and the hope that I could somehow find its match.

The blind need to exact my revenge led me to the fighting pits of Glacium, where I met the Bruma of Alzona's barracks. Looking back, I guess the Outer Rings forced me to grow up. It banished the last of my naivety, the last embers of the girl I used to be. I overcame much of the darkness from my childhood, and pulled through with greater perspective on what I needed to do.

The thought reminds me of what I must do tonight. I look toward the door of my room and grimace. At least my friends from Alzona's barracks will be here. I'm guaranteed *some* friendly faces.

Actually, I'm surprised Jovan hasn't stormed up here to demand I go down.

I sigh. The king of Glacium. The man who complicated everything.

He got under my veil—literally. After spending a night with him, I fled and discovered a hidden community tucked away on the Great Stairway between our two worlds. The residents of this community were of mixed blood. It was here I began to accept who I was: part Bruma, and part Solati.

The real, unanswered, question is *how* I am half Bruma.

My assumption is that my mother had an affair with a delegate from Glacium during a treaty negotiation. I can only imagine the heart attack the Tatum had when she saw that my eyes were blue.

Instead of admitting her error and supporting her child, she had me veiled at birth. Her secret was covered, hidden just under the surface.

The physical problems of this made me a laughing stock within the court. That would've been bad enough, but my mother also had me locked in a tower for most of the first ten years of my life. She had me beaten and abused, inflicting mental warfare to bend me to her will and make sure I would never want to remove my veil.

Her plan had almost worked.

The veil became a looming fear in my mind, a heavy weight I couldn't shift. The thought of doing so brought on instant panic. If I'm honest… it still does, though I have learned to control it.

A loud crash from the food hall makes me jump. It is followed by uproarious laughter. My heart thumps in a wild beat.

…At least, I *think* I can control it…

The younger version of myself would have never imagined she'd take the veil off one day.

I'm not sure I would've removed the veil if not for Kedrick. He remains in my heart as the only person who wasn't afraid to get to know me because of who my mother was. He died to gift me life. Somewhere along the line I realized that. My revenge-filled mind cleared and I decided to treat his sacrifice with respect.

Make no mistake—whoever is guilty for his murder will meet their end. I'm just wise enough now to understand there are other things that take priority.

The door is flung open; perhaps ripped from the hinges is a more apt description. The heavy wood crashes against the stone wall, and in the entrance of my room stands the king of Glacium.

We stare at each other wordlessly. It's like this every time. I can't imagine getting over how he makes my heart stop, or how all words disappear from thought when I set my eyes upon him. His piercing blue eyes peer into the very corners of my being.

"Get up," he says. "You're going downstairs."

With all that said, he can be overbearing and pig-headed.

"I'm not going tonight. I'll go tomorrow," I reply.

The king strolls into the room and I tense. Jovan never strolls.

The towering man of muscle circles the bed with lazy steps, never removing his gaze from my face.

I lick my lips.

"And what is your reason tonight?" He waits for my answer from the end of the bed, resting one arm against the stone framing.

What is my reason? I'd used pain a few times. Then faked illness another. Fatigue at the start.

"I... I don't feel—"

He chooses that moment to strike. My reflexes are still sharp, but my muscles are weakened from bed rest and injury. One arm is under my knees, and the other encircling my back before the gasp has left my throat.

I glare up into Jovan's face as he swings me up into his arms. I'm glad to see he's finally shaved. For a while after I first awoke, his stubble had become unruly.

His jaw is set. "You're coming to the food hall for dinner, whether you like it or not."

Damn my breath for coming fast, but it does. I can't maintain my glare and I feel my eyes widen of their own accord.

Jovan's eyes lose their glacial edge. "Lina, you have to do this."

My insides melt as he drops the "O" from my name. It is a form of endearment on Osolis.

He hoists me into a better position and heads to the door. "You might hate me for forcing this, but it needs to be done. You're worrying yourself sick."

I lift my arms to wrap them around his neck. I don't place him in a head lock, but the thought does cross my mind. "Jovan. It's not a good idea."

He stops in his tracks. "So what would you do then? Do you wish to leave?"

I blink. "W-what?"

"We can leave and never return."

It's hard to be angry when I'm reliant on him to carry me. "Don't be stupid."

Jovan continues down the stairs. My chest scars pull painfully, though I can tell he's trying to lessen the jarring.

"Those are your choices," he says firmly. "You enter the food hall. Or we leave. What would you like to do?"

He's manipulating me and not even trying to hide it. Jovan would make a terrible Solati. He is skilled at hiding the emotion from his face, but has no subtlety in the way he speaks. That's not to say his way is ineffective.

He knows I won't run. He knows that I care too much about what others think of me; that I have come too far, have borne too much to give up. "You're right," I say quietly.

I wince as he wrenches to an immediate stop.

"What did you say?" His eyes are wide; an incredulous smile lights his face.

A small smile creeps across my face against my will. "I said you *might* be right."

He snorts. "I'm definitely right."

I make sure he sees me rolling my eyes. But the reality of what I'm about to do rushes back as he reaches the bottom of the stairs. My breath catches. I can't do this!

"Put me down," I demand. My hands are no longer clutching his neck; they're pushing him away. "Jovan, put me down, now."

His grip tightens. He turns, heading into the shadowed cover of a smaller hall. The torches flicker as we disturb them with our movement. The hall is empty.

"Lina. You need to get yourself together. This is happening. I know you feel weak; I understand you've been in pain. But you need to be strong in there. I have no doubt you *will* be."

A tear trickles from the corner of my eye. Not wanting him to see, I lay my head against his chest. Strong. I can be strong. I've spent my whole life doing so. With a sigh, I grab a piece of his tunic and roll the fabric between my fingers. It is supple and thick. The typical worked leather most Bruma wear. Being for royalty, the king's clothing is soft and embroidered with intricate designs. I close my eyes as I inhale the smell of him. The scent of soap and man.

My breathing evens once more.

This is no worse than anything else I've been through. Good or bad, there is no escaping my next move. If it's bad? There is always my plan to retreat to the Ire. But if the reaction is platonic? It could be the start of a new era for our worlds.

I represent everyone of mixed blood in the coming moments. And, I remind myself, the decision to show my face to the assembly wasn't entirely unplanned. To forge an alliance between myself, Glacium, and the Ire, I was forced to reveal my face to the Ire's leader, Adox. My actions started an inevitable cascade I knew could only end one way.

That is when I decided Glacium and Osolis would find out on my terms. Most of my friends responded well. But Jacquiline, whom I once counted as a loyal friend, now despises me.

My insides quail as I think of her reaction, multiplied by hundreds.

If the disgust is only mild, I'll have a chance to challenge my mother for the title of Tatum and to end her tyranny, once and for all. I could save my people from starvation and slavery; forge a true peace between the—now three—races of our worlds. *If* I can go through with the next few moments, the Accords will be tainted no longer. They will be a code. A practice. A change in the way we live our lives.

It will be what Kedrick and I first dreamed about years ago. What Olandon and I conspired about as children.

What Jovan and I might die trying to make an eventuality.

He is looking at me with a peculiar expression when I raise my head. His eyes flicker to where my hand still rolls the material of his tunic. Cheeks heating, I smooth the fabric. Several large wrinkles mar the front. He nudges my head back gently and touches his smooth lips to my own. My mouth melds to his firm lips. The movement is more familiar than it was, though it always takes my breath away.

A moan slips through my teeth and Jovan pulls back, a glint in his eye.

"You ready?" He arches a brow.

Am I ready to change the world? No. "Yes," I answer.

The king grins and kisses my nose. He doesn't believe me—*I* don't believe me—but we are both practiced at making *others* believe us.

In this deadly game, that is all that counts.

CHAPTER TWO

"**P**UT ME DOWN," I whisper in Jovan's ear.

My legs wobble and I try to convince myself it's not from fear as I stare at the entrance to the food hall.

I hate this archway. It lures you into a false sense that you're safe. For the three seconds it takes to walk underneath the carved stone, the sound bottlenecks and you cannot see what lies behind—or ahead.

I take a few staggering steps forward, barely hearing Jovan's whispered encouragement before the curved archway above me opens into the beamed ceiling of the food hall. Last time I saw those beams, I was sprinting over them to kill Brovek and prevent him from lighting the signal for my mother's army to march upon Glacium.

And last time the women and children were huddled, terrified, down the far end of the hall.

Tables and benches are set systematically throughout the room. The throne platform sits on a raised dais at one end of the rectangular space, and those of highest position in the assembly sit closest to the king. The watchmen who aren't on duty occupy the tables at the back. I once sat in these seats when I came to the castle after the Dome as Frost. The assembly knows me as this fearsome Outer Rings fighter.

…They saw their king showing a particular interest in me at a ball last sector.

With a jolt I realize the implications of this moment are twofold: The assembly know who Frost really is, and understand the Tatuma of

Osolis and the king of Glacium are closer than any Bruma or Solati have ever been. Openly.

My palms are slippery with sweat as I hold onto my blank expression with the last of my control.

They stare as I slowly make my way through their midst.

I should be used to it, but this is… different. This time they stare in shock. Not because of my position, or what I'm wearing.

Because the Tatuma of Osolis is a half-breed.

A dog whines from the back of the room and it is by far the loudest sound as I gaze impassively around me. It is the worst kind of agony. My heart beats in my ears. Jovan approaches and slides an arm around my waist, squeezing me tightly to him. As we walk through the midst of his people, my careful control starts to slip. Nothing could have prepared me for this moment. And if it had not been thrust upon me, I can't be sure I ever would have reached this point. I would rather come face-to-face with my mother.

Heads turn to follow the king's path to the throne table. We pass the delegates' benches. Fiona gives me a tremulous smile and makes me wish I'd never looked. The other faces there are grim.

Three steps up onto the throne platform.

My body is shaking so hard, I simply can't do it. Before I can look up, Jovan sweeps me into his arms. There was a time this would have embarrassed me, being so weak.

I fix my eyes on the king's handsome face and his eyes widen slightly—I must look terrified.

He comes to a halt in the middle of the throne platform, facing the assembly.

…And looks out across the awful, silent crowd.

The king of Glacium speaks. "In my arms, I hold a woman who is unlike any other." He pauses and my own fear is interrupted as I see him swallow.

"She has faced a life of… *unspeakable* cruelty." His words are hoarse.

I stroke the base of his neck where my thumb rests under his hair, heart breaking as he shows this hidden face to his people.

"You have known her first as the means of Kedrick's death," he states.

There are a few gasps.

He meets my eyes. "Though it has been many months now since we found out my brother died to *protect* her. As you can see, his death was more complicated than we could imagine."

A burning is building behind my eyes. Because I miss my friend. And Jovan unmistakably misses his brother.

"You know her as Frost, the woman who defied me in the Dome and saved the lives of her men."

There are a few chuckles. I peek and see Sanjay is one of them. He gives me a wink, one hand on Fiona's pregnant stomach.

"You know her as the Tatuma of Osolis. A position held by those who have been our enemies in the past. Many of you have experienced her unfaltering kindness. And many of you have given her your loyalty and respect, looking past the views ingrained in you from a young age: that Bruma do not mix with Solati and Solati do not mix with us."

I watch Jovan, enthralled by his words. He is transforming before my eyes, showing the first signs of the great king he is destined to be.

"Three weeks ago, you came to understand Frost was none other than our own Olina. A fact I have known for much of her stay here." He swallows thickly. "I could carry her in my arms all day, she is so slight. But this woman saved the lives of your wives and children. She did so at great risk. And as you saw, nearly paid for this with the ultimate price."

The sound of scraping wood tears my attention from the king. I blink out at the assembly as they stand from their tables. Some are crying. Those not staring at me are entranced by their king's words.

"Jovan," I whisper. "I need to stand."

Carefully, he places me on both feet. Never moving away. My legs shake, from weakness and emotion. I cling to Jovan's arm as he faces his subjects, using his free hand to push the hair back from my face.

"Tatuma Olina is of mixed blood. And I tell you it does not matter," he announces. "Bruma say they judge a person by their actions, not their words. In revolutions gone by we have wielded this as a shield. But I say, as your king, we stick to this code. This woman has saved you. She has proven herself time and again. We owe Tatuma Olina a great debt."

Twin tracks of tears trickle from my eyes. I make no move to dash them away as chairs are pushed back behind me. I glance toward the noise and see the advisors are… kneeling. More scraping sounds and I'm unsure where to look as, in a wave, from front to back, the assembly kneels on the cold stone floor.

There are those who might not agree with what Jovan is saying. But how can they stay seated when everyone else shows their respect? Their king has told them they owe me a debt. They obey him, or they forfeit their lives. I *do* notice Jacquiline isn't in the room—one person who will never kneel to me.

My legs nearly buckle as Jovan untangles his arm from my vise-like grip. Through my steadily blurring vision, I watch as the king of Glacium kneels, holding both of my hands in one of his.

His eyes blaze as his jaw works to control his own reaction. "I, the king of Glacium, kneel before the Tatuma of Osolis."

There is a clamoring of whispers.

"I give you Glacium's loyalty. I pledge that your deeds are worthy of earning our trust and our unwavering gratitude."

I cannot speak. Nothing I could say would ever be enough. So, tears streaming down my face, I nod and attempt to pull the king back to his feet.

It doesn't work.

My shaking legs buckle and I fall into Jovan, who steadies me. I place my hand over my heart and stutter something vague. Thank Solis no one hears my incoherent words. The king of Glacium's eyes glint with amusement, though he doesn't laugh aloud. I wipe my eyes to glare at him.

The shocked whispering provoked by Jovan's surprise dies down.

I fidget as the assembly's attention lands on me once more.

"I bet all her good qualities come from her Bruma side," a voice calls out loudly.

The hall explodes into tumultuous noise at the remark. Sanjay bows to the assembly before wincing at Rhone's crushing punch on the shoulder. I grin at the red-haired man. I've lost count of the number of times he's saved the day for me in this manner.

Jovan carries me around the throne table and I'm grateful for the help, sagging in exhaustion now that the worst part is done. A warmth spreads from my chest. I've survived the initial test; I'll be stronger next time. It will become easier, just like removing my veil in the beginning. The Bruma might not like my heritage, but the sight will still become familiar. With this first step, in generations to come, the Ire folk might find acceptance.

Could we achieve peace? After so much bloodshed?

My mind is a whirl after the emotional cliff I've dived off. It takes a minute to realize where I am.

On Jovan's knee. On his throne.

His advisors will hear me. I'm well past caring. "I want to sit on my own chair, Jovan."

He ignores me, sipping from his goblet. I glance down the table left and right and find Olandon watching with angry eyes. Rian stands behind him.

Rian. The sole surviving member of my mother's Elite. The young soldier switched sides before we fought the Elite and I accepted his pledge of loyalty. I remembered him, only vaguely, from my time on Osolis. He'd pulled his punches during one of my beatings. He'd risked doing so under the Tatum's watchful eye. To me, this displayed the soundest of moral strength. But Olandon wasn't so trusting. During his visits to my sickbed, he'd frequently expressed concerns over keeping Rian alive. By now I trusted my gut, and understood Olandon's faults, too, and that his wish to protect me overshadowed all else. Rian was on my side. Or rather, he was on the side that would help Osolis prosper once more. I didn't have enough friends that I could be picky with my enemies.

Drummond is peering at the king and I with undisguised annoy-ance. He's not the only advisor uncomfortable with the closeness between me and Jovan, though most seem happy enough. I raise my eyebrows and Drummond's expression swiftly disappears. If there's one thing the advisors understand, it's that they should be careful what they reveal in front of me. The memory of Blaine's severed head is still foremost in their minds.

I'm jostled between Jovan's arms as he cuts a pear into chunks.

"Eat," he orders, holding a slice up.

I let my hair slip forward as I glare at him, refusing to open my mouth. "I am not eating from your lap. Nor your hand."

Someone is chuckling. "She's not going to make this easy on you."

Jovan doesn't look away.

"It is a Bruma custom," he explains. "If you reject the food I offer you, you reject me and all I offer."

My face falls. "I do?" This man had humbled himself before his entire people for me. He'd offered peace.

Jovan nods. Someone is choking behind him, but I don't move my eyes from his.

"If I just eat one bite, is that enough? You feeding me is… strange."

His eyes gleam and I relent, glimpsing at the men. Their faces are carefully neutral.

Jovan holds up the pear, eyebrow raised, and I brush my hair behind my ear, opening my mouth. If this is going to be done, it's only happening once. Everyone needs to see.

My lips close over the juicy pear, brushing against his fingers. His expression has never been so focused on my actions. Or maybe I notice this more because of where we are and who is watching. I chew quickly, avoiding the gaze of everyone. Juice escapes and rolls down my chin. But when I move to wipe the juice away, Jovan grips my hand and leans forward. As I sit frozen, the king licks the juice away and then presses a deep, breathtaking kiss to my mouth.

I gasp as he pulls away.

The hall cheers, to my mortification. I've never been more relieved when the assembly's usual bustle and clang resumes.

Until…

"Finally." The word is breathed on a sigh.

My eyes narrow at the word I clearly was not meant to hear. "Jovan," I growl. "What did that mean?"

He beams down at me, and so much happiness pours from him that I can only blink at the sight.

"Want some more?" he offers, mouth whispering at my ear. Pleasant shivers ripple through me even as I snatch the chunk of pear from him and shove it in my mouth before he can try to feed me again.

"What did it mean?" I press.

But he is no longer listening. He's talking to Roscoe on his other side. I glare at him and know he feels its weight, yet he keeps up forced conversation with his kind right-hand man.

We will be having words later.

Once I've fed *myself* from the socially awkward position of Jovan's lap, my eyelids begin to droop. It's the first time I've been out of my room since the Elite nearly killed me. And the night packed an emotional punch.

"I'm so happy for you, my King," comes a quiet voice.

"Thank you." Jovan's chest rumbles under my cheek, lulling me further into a boneless sleep.

"But how will it work?"

My eyebrows draw together in my mind. What are they talking about?

"That is something we will figure out together. For now, there are more pressing matters to attend to."

I'm lifted as he stands. I briefly ponder whether it's best to stay asleep or crack my eyes open for the walk out.

I choose the coward's way and keep my face smooth.

"Tomorrow evening we are to host a party from the Ire." His announcement makes me regret my decision.

I should be awake to show my support. Too late.

"I have spoken further with you about the mixed race on the Great Stairway. When their leader and his delegate arrive tomorrow, you will treat them with respect. They are Glacium's allies. And the Tatuma's."

The Ire are coming for a specific reason. Jovan and I have spoken at length about it. He has discussed the matter with his advisors as well, but this is the first time he has broached the subject with his people.

He does it with his usual blunt tone, in the voice which brooks no argument, only deference.

"Tomorrow evening, my guests, the Tatuma, and I will plan how to kill the ruler of Osolis."

CHAPTER THREE

*T*HREE SHORT, SHARP knocks sound from the door of my dungeon room. It's not really a dungeon, but it is where I was locked upon reaching Glacium half a revolution ago. It isn't that bad, though nowhere near as luxurious as the bedroom connecting with the king's that I used as Frost—but better than a tent any day.

Olandon enters, drifting forward with graceful steps. Though he wears the mix of leather and fur that makes up Bruma clothing, you can tell at a glance he is Solati. My brother and I have the same blue-black hair, but that is where similarities end. His eyes are brown, for starters, and he towers over me by a good three heads—a typical difference between males and females on Osolis.

Things were always simple between us as children. My mother hated me, I protected my younger brothers, and Olandon—the eldest of my three siblings—shared what he could of my burden. We trained together and told each other everything.

That changed when Kedrick arrived. And has continued changing as I spend more time on Glacium.

Deep down, I wonder if being mixed alters the way I see problems and solutions. I love my brother. I'd walk through fire to save him. But his constant questioning of the decisions I make causes me to doubt myself, and his reasoning. The ease of our relationship has suffered for it. The fundamentals are there; the undying loyalty and love. But everything else seems changed. However, I have seen growth in him from the time he's spent on Glacium—I suspect his friendship with Ashawn has broken through many of my brother's prejudices.

"You are not joining in on the discussion of the day," he says.

Olandon is much better at sticking to the "no questions" rule from our world. I gave this up long ago.

"I'm afraid I've just woken." I look out the small window and see Glacium is bright with firelight from Osolis. I've slept until midday.

"Dinner taxed your strength."

I meet his eyes with a tight smile. He deserves an explanation. Or maybe I'm still trying to convince myself. "Landon... about Jovan and I..."

His face smooths and he crosses the room to sit on the long bench at the base of the bed.

I begin a few sentences in my mind, but nothing fits. How do I make a person understand how I feel when they find Bruma disgusting?

Olandon watches my debate for a moment. "You love him," he supplies.

I exhale loudly. "Yes. But that doesn't mean I'm abandoning our people. My people come first. It is the same for Jovan. He understands what must be done. I want you to see that."

"You are sure on this."

I blink. "Well, yes. I mean, we've spoken about it." My brows pull together as I attempt to recall my conversations with Jovan over the last few weeks. There were a lot of "I love you's," and we had discussed removing my mother from rule, then hours of kissing.

But had we directly spoken about what would happen after?

I sit down next to Olandon. "No. That is untrue. We haven't."

He grips my hand. "You need to."

I nod absently.

We are both quiet. The only show of our emotions is how our hands interact, the grip tightening and relaxing at intervals.

His breath picks up. "And you were right, sister."

I tilt my head to him and watch as a red color steals across his high-boned cheeks.

"For some reason, her actions still take me by surprise. Mother's. I never truly believed she would kill you until I heard Hare's orders."

Hare, now dead, had been the leader of the Elite. The Elite were my mother's best soldiers. Usually they acted as her personal guard. But this time she had sent them on a special mission: to kill her daughter. I'd particularly enjoyed breaking Hare's neck. Though probably not as much as he'd enjoyed breaking my leg when I was a child.

"You did the right thing by helping Glacium defeat our army."

I gape at him, and a ghost of a smile appears on his face.

"You never thought to hear me say this," he prompts.

That was one way of putting it. "No," I say. "I thought you doubted the decision and hated me for it."

I survey his face as he takes in my own. His admission astounds me. And gives me hope.

His words are stilted. "I am beginning to learn that when you lead, sometimes you must make decisions others won't like. That you must assess the long-term situation and possibly make short-term sacrifices to get there."

"I…" My heart swells in my chest and prevents me from talking. I pull Olandon toward me and squeeze him tightly. "That means more to me than you know."

He stays where he is, in my arms. "I apologize for questioning your motives, Tatuma."

"Lina," I correct, pulling back.

He smiles and ducks his head. "Lina."

I laugh. "You're eighteen. Don't be too hard on yourself."

His smile grows to a grin. "You are only one year older."

"Or two."

He straightens. "We still do not know your true age." He draws a rolled scroll from his coat. Olandon still wears additional layers, though there's only the occasional blizzard in the Sixth. I quickly got over the cold while living in the icy Outer Rings.

He holds the scroll out to me.

I arch an eyebrow and raise my hand to take it. "And this is?" A message from Jovan? It looks too big for that.

His tone is somber. "A list of the men who might be your father."

Shrieking, I drop the scroll as though it is aflame. I'm on my feet staring between the bound roll of paper and my brother in the next instant, circling the offending document warily.

He rises. "You tasked me with looking into the matter."

My mouth dries as I stare at the roll. My father's name is on that list?

Olandon is waiting for me to speak.

I clear my throat. "Yes." I wave a hand. "Yes, of course. I did, you're right." I crouch beside the scroll, ready to jump away.

...I can't take my eyes off it.

A name on this list belongs to my father. The other half in my mother's forbidden affair. The man who left me alone, at the mercy of my mother's abuse. I'd yearned for my father to save me, to take me away from the palace. And he never came.

Olandon is speaking.

"Sorry," I mumble. "What did you say?"

He crouches beside me. "I said, this is just the list of the delegates in the revolution closest to your age. I've added the delegate names from the revolutions either side as well, down the bottom, but the names at the top of the list fit best with the timeline of what we suspect your age to be."

I take a long inhale through my nose. "Okay."

"It does not account for your father originating from the Ire."

"W-what?" My voice sounds thick. It annoys me.

Olandon pulls me back to the bench seat. "It is possible he is of the Ire folk. If so, finding your father will prove more difficult." He puts an arm around my shoulders. "Your reaction is concerning."

I untangle myself and focus my thoughts. "I'm sorry. I asked you to do this. But I'm thinking I only asked because it was the next logical step."

"You don't want to find out." He bends forward to pick up the list.

I shake my head. "No. That's not it." What do I feel? The better part of three revolutions on Glacium and I still have to manually process my emotions. "I think I'm afraid once I have the knowledge I won't be able to forget it."

"You are worried it will be someone you dislike."

I sigh. "Yes."

He taps the rolled paper against my knee. "I can keep it safe until you are sure."

Do I want him to take it away? With another sigh, I hold out my hand. There are already enough uncertainties in my life. Olandon grins as I take the scroll. He lifts a shoulder in response to my accusing gaze.

I was just manipulated. By my younger brother.

Palms sweating, I undo the fabric tie and open the list.

Olandon makes to stand.

"Stay," I request.

He nods and remains next to me.

My eyes dart across the names on the list. The first names are the most likely, using Olandon's reasoning. I know most of the men there. But there are fewer names than I thought there would be.

"There are only seven names," I say. A peace delegation consisted of twelve members.

"I removed those who were more than double the Tatum's age. Or who already had families."

That made sense.

I read the entire list, my stomach alternatively dropping or lifting. "What does the 'D' mean?"

"Deceased."

Would I prefer that? If I never had to come face-to-face with the man who'd impregnated a woman and left?

"Roman," I say aloud. "I never knew he'd been to two delegations. He would have been the right age, I suppose. I wouldn't mind that so much." A thought occurs to me. "Except…"

"The fool Jacquiline would be your step-mother."

Jacky was a lot younger than Roman. He wouldn't have been with her at the time.

I shudder and read the next name. "Cahter. Who is he?"

Olandon cranes his head to read the notes next to the name. "He left the assembly and resides in the Middle Ring."

I'm impressed with the depth of information in Glacium's archives. "Their records are thorough."

My brother wipes a hand across his face. "I asked questions here and there."

I frown. "Someone helped you?" Was the person helping him the same woman who "took care of him" while I traveled to the Ire? I'd overheard a lewd comment from Ashawn that left me wondering if Olandon might have overcome his aversion to Bruma more than I thought.

Does he think I'd judge him? I'm in love with the Bruma king, for Solis' sake.

He points at the list. "What about Drummond?"

His distraction is blatant, but successful. Drummond is one of the names making me feel sick.

I let the scroll close. "I am *not* Arla's sister."

"You don't like her."

I snort and hide my smile as Olandon's eyes tighten. He hates the sound. "I don't like either of them. Though Drummond is loyal to Jovan. And isn't Arla the same age as me?"

"Drummond married immediately after the delegation year."

Nearly wider than he is tall, Drummond is outspoken, and more likely to judge a female on her looks than her intelligence. Could this man be my father? "So what would you recommend doing next?" I ask him.

He takes the list and studies it. "We whittle these names down by discerning whether they are singers. My... informant didn't know this. I think we need someone older."

Aunty Jain's hint resurfaces.

I hadn't known I *had* an aunt until Olandon discovered her after my kidnapping. Mother had banished Cassius's wife to the Fifth because Jain had knowledge of the Tatum's affair. My brother guessed our aunty had gone insane from torture—judging by the scars—but in a lucid moment, she'd revealed my father was a beautiful singer.

I smile at my brother. "You're good at this, Landon."

His returning look is dry. "It has been my sole task."

My grin fades at the undercurrent of sadness in his tone. "It won't be long until you are back home. You miss Osolis and so do I." I squeeze his hand. "I promise you will see your friends again."

He fixes his eyes on my face. His mouth opens and closes twice. But whatever he wants to say remains unspoken as he delivers a curt nod, making to leave.

"I'll ask Jovan about the names," I say softly.

He bows. "If I can be of further service, Tatuma, you need only ask."

The conversation with Olandon blindsided me. As I stand outside the king's council room, I work to push the matter to the side and catch my breath. The stairs had just tested the limits of my fitness.

The Ire delegation and Jovan's council have been discussing war plans all morning. I truly had intended to be here on time, but of course everyone let me sleep. This doesn't bother me as much as it should, which surprises me. Jovan and I had spoken at length about the best way to usurp my mother. And I trust Adox. Which surprises me again. The older Ire leader has proven he's committed to seeing this out to the end. Perhaps, like me, he senses the possibility of a better future.

I lift both arms and push against the double doors. Pain shoots through my chest and I drop my trembling arms with a gasp.

This has to be a joke. I can't be this weak.

I wedge my shoulder against the wood and push.

Nothing.

"Need a hand?" a quiet voice asks.

I whirl, sagging in relief when I see Adnan—I'd never live it down if Sanjay witnessed my unsuccessful attempts to open a door. The damn thing is stuck. Jammed shut from the inside, or something.

Adnan steps forward and I move aside. He places both palms on the entrance and opens it with a light push.

I peek at Adnan, wiping perspiration from my forehead. "Thanks."

It's a testament to how kind he is that the inventor—another of Kedrick's delegation—has no discernible laughter in his gaze.

"Don't tell Sanjay," I beg.

He chuckles and pushes the door open a little wider. "I promise."

He tilts his head to the meeting room. "Haven't you got a few worlds to save?"

I grin at him. "I believe I do."

I was first brought before the king to be tried in this very room. Then I became an unwelcome addition to his council. I'd even been in here as Frost.

Today, I take my seat opposite the king of Glacium to discuss how best to murder my mother.

The talking decreases in volume as I enter, then picks up again.

Adox and his two hulking guards are present, along with a recovering Hamish. He survived attack from Mother's army to bring us warning.

Jovan's advisors are also present. Among them is Drummond, slurping from his goblet. I grimace as the liquid spills onto the front of his tunic.

"Tatuma, how do you fare today?"

Pushing the mystery of my father to the back of my mind, I smile across at Roscoe. "I'm afraid I paid the price for coming to dinner last night. But I am rested now."

"You're sure?"

Jovan's voice cuts across the stone circle from his throne. I meet his suspicious expression with an arched eyebrow.

"Yes, King Jovan. I am sure." I settle back onto the cold seat. Adox sits halfway around the circle at equal distance to the Osolis and Glacium leaders. How diplomatic. "What decisions have you reached?" I ask.

I nearly laugh as irritation flashes across Jovan's face. It gives me my answer.

Adox leans forward, expression bland. The leader of the mixed has seen many revolutions. His skin is weathered and lined, though his brown eyes hold wisdom, and remember much pain. Pain that has clouded his decisions in the past.

"Tatuma Olina, well met."

I have found the Ire folk are a mix of the traits of the two other worlds, just like their blood.

I dip my head. "Well met, Adox. Did you leave the Ire in good health?"

His mouth thins. "For now."

I look into his brown eyes. "I promised you if the Ire came to harm, I would do my best to remove Tatum Avanna from rule. And I will."

Jovan speaks. "The main dilemma we have is when to launch our attack."

His advisors erupt simultaneously.

"We should leave. At once!"

"Don't be an idiot; we'll miss out on valuable training."

"We must follow tradition."

"Does anyone care to explain to me what the fuck is traditional about this situation?"

I watch as the room explodes into chaos, trying to decide if the situation is too life-threatening to be amusing.

"This makes me wonder why I accepted the role of advisor," a voice murmurs to my right. I share a grin with Shard, one of the fighters from Alzona's barracks. His blue eyes twinkle back at me over the sharp features of his face.

"Too late now," I mutter back. "Update?"

He leans toward me. "The king wishes to launch an immediate attack. Adox thinks we should wait. Since Osolis now knows the Ire and Glacium are in alliance, we do not need to wage war. He does not believe they will attack us again."

I'm already shaking my head. I stand and raise my hand. The room gradually quietens.

"The longer we wait, the more time my mother has to put defenses in place. The army needs to leave now."

Adox pulls himself upward. "But why wage unnecessary war? You enlisted my help to save lives. Now you are asking me to support you *taking* them."

"My concern is with removing my mother from power," I say. "That is of the utmost importance."

"But why? Why do you wish to remove her from rule?" the old man asks.

My eyes widen. What is he suggesting? He knows of my mother's tyranny. "Because my people suffer under her hand. Because I wish for three worlds united in peace."

Jovan is rising to his feet. I caution him with my eyes. Threats won't work with this man.

Adox watches me with shrewd eyes. "Tatuma. I do not question your motives. Your heart is unquestionably kind. But if we attack Osolis, innocents will die. They will look to blame someone." He hesitates and I tense as I realize what he is about to say next.

"You are of mixed blood. If we declare war and usurp your mother, will the Solati people support you?" He resumes his seat.

My ears ring from his words.

"War has already been declared. If you do not understand that the Tatum will keep coming until she kills us all, then you are deluded," Jovan interjects.

The men either side of Adox stand at Jovan's insult.

I move around the table and stand directly in front of Adox. I can't fathom why he suddenly doubts me, but I will convince him otherwise.

He waits expectantly.

My eyebrows draw together. "When I first spoke to you, you told me that by helping Glacium, the risk was great and the consequences sizeable."

He nods slowly.

"This is no different. Your concerns are warranted. You, better than most, are aware of the discrimination against those of mixed blood. You're also a man who assesses both sides, not just the negative. You have discerned what this could mean for your people if we win."

"I have," he whispers.

I reach across the circle and grip his hands. "A Tatum of mixed blood. A representative of those who have lived shunned and exiled. Hidden no longer, disgraced no more. The start to a better life, generations from now."

I implore him with my eyes. "A unified world where no person is kept to the shadows. Where no person is deemed less than another. Can you *see* this world?"

Tears gather in the old man's eyes. "I can."

"The risk is great. The consequences sizeable. But the potential for better lives for all people is also there. Do not lose sight of that," I breathe.

He pats my hands and gestures to the two men, standing at his side, bunching their muscles at Jovan. They help him up this time.

Adox gives a curt dip of the head to the king. "I agree to your plans. Your army should be mobilized without delay. My men will commence Soar training with a select party of your watchmen. The Ire will begin repairs on the pathway immediately."

Cassius had destroyed the supports connecting the stepping islands of the Oscala during their retreat, trying to delay our retaliation.

Jovan flashes a confused look before smoothing his features. "Why are you suddenly in agreement, leader of the Ire?"

Adox fixes me with a stare. His eyes still appear moist. "I was already in agreement, King Jovan of Glacium. But I was not convinced."

I tilt my head.

He smiles. "You are about to embark on a mission that no other has. If you could not convince me of your right to be Tatum, how could you convince your people? If you can show them what you just showed me— that unshakeable belief—then the Solati will follow you into the fires of the Fourth." He peers at the king. "That is what I was waiting for."

He bows and I return the gesture, my throat working at his touching words. Because I haven't even begun to analyze the terror that awaits me when I next set foot on Osolis. I've purposely denied it. The thought of standing before another Solati, the most judgmental race, and showing my true self is a harrowing nightmare.

I've convinced the leader of the Ire I can do it.

But doubt wrestles with my own convictions.

And I can only hope no one will see.

CHAPTER FOUR

"MY KING, I caught her exercising." Sadra is quite terrifying when she's mad.

Her husband, Malir, the commander of Glacium's army, stands at the door just behind Jovan. I haven't looked at *his* face yet. But Malir's shows plain amusement.

Malir has held my respect since the early days on Osolis, when he was Kedrick's personal guard. The middle-aged and highly skilled fighter saved my skin on the journey here, too. He'd challenged Blaine en route to Glacium and saw I was well treated. If my fate had been left to Blaine, I don't know if I would have made it through the Oscala alive.

I sit on the bed, panting, and try not to appear guilty. I know the sweat soaking my shirt could be giving me away. I can't believe Sadra told on me!

Jovan's icy voice hits me. "Did you now?"

Maybe he's not as angry as he sounds. I peek at his face.

He is.

"Leave us," he orders.

Sadra throws me a final disapproving shake of the head before leaving. She whacks Malir in the chest and the grin drops off his face.

Jovan stares at me, bulging arms crossed.

I cover my face and flop back onto the bed. "Don't start."

"Believe me, my life would be a lot less stressful if I didn't have to."

I push up on my elbows. "What's that supposed to mean?"

He stays put by the closed door. His jaw is tight. It is the expression he keeps when he wants to shake reason into me.

"You are not ready to train."

I wipe a forearm under my chin. "I have to get my fitness up if we are to leave in the next week."

Silence meets my remark.

When I glance up, Jovan has his expressionless mask on. Great. He circles to my side and crouches before me. A small drop in my gut warns me I'm not going to like what he says next.

He grips my hands. "You are too sick to leave with the army."

My mouth drops open and he hurries on.

"You will work yourself to exhaustion. And slow the men down."

"Excuse me?" Outrage makes my voice shrill.

"It will take us six weeks to get to Osolis."

"How am I meant to overthrow my mother if I'm not there? How am I meant to convince the people to follow us?" I blurt. This is unbelievable.

Jovan swallows. "You can stay here for five more weeks and catch up."

"And how—?"

He raises an eyebrow. "A Soar."

My cheeks heat. It was possible I'd forgotten about that. With the Soar I could traverse the Oscala in a handful of days. But that wasn't the point!

"I can do it." I pull from his grip and fold my arms across my chest. His gaze dips downward to where my shirt is wet and clings to me.

He clears his throat and meets my narrowed glare. "And then you will be so exhausted you won't be able to lift your arm, let alone swing a sword."

"So *you* will be there. The leader of the Ire will be there. And the future leader of Osolis will just lay in bed?"

His eyes flicker as the lines of his face harden. He's about to change tactics. Jovan rises to his full height.

"Then you will have no problem ordering Hamish to leave with you."

I roll my eyes. "That's different."

"He nearly died. He's been in bed longer than you."

I am on my feet. "And he is not the leader of a people!"

Jovan grows predator-still, and I tense before remembering he's ordering me to stay behind. The king of Glacium has some twisted notions of what the female sex should do. "You're only trying to make me stay here because I'm female. Again!"

His roar is so loud I jump, just barely clamping down on my squeal as it tries to leave my lips.

Jovan's eyes are blazing. "I came in here thinking you might be reasonable. This is not a request. You will remain behind and heal!"

"I am the Tatuma of Osolis. You cannot order me around like a subject," I state.

Jovan throws his hands in the air and stalks to the door, nearly ripping it from the hinges. "Guards!" he bellows.

There's an urgent clatter of men and spears in response to his booming shout.

Anger boils within me as Jovan throws me a triumphant look before turning to face the ten or so watchmen who have gathered outside my chambers.

He points a finger to where I perch on the bed. I glower at the watchmen until they avert their eyes.

"The Tatuma does not leave this room until she can be trusted to stay where I damn well put her."

The watchmen exchange confused looks as their king stalks off.

Summoning as much dignity as possible, I rise to shut the door. Two of the younger watchmen scramble away from the entrance as I approach. Frost is pissed off, and they don't want to get in her way.

I can't believe Jovan locked me in my room. He knows I hate being confined. He knows what my mother did to me.

But even in my rage I recognize the difference between his actions and my mother's.

I flop back onto the pile of furs atop the bed with a long sigh. My muscles are shaking, and I'd only attempted two sets of a strengthening regime.

With a groan, I realize how ridiculous it was to protest Jovan's request. Thinking of his order as a "request" makes it feel more acceptable. He'd come in here to discuss the matter with me, too. When had he ever done that before? And I threw it in his face because I'm afraid I won't be back to fighting fitness in time for the battle of my life—for my life.

I whack the bed beside me. I'd gotten caught up in the argument. But why is he so infuriating?

I glare at the guarded door. *That* I can't excuse. He might be right about me waiting behind. But he should know better than to try to keep me in my chambers by now.

———

I glance toward the archway just in time to see the king stop in his tracks. I don't conceal the large smirk on my face from where I sit with the delegates. Fiona edges away from me as Jovan bears down on our table.

"You're in trouble," Rhone observes.

I cross my feet. "Looks that way."

He snorts and bends back over his food with a shake of his head.

The king doesn't speak a word. He just bends, picks me up, and places me over his shoulder. My wound doesn't appreciate the treatment. Kaura trots after us, whining at the sight of her chief ear-scratcher being carried away, until Rhone whistles her back.

"Put me down," I hiss. I swear he's carried me more lately than I've walked.

He answers with a stinging slap to my bottom. The food hall rings with the assembly's laughter. Jovan is going to pay for that. I wait patiently for him to enter my trap.

"How did you get out?" he asks once we are free of the food hall.

I grin into his back. Bait taken. "You left ten men and only one brain." Luckily for me that brain had belonged to Wrath, now Warren, former pit fighter.

His voice cut through the space to me. "They defied a direct order. They will be dealt with."

The muscles in his legs are slightly distracting. "They didn't defy your order," I correct. "You told them I wasn't to be let out until I could be trusted to stay still. I merely opened the door and told them I could be trusted."

Along with some helpful persuasion from Wrath, but I can't tell Jovan that.

"You're kidding me," he mutters.

I smile into his back before it strikes me we should be in my room by now.

"Where are you taking me?"

He slaps my bottom again.

"What was that one for?" I demand.

I can hear the grin in his voice. "Because your very enticing ass is right next to my face and I can't think straight."

"Oh." I wince as it comes out as a squeak.

"I'm taking you to the baths."

Hot water. Relaxation. I nearly melt on top of the king's shoulders. But then I remember he will be there. "Why? I can just have one in my room."

"I thought you didn't want to be in your room?"

"I don't want to be *locked* in my room. There's a difference," I bite.

We move around the kitchens, ignoring the wide-eyed staff. Jovan pushes the door open into the stone tunnel that branches from the main castle to the baths.

He squeezes my thigh. "Your muscles are sore."

How did he know that?

"And I'm sorry for losing my temper," he adds.

I wait.

"…And locking you in the damn room." He places me back on my feet as we reach our destination.

"And I'm sorry for losing my temper, too," I say. "It will be hard to be left behind. But you're right—I will only slow you down."

A finger tilts my chin up. "If it were possible, I would wait."

I push up to kiss his cheek. "I know."

He looks around. "Get out," he barks.

My breath hitches as a dozen people pull themselves from the water. Each of them naked. Not all of them behaving. I turn my face toward Jovan's chest so I don't glimpse more skin than I already have.

After a whirling flurry, the door bangs closed.

"That was rude," I reprimand him.

The king shrugs. His hands go to the ties on my tunic as he begins unfastening them.

My eyes widen. "Jovan."

He pauses and takes in my hesitancy. Dropping his hands, he crushes me to his chest. "Lina, these past few weeks have been among the worst of my life. Blaine, then watching you in that bed, near death. I'll be leaving in a few days. I want to take care of you. I *need* to take care of you. Nothing else."

There's a twang of disappointment at his oath. But I'm not brave enough to contradict him.

His hands busy themselves once more. I grip them and stare up into his open face. I love it when he drops the mask.

"You can take care of me," I say. "But I will undress myself."

Jovan begins to argue.

My face reddens. "I'm not ready for you to do that."

He blows out a breath and turns away. "All this waiting isn't good for my health."

Solati are a lot more conservative. Clothing is an inconvenience the Bruma suffer because it's rather cold most of the time. I shudder to think what they *wouldn't* wear if they lived on my world.

I hurry to remove my clothing while the king's back is turned.

As I reach the water's edge and the warm water laps at my feet, I hear a muffled sound behind me.

A part of me knew he would watch.

I wade into the bath until the water covers me like a blanket. Torches on the walls illuminate the cavern, and he'll see me when he gets close. At least with the water there I can pretend I'm not naked.

I avert my eyes until he's waist deep.

His deep chuckle floats across the water before his hands reach for me.

CHAPTER FIVE

I'M WOKEN BY a disturbance. With a sigh, I roll toward the rustle.

A hand strokes my hair back.

"I didn't mean to wake you."

I give Jovan a sleepy smile, my heart threatening to burst at the soft expression in his eyes. Nothing happened in the baths—except for the best massage of my life—nor in the three days since then. But there is an intimacy between me and the king that had only been present in brief moments beforehand. There's a mutual acknowledgement of the attraction we feel. It's made me unaccountably shy around him. Silly, after all we've been through.

My happiness evaporates as I take in the heaviness in his expression. He leans over to pull on his thick boots and I hug him from behind, resting my head between his shoulder blades.

"This is it, isn't it?" he says.

Glacium's army marched for Osolis this morning.

"When the Tatum's forces watched us from the Great Stairway there wasn't this... finality." He draws the last word out. "I knew then, if we beat Cassius and the Elite, I would return to my castle. This battle we're embarking on feels different."

"You're leaving your home world for the first time," I say softly.

He shakes his head. "Yes. But that's not it. Even if we win this battle..."

I understand what he means. "Things will change."

He pulls me around to his lap. "Our lives will never be the same again. They will never be as they are now."

The firelight is just stretching through the Oscala to Glacium as I stand on the giant steps overlooking the front courtyard.

The majority of the people I love are milling below.

Jovan's army spills out of the courtyard into the space beyond the castle's portcullis. Olandon, Shard, Blizzard, Ice, Avalanche, Malir, Rhone, Sanjay, and Adnan are garbed in travel cloaks, burdened by heavy packs. I spy Jovan, his heavy war sword strapped to his side.

Though early, it seems all the assembly and Inner Rings members are present. In fact, people of all descriptions line the paved road leading away from the castle. Jovan welcomed any man who wanted to join the war effort.

It was Glacium's way—to try to overwhelm the Solati army with sheer numbers.

The poor saw this as a way to get fed for a couple of months. And no doubt to pilfer what they could from their enemies. I wasn't complaining at the additional help—as long as they didn't hurt my people without cause.

I make my way down the stairs with some effort. Roscoe sees my struggles and rushes forward to lend an arm. I head for my brother. He and Rian will be the Solati presence in this force until I can join them.

"Be safe, brother." I pull him into a hug.

He untangles himself with a small cough.

"You'll be fine," I say. It hasn't escaped my notice that a journey through the Oscala might rub at his freshly healed wounds. My brother had attempted to navigate the pathway without a map, to save me. The foolish action nearly cost him his life.

"Of course," he responds.

I scan his face, trying to understand his melancholy.

He grips his large pack and swings it over one shoulder. It reminds me how big he has become. Nearly as tall as Jovan, though lean where the king is muscled.

"I never thought I would be sad to leave this hellhole."

My brows lift of their own accord. Olandon is going to miss Glacium? I watch as he looks past me, to the castle. His eyes alight as he recognizes someone.

I hold myself back from spinning to see. It makes me realize just how much I've neglected my brother. And just how much he's changed. Could Olandon love a woman of Bruma descent? I never thought I'd see the day.

Out of the corner of my eye, I see Ice is up to no good. I grab his wrist as he tries to relieve Adnan of his goldies. Blizzard does the honors of clouting the slinking man around the head for trying to steal Adnan's money.

"Ow. It wasn't what you think, girly."

I roll my eyes. "Sure. Just don't do it where people can see. Or to my friends."

Ice mumbles under his breath with what sounds like, "You think I'd get some thanks, spying for the king and all."

Shard is tugging his own supplies on. A series of daggers hang from his belt. He's lethal with these weapons. "You'll be catching up, I hear?"

I kick at the ground. "You heard right."

Blizzard pats me on the head. "That's a good little girl."

I grit my teeth.

"Minister of the people," Avalanche rumbles, patting Blizzard on the head.

I laugh with the barracks as the tips of Blizzard's ears turn pink. Any guilt I'd felt for foisting the role onto the Outer Rings man is long gone. As much as I love Blizzard and am awed by the extent of his selflessness, he has a tendency to be a little annoying. I have no qualms about joining in the laughter. When Sanjay opens his mouth to comment, I hurry to intercept.

Fiona's red-haired husband can't resist baiting the passionate pit fighter. And after hearing tales of two of their fights already, from Shard, I'm in no hurry for another to occur.

It wouldn't be a problem if Sanjay had more skill in combat.

Adnan covers Sanjay's mouth and I throw him a grateful glance.

Roman is there talking to the delegation of the previous revolutions. It must be strange for the group. They've been with me the whole time. When they first reached Osolis, it was supposed to be a once-in-a-lifetime trip—twice for Roman. A job they'd been selected to do. And not one they'd enjoy. When they left Osolis, they had me in tow. They returned to Glacium soil in the knowledge their actions had likely started a war.

Now most of them were to return. Except Roman. He, along with five of Jovan's older advisors, will stay to run Glacium in the king's stead.

Jovan left a small force behind, but this was only meant to give off the sense of security, rather than security itself. If the force is ever tested, it will mean the rest of Glacium's army is dead.

I hug Rhone and catch Malir as he leaps around shouting orders to the watchmen.

Sanjay gives me a wooden hug—he's not good at emotions. He rubs his nose. "Can you do something for me while you're here?" he asks. I follow his gaze to Fiona. She's halfway through her pregnancy. How does Sanjay feel, knowing he may never meet his child? The young couple has struggled through so much to be together. The thought of Fiona having to raise her child alone is unbearable.

"I'll make sure she's looked after," I say.

His eyes grow bright as he nods and turns to his wife. He sinks down and spreads his hands wide on her swelling belly. And with infinite tenderness, he kisses his unborn child. Fiona cries as Sanjay pulls her close, then, without another word, he joins the parade of men leaving for battle.

I grab Fiona's hand as she moves after her husband. "Shh, Fi. He's all right."

"B-but what if I never see him again?"

I can't answer the gentle blonde sobbing in my arms, but I know I'll do my best to ensure she and her child see Sanjay again. I won't let my mother take this. She won't separate this family if I can prevent it.

A shadow falls over us. Sadra leads Fiona away as the king approaches. Sadra has shed a few tears, but I imagine she is more used to seeing Malir in precarious positions in his line of work.

It's ridiculous. I will see the king in mere weeks, but the emotion of the last hour has me remembering all over again how easy it is for everything you care about to be ripped away. I memorize every inch of Jovan's handsome face.

Three hand spans separate us. We don't move. We just stare at each other.

Finally, I speak. "It's so real."

He doesn't reply, but I hear what he can't say. I sense the same urgency in him as myself. And the fact that *he's* not calm completely unsettles me.

With a slow motion, he lifts his hand to cup my face. I take a step forward and close the gap as he brushes his thumb over my lips.

"Five weeks," he whispers.

Then he is gone, ducking under the lowering portcullis, with only a single look back over his shoulder.

CHAPTER SIX

*W*AITING BEHIND IS harder than walking into battle. Messages from the marching king arrive in a tedious trickle, the only update as to whether the army is alive or dead.

A nervous kind of stupor descends upon the castle. It's like Jovan took all hope with him. As much as the women still laugh, it doesn't carry the same humor or lightness.

It's the not knowing; the wringing uncertainty is torture.

A week after the army departs, Sadra gives me clearance to resume light training. She grumbles it is still too early. As much as I like the older healer, I've been itching to begin for days.

The training yard doesn't hold the same allure without the thudding and clanging from the other watchmen. Only Hamish joins me there in the following month, though he sticks to archery—maintaining it's too late to learn how to fight and that his ego can't take learning it from me.

The ladies of the castle peer over the parapet to watch us train. I have no doubt it's Hamish who draws them in. Even skinny from spending too long in a sickbed, he is handsome; bright green eyes dance under thick black hair. Now a ropey scar mars his torso where a Solati scout pierced him with an arrow. Like me, he's doing his best to overcome the weakness from his injury.

We both collapse on the stone stairs on the side of the yard that leads down from the walkway above.

I'm frustrated with my low stamina. I can feel my muscles reform-ing, and some of my speed has returned... I guess I'm near half-strength.

It's nowhere close to where I need to be.

"Have I told you how surprised I was to find out you're the Tatuma of Osolis?" He pants and pours water over his face.

I roll my eyes and pretend to think. "Yes, you might have mentioned it yesterday."

He taps his temple. "I thought it was the day before that."

He's mentioned it every day since we commenced training.

He dashes a hand across the surface of the trough next to him. Freezing water splashes over me. "I'm not sure if I've forgiven you, yet."

This also gets a daily mention.

"Even though the fate of an entire race rested on my shoulders?"

He picks up his bow from the rack and flexes the string. "That does change things," he decides. "Consider yourself forgiven."

I repeat my daily show of gratefulness and select my own bow. I couldn't do any more squats if my life depended on it. We shoot in com-panionable quiet. I'm glad we've recovered the ease of our friendship. It was strained for a while when Hamish told me he held stronger feelings for me.

The calm is only interrupted by the twang, whir, and thud of the arrow. And the distant noise from the women above.

"So he's it? The king."

I groan inwardly, almost able to see the ground we've gained crumble under our feet. "Yes, Hamish. He is it." I press my cheek against the tense bowstring and release. The scar on my chest gives a savage pull. The arrow hits the target. Barely. My trembling arms fall to my sides in relief while the scar continues to throb.

He passes me another arrow and I nock it, pushing aside the pain and rolling my shoulders to shake off the fatigue.

"What happens when you defeat your mother and become Tatum?"

I face the target, swallowing my reaction. A part of me can't help playing Jovan's words over in my mind: *Our lives will never be the same.*

I know they won't be. Either way, Jovan and I lose the battle. It isn't something I'm ready to think about. I want my delusions a little longer.

I toss my arrow into the basket and jam my bow back on the stand. My breath catches as I face the Ire man. "Then we will do what is right for our people."

And I wonder if I will have the strength.

I stand on the roof of the castle looking over Glacium. In less than one revolution, this world has become so dear to me. It is the first place I was truly free. In my heart, it will remain the home where I grew into myself and found the strength to remove the veil.

My boots fill with a heavy weight as my departure draws near. My feet drag me to and fro. And it is because my life here has been wonderful. I've met people—and dogs—I love. And I have no idea how I will go on without them.

The happiness I experienced here was more than I ever thought to have. And while I will be able to visit with ease, using a Soar, I will never live here again, or be a part of this place. If everything works out in my favor, it could be a revolution until Osolis is stable enough to leave in someone else's care. And when that happens, I'll be visiting as the Tatum, not as Olina.

Kaura whines as I scratch under her chin and pull her close. I turn my head to the side as she licks my ear and I smile. But I cannot laugh as I usually do. My eyes find Cameron, one of the young boys in the castle.

"Will you play with her every day?" I ask.

Kaura's whine grows louder as my voice cracks.

"Sure thing, Lina," Cam says proudly. "Rhone says I can help him with all the dogs."

Perhaps it's the morose nature of my thoughts lately, but as I study Cam I feel he's different as well. That the child-like chubbiness has faded, and knowledge is present in his eyes that wasn't there before. I guess watching the Elite kill fifty-six of your people and abuse your mother would do that to a child.

Cam had been forced to grow up.

I kiss Kaura on the nose, recalling the joy of first discovering her. Of protecting her from the thugs. And of the peace she brought to me after

Kedrick's death. She can't come to Osolis. Rhone told me in no uncertain terms that it would be far too hot for her. Rhone and Cam would care for her well. But that didn't make this any easier.

My tears fall onto her fur and I give her a final squeeze. "Goodbye, girl."

I direct her to stay with Cameron and walk back to the castle.

The others wait for me in the food hall. The only men in the room are Roman, Merc, and Jak. I climb the steps of the throne platform, weary beyond physical measure. I turn and gaze into the faces of the women and children of the assembly. Not all of them have made this journey easy for me. Arla. And through my trials I have lost the friendships of others. Jacquiline. But my gaze settles on Sadra and Fiona and the females closest to them.

Crystal waves to me from the side. Her presence is almost my undoing. She has traveled here from the Second Sector to bid me farewell.

"I never had female friends before Glacium." I'm startled as I say the words aloud. "I thank you all for your generosity and your open-mindedness. It must be off-putting to welcome a stranger who covers her face. So I thank you for accepting me as one of your own during my time here." I smile fondly at Fiona as she cries again. Anyone who didn't know her would blame the pregnancy, but that's just Fi. She wears her heart on her tunic.

Macy shifts, drawing my attention, and I beam at the shining woman. Her hair is pulled into an elegant up-do. She stands tall, the proud bearer of new muscles after her training at Alzona's barracks.

"I can only speak for myself when I say each of you is welcome to visit any time," I say.

Macy smiles shyly.

There are murmurs of assent from most of the others. Arla doesn't bother. But she doesn't interrupt either, which I'm glad for.

I bow to them. "I'll do my best to ensure your men return home safe to you. If we succeed, you no longer have anything to fear from my people."

I'm breathless by the time I reach Crystal.

She grips my arms. Crystal is mixed, a girl of my own height who left the Ire as soon as she could. Unfortunately, Glacium was cruel to her, but she has found her reason to go on in Alzona. By Avalanche's account, the pair have sorted their differences—or rather, revealed their secrets—and are stronger than ever.

"Zona couldn't come," Crystal apologizes. "She said we'll probably never be rid of you anyway."

"That sounds like something she'd say," I reply.

Crystal giggles.

I pull the strawberry-blonde girl close. "I'll miss you." It's the first time I've said the words to anyone and I want to bawl like a scolded child.

Crystal squeezes me and runs a hand through my hair. "Your split ends are beyond control. You'll have to come back for a haircut."

It's the weakest excuse to travel between Osolis and Glacium ever to be uttered. And hopefully a sign of new times. "I will," I say softly.

"Oh," she blurts. The petite woman draws a small piece of black fabric from her pocket and hands it to me. "This is from Willow."

I stare down at the material. Willow was the top whore in one of the Outer Ring's brothels.

Crystal screws up her face. "She said, 'Is this what you were looking for?' and then did that weird chime laugh."

A laugh bursts from my lips as I understand. I'd pestered Willow for material to replace my veil when it was ruined beyond repair. I shouldn't be surprised she'd heard who Frost really was. Word in Glacium doesn't travel fast, but Willow… *worked* with some affluent Bruma. I'm happy to have this memory of her to tide me over until we meet again. When I next see her she'll probably be running the brothel!

I shake my head and pocket the fabric.

With a final kiss on the cheek for Crystal, I leave the room. The men, Fiona, and Sadra follow me.

Hamish waits on the roof with our Soars. I'm grateful when Fiona and Sadra give me quick, tear-free hugs and go. It makes leaving seem less permanent. Roman eyes the Soar with wariness as I snap the rods into place. Hamish is already perched on the parapet to leave. We'll be stopping at the Ire on the way to pick up messages from Adox.

"Here," Roman says. "These are for King Jovan."

I tuck the sealed messages into my small pack, already aware of the words inside. The pack only holds my bedding, two short swords, my Solati robes—which I've kept all this time—Kedrick's fletching, and a bit of Kaura's fur. There don't seem to be enough possessions to represent the last year and a half of my life.

"Take care, Roman. And tell Jacky I'm sorry it didn't work out between us."

A sadness passes over the man, who is on the greater side of middle age. Jacquiline's mother was killed by someone from the Ire—though no one believed her tall tale of a flying man at the time. She now possessed a blind hatred of anyone of mixed blood.

"*You* don't have anything to apologize for," he says, bumping my chin up with a finger.

I'm so weighed down with heartache, I'm not sure my Soar will hold me. I dip my head to the other advisors and climb atop the wall.

Despite myself, I chuckle at the expression on their faces. They clearly think I'm about to plummet to my death despite the frequent visits from our flying friends over the last two months.

"Goodbye," I say.

And though I speak the words to the Bruma watching me, I am really talking to Glacium itself.

CHAPTER SEVEN

*W*E HEAD TOWARD the First Sector. From there we will head straight to the Ire.

I wave down to the watchmen guarding the ground entrance to the Great Stairway. They are pinpricks on the ground.

The six semi-defined areas the Bruma call sectors are clearly visible from up here. My world is also separated into six wedges, but Solati call these rotations.

The area closest to the other world has the label of "First Rotation or Sector" and this space remains "the First" even as the worlds rotate around their three-year revolution.

The areas are then numbered in a circle from one through to six. Not all of these are livable, however; the Fourth—on each planet—is fatal to any who enter. Either so cold, you can freeze in minutes, or so hot it would cause your clothes to burst into flame.

Hamish races ahead of me as we enter the treacherous labyrinth of floating islands that makes up the Oscala—or Great Stairway.

If you stand on either world, it is clear that Osolis and Glacium sit side by side in a flat line.

This space is filled with a maze of floating islands of all shapes and sizes. Long ago, a pathway was forged through the islands and recorded on two maps. These maps were held by the ruler of each world.

Without a map, the pathway is a death trap. Or was. Soars make the journey *much* easier.

I throw myself to the side to avoid a jutting rock, cursing the fast pace. Hamish weaves and banks past cliff faces with skill, eager to get back to his family and friends. Tightening my grip, I give the task of keeping up my full attention.

We reach the Ire at midday.

Hamish veers off to see his family and I continue onward to Adox's rock, the main island.

The homes of the Ire are named after the eldest female in residence. I haven't quite figured out if Adox's rock is named after him because he's leader, or because he is widowed.

If no one lives permanently on an island, a generic name is given to the space depicting its role in the Ire: nursery rock, meeting rock, and training rock are a few. By now the people of the Ire know who I really am. But this is the first time I've been back since they've been told. The folk keep their distance, but I return a couple of smiles here and there. Could be worse.

Adox is waiting for me on his cushioned seat.

"No, don't stand," I implore.

He shoots me an amused look and rests back. "I trust your flight was a good one?"

I take the seat opposite him. "It was. What news?"

"So eager," he chuckles.

I grace him with a dry reply. "I have a new appreciation for those who remain behind."

He waves one of the burly men forward. The man eyes me as he passes Adox a message. The two bodyguards haven't trusted me since they attempted to stop me from leaving the Ire. I'm afraid they lost rather badly.

Adox passes the message across the low fire. "There have been a few incidents."

I add the message to the others in my pack. "Like?"

"It seems your uncle Cassius left a few surprises on the pathway for the Glacium army to find. We set out to fix the ruined supports, but the thought of checking for traps never crossed my mind."

"How many?"

"Twenty," he answers with a grim set to his mouth.

I gasp. Twenty.

Adox gives me a few minutes to absorb the news.

"It is not my intention to come across as uncaring," he says hesitantly. "But the effect this has had on morale holds a greater threat than the loss of numbers. The pathway is mentally tough at the best of times. You will be aware of this. Many of the Bruma have already lost friends. And the intelligence of the Solati army has them on edge."

The Osolis army is something to be respected. But open fear within our ranks is a big problem. "I should leave immediately." I rise, already thinking of reaching the others.

This time Adox does stagger to his feet with the help of the two men at his side. "I thought you would wish to press on. But before you go..."

The old man takes a small parcel from one of the men and limps toward me. "Some food to help you along."

My smile is genuine as I take his offering. I turn to leave again and am stopped by a gnarled hand around my wrist.

"I have firsthand experience with the fallout of the path you mean to take," he says. His brown eyes hold the wisdom of age. "Remember you are always welcome here, no matter whether you are welcome elsewhere."

He keeps his grip tight until he is sure I understand.

"Adox, I am honored. Thank you." I bow low. His offer is worth one thousand food parcels.

There is no further delay as I stride to my Soar and slip my feet into the loops, buckling the contraption around my chest.

The wings of the device spread wide behind me as I tilt over the edge of Adox's rock.

The conversation with the Ire leader has me worried. He wouldn't mention concerns over the state of the men's morale if they weren't warranted. But I'm hopeful the situation is better than he has reported. Much can change in a few days.

Jovan should be reaching the edges of the smoke layer by now. I might be able to join the head of the procession by midday tomorrow.

I pick up the first signs of Glacium's army as the firelight begins to fade.

There are shouts from the sentries as I'm spotted. Shouts of welcome, not alarm. The Soars are probably a regular sight by now.

I land a few islands into the procession on shaking legs. A ragged-looking Bruma approaches. Outer Rings, by the dress of him.

"You looking for the fancy men, Frost?" he asks.

I guesstimate the man remains in possession of a third of his teeth. I slip into Frost's crude persona. "What do you think? Which way?"

Not offended in the slightest, he points down to the left. I can see a small party gathered at the edge watching the exchange.

I toss Adox's food parcel to the man and soar toward the "fancy men." Can't wait to share that one with Jovan and the barracks.

It turns out the waiting group consists of Roscoe, Adnan, and Sanjay, as well other Inner Rings Bruma I don't recognize. Jovan's most trusted men will be dispersed throughout to maintain order and direct the march. There doesn't seem to be any logic to the remaining stream of soldiers; Middle, Inner, Outer, and assembly are all mixed.

I haven't even snapped a single rod of the Soar before Sanjay is upon me. He waits anxiously for news while I pretend not to understand what he wants. It's cruel. But quite satisfying.

"How goes the march?" I ask Roscoe.

"Olina!"

I frown at Sanjay. "Don't interrupt."

Red begins to creep up his neck and I catch an amused glance from Adnan.

I wait until he looks about to burst before relenting. "Oh, I forgot. Fiona gave me this message for you." I rifle through my bundle and give him the right note. It can't be missed due to the tear stains.

He tears off the seal and scans the missive, grinning as he reaches the words halfway down the page. He clears his throat and talks loudly. "'Sanjay, it is worse than when you were last gone. I catch myself thinking a lot about that time in the food hall, after everyone had gone to bed. Do you remember? You sat me on top of—'"

With a jolt I realize he's about to read the letter aloud.

Roscoe touches my shoulder. "Would you like to move elsewhere?"

I nod. It's either that or clap my hands over my ears and scream.

Roscoe takes my pack, and I tuck the Soar under my arm and follow Jovan's right-hand man through the bedrolls and Bruma, hearing shouts of, "What happened next?" and "Shh, I'm trying to hear," echoing behind me.

Drummond is in the cave. Great.

"What's going on out there?" he asks.

Roscoe coughs politely. "Sanjay has received a message from Fiona."

Drummond leaves without another word.

That. Might be my father.

My eyes fix on the spot where he sat. "Hey, Roscoe?"

"Yes, Tatuma?"

I give him a false angry look. "Surely you know to call me Lina by now. I've given you permission to do so."

"Possibly because I was the only Bruma who bothered to ask," he added.

I can't argue with that. Dropping the first letter of someone's name is meaningful on Osolis. On Glacium, the Bruma just see it as a way to save time. Plus, it's easier to say when they're drunk. He passes me a bowl of stew. I'm glad because I'd started to regret giving the toothless man my food.

"What an interesting time you've had since arriving on Glacium," he remarks.

I spoon the meat into my mouth. The stew isn't so bad. Better than the food I got on my first journey through the Oscala. What a difference food deliveries from the Ire make to the menu.

"That's one word for it." I smile at him.

Adnan pushes through the material covering the cave entrance. His face is bright red. I gather Fiona's tale grew too graphic for the inventor. Like his father, Adnan is unerringly kind. He must be in his mid-twenties now. I wish he'd find someone to love. But unless he has a decent amount of brew in him, he seems unable to talk at all, much less to females.

I recall my initial question. "Is Drummond a good singer?" I ask Roscoe.

He chokes on his stew and Adnan hurries to take the bowl from him.

Adnan is chuckling quietly. "Drummond is as tone deaf as a donkey on wine."

I pause to appreciate that picture while my insides collapse in relief. My father was, or is, a singer. *Drummond isn't my father!* I don't dance around the cave as I wish to, but it is a near thing.

Roscoe and Adnan watch me, waiting for an explanation.

My breath catches. I swiftly decide to take them into my confidence. They're discreet. If Sanjay were in the room, it would be another matter. "I'm trying to find my father," I say with a shy smile. I lean forward and rummage through my pack and brush past Kedrick's arrow, drawing Olandon's scroll from the depths.

Adnan passes his water skin to Roscoe and then peers over my shoulder.

He whistles long and low. "That's a long list."

"The top names are more likely. They were from the delegation closest to when we believe I was conceived."

Adnan's brain starts working. I can almost hear it. "Have you considered it may be someone from the Ire?"

Roscoe joins on my other side.

"Yes, but a relation told Olandon that the man was a good singer."

Roscoe draws my attention away from the list to ask a few questions. I'm markedly happier to talk about the matter now that I know it isn't Drummond. A thrill shoots through me as I wonder if I'll know who my father is by the end of the night.

Instead of dread, there is now something akin to excitement. Adnan suddenly stands, startling me. I glance up at him in the dark cave.

A burst of clapping and laughter breaks in from the surrounding islands.

"You'd best go and see if you can tame your friend a little," Roscoe suggests.

Adnan gives a curt nod and leaves us to the list.

Roscoe smiles. "He misses his workshop. This break will be good for him."

"Let us hope it will be good for all of us."

A fleeting expression settles over the considerate Bruma's face. It is impossible to dissect. "Yes," he says. "Let us hope."

CHAPTER EIGHT

I SET OUT THE next day, eager to reach the others.

Olandon will be interested to know I've whittled the names down to four possible Bruma with Roscoe's help. I don't know any of the four men well, but there are no objections to what I do know of them. A tiny part of me can't help the weight of disappointment I feel. As a child, my mind turned my father into an undefeatable hero. None of the four men quite fit that image.

And, I remind myself, there's a chance it's not one of the four men at all. It could be one of the deceased on the list. Or someone of the Ire. I shouldn't get my hopes up.

I wave to all I pass—where I can avoid crashing into a cliff. I spot Malir and Rhone, and Wrath, Blizzard, and Ice along the way. Most of the others will be with their king. Some of the men shout at me and I shout back, varying politeness and insults depending on where they appear to be from. I'm sure I get it wrong a few times. But I'm sure they'll appreciate any change in the repetitive scenery.

Smoke unfurls far in front of me, warning me to stop—if I enter the smoke layer surrounding Osolis at the wrong time, I risk death through smoke inhalation, or from lack of visibility. The smoke layer is only present at night.

My heart sinks. Another night away from Jovan.

I don't recognize anyone on the island I touch down upon. No one points out the direction of the "fancy men" so I imagine there are none close by.

Folding the Soar, I ignore those around me as I set up my bedroll in the middle of the rocky clearing. This island is wide and flat. There is plenty of room to sleep. Which is probably why the Bruma are separating into three different camps. I shake my head as folk from the Inner and Outer rings throw disgusted glances at one another from opposite sides.

It wasn't long ago that the Outer Rings had threatened to rise in rebellion; the uprising was orchestrated by Blaine, Alzona's father and traitor to the Crown. The one perk to bringing the poor of Glacium along—because it certainly isn't their ability to follow orders—is the king can keep an eye on them and lessen the likelihood of a civilian attack while we are gone. I doubt it will be a problem. Regardless of what ring you come from on Glacium, I find most Bruma are bred with a sense of loyalty. A move against their king while he fights to save their families wouldn't sit well with most Bruma.

No, with Blaine gone, the weapon caches emptied, and the whore-hounds eliminated, the rebellion is truly extinguished, and the addition of Blizzard as the people's spokesperson has gone a long way in showing the poor their king is taking them seriously, where his forebears never did.

"Tatuma Olina. Won't you join us?"

I glance up at an Inner Rings man. He looks at the people around me and arches an eyebrow like we share some kind of joke. I look at the same people and see nothing wrong with them.

"No. I believe I'll stay where I am."

The Bruma is affronted, there's no doubt of that. I tilt my head to the side and watch him until he backs away, returning to his snobby friends. The sniggers from behind tell me the Outer Rings appreciate my snub—but I'll still be keeping my pack close and my dagger ready. Loyalty is a Bruma trait, but it doesn't preclude theft.

The last of the firelight is obscured by the smoke layer far below us. I'm drifting to sleep when a ruckus from a neighboring rock alerts me. The men quieten their low conversations, each straining to listen.

"Where is she?"

Why is it that the first emotion I feel is guilt? It must be because normally at our reunions I've done something I shouldn't. The king of Glacium has come looking for me and the knowledge sends me into a spin. It has been over five weeks. Has he thought about me each day? Should I pretend to be less excited than I am, or kiss him for hours like I truly want to?

I recall the surrounding men and Sanjay's letter and decide on the first course.

"She's over there, m'King."

"Lina?" Jovan calls. He makes no effort to lower his voice. Never mind that he's waking several islands of soldiers who have marched all day.

"Over here," I call. My voice is mostly calm. I roll to my side and watch as he picks his way through his subjects. He tramples a few people, but they don't say a word, and I can't say I blame them.

I see the gleam on his light skin, then the motion of his hands. As he draws closer and smaller details are revealed, a warmth begins to spread deep in my stomach.

The king kneels by my side and I rise to sitting and fall into his arms.

It would be nice to tell him how much I missed him. How much I love him. But we are in the midst of some very interested men, so I just breathe in his scent, happy to see he's felt the same while away from me.

Something wet brushes me. I reach up to his neck where a saturated cloth sits. I recognize it immediately. It's a safeguard against the smoke.

"You came from below the smoke layer?" I accuse.

He pushes me off the blanket. I land on the cold rock next to the bedroll. Before I can punch him in the kidney for it, he shifts into my spot, picks me up, and places me on top of his chest. "I did," he says.

Jovan brings my hand to his mouth and kisses my palm. I flip his hand and draw it down to my mouth, returning the gesture. If there weren't roughly fifty men on this island, our reunion could be going very differently judging by the raggedness of his breath. The desire to touch him is almost painful. We both lay there, tense. Unmoving.

This is going to be a long night.

A whisper interrupts the silence, reaching us from where the Outer Rings Bruma sleep. "Beri, I think the Frost girly might be the fire princess."

Jovan's snort is hardly quiet. I pinch him to shut him up.

"Well, duh. Ain't you been hearing the stuff? She was as snobby as anything before we corrupted her in the Outta Rings. We fixed her."

The king's body begins to shake underneath me. I close my eyes, wanting to hear the rest.

"That makes sense. Didn't think I could like a Sluti."

"It's a Soolatee, you stupid shit."

My own body begins to shake. I muffle my laughter against Jovan's chest.

Just like that, the Outer Rings create their own version of my story.

"Give me a rundown," I grumble.

It is barely morning and I'm chewing on a chunk of stale bread. I glare around me, tallying my list of aches and pains. The castle beds have made me soft. And the king keeps throwing intrigued looks at my hair. My mood sours further as I imagine the utter mess it's in.

"I heard about the losses," I say.

His jaw clenches. "The cowards left traps along the pathway."

At Cassius's orders, I want to say. But I refrain.

"We sent a team ahead of the rest to spring any traps. The men in the team are rotated. Thankfully there haven't been any further surprises. Your brother thinks the army might have been low on food supplies and couldn't delay any longer."

"Any other fatalities?" I ask. I spot my brother's dark hair ahead.

"We've lost three to the stairway. All from fights."

Idiots. What a stupid reason to throw your life away.

Olandon clasps my forearm in greeting. "Well met, sister."

I return the welcome.

Olandon turns to Jovan. I grit my teeth at the disdain in my brother's eyes. I'm sure Jovan must see it. The difference is, the king doesn't care.

"If we are to make the next cave, we will need to make haste."

This is where it gets tricky. To survive the next week of travel we will have to reach each of the caves. The caves contain large fans that keep the thick smoke at bay. The army will need to separate into parties of fifty.

There was a good reason my people had never lost a fight on their home world. And it came down to the smoke barrier. The Glacium army could only trickle into our world, forced to use the caves. No matter if they crammed two hundred watchmen into a cave overnight. The Osolis army would merely pick the Bruma off as they were forced to wait for their comrades to arrive behind them.

Usually.

We have the advantage of the Ire.

While the army filters through as normal, the Ire folk will work to transport the remaining men. It is the sole advantage that might win us the battle.

We will flood in at twice the speed, *and* due to Jovan's foresight, we will have archers to keep the Tatum's army at bay. We only need two or three days. In that time our army will swell from a few hundred to full strength.

This will be a war like no other in history.

Jovan stops me and pulls me to the side. "I want you to fly ahead to the cave and conserve your strength."

Ashawn stops beside us. His eyes dart between Jovan and myself, anticipating an argument.

Jovan sighs. "Ash."

"Yes, dear brother?"

"Fuck off."

"On it!" Ashawn resumes his trek down the roughly cut cliff steps.

Jovan's youngest brother has come a long way from the bitter, revenge-seeking man I first knew. Ash is prettier than Jovan, an exact replica of Kedrick; charming where his remaining brother is blunt. I can see he'll become a favorite amongst the assembly ladies in a few years. He already does fairly well for himself from what I hear. Looking at him used to be a red-hot poker in my chest, but I no longer see Prince Kedrick when I look at him. Just Ashawn.

If I fly to the next cave, I can spend the day training, instead of expending all my energy on the walk.

Jovan is holding up his hands. "Now before you—"

"That makes sense." I untuck my Soar and begin assembling it, stretching the shiny fabric tight over the Seedyr wood frame.

I realize Jovan hasn't made a sound and crane my neck to witness his incredulity.

"That was," he deliberated for a moment, "easier than expected."

I grin as I strap myself in. "Maybe I'm too happy to see you to give you trouble."

The last men in our party of fifty wander past. And finally, his lips are on mine. I can't touch him because I'm holding up the Soar. Frustrated, I press myself upward, kissing him hard to the point of pain.

We break apart, both breathing harder.

He kisses my eyelids. "I hope today goes quickly."

I tuck away my shy smile, using the task of stepping into the loops to break away from his gaze. He's always been able to see right through me with those piercing eyes. I don't know why I bother hiding my embarrassment.

"You'll be careful," I ask.

"If I'm not, will you kiss it better?"

I twist to the edge and lean forward. "Probably not," I throw over my shoulder.

Mischief sneaks through me and I fly as quickly as I can toward a cliff face before spiraling off to one side at the last second.

"Watch where you're bloody going!" The words are roared.

I laugh, the carefree sound echoing through the Oscala, and surely reaching the ears of the man I've just frightened half to death.

There's definitely some guilt as I spend most of the day atop an island overlooking Osolis, training while the others risk their lives on the pathway. The sight of my home world puts new sharpness into my kicks and punches. I work myself harder than I have since my injury. And for the first time I don't feel wrung out afterward.

I set out with several hours to spare. Jovan would have pushed the men so hard they'll reach the cave early. I want to be there when he arrives.

I'm a fair way from the pathway, but it doesn't worry me. I know how to navigate the Oscala, and the Bruma are impossible to miss with the amount of noise they make.

I smile as I remember my stunt from earlier. No doubt Jovan has spent the day plotting how to exact revenge. My thoughts turn to whether I'll get alone time with the king tonight when a tearing sound wrenches me from my daydream.

I don't immediately understand what has happened. But as I begin to lose altitude, it becomes clear.

I glance at the material behind me. My heart pounds as I discover the tearing sound did indeed come from the device keeping me in the air. My fear chokes me. I push and pull on the bar underneath my straight arms. But the Soar relies on the sails between the rods.

I'm not falling too quickly. I need to get to an island before the tear gets any worse.

Another rip sounds to my left. But this time when I wrench around to survey the damage, a glint catches my eye.

An arrow is embedded in the framing of the Soar directly above my head. My eyes widen. I recognize the arrow as though it were a part of me.

Seedyr wood. Kedrick's assassin.

Now he's trying to shoot me down!

Forcing my mind back to my rapidly impending death, I take a few precious seconds to analyze the situation. There's only one island close enough to get to. The assassin has chosen his spot well. A large hole gapes beneath me.

If I don't reach it, I will fall into oblivion.

I push forward on the bar underneath me with all my weight. The Soar continues to fall faster and faster. *Veni*, I'm not going to make the top of the island. Crashing into the side is looking more likely. Desperately, my end staring me in the face, I scan the cliffside. I have no idea where the archer is. And that's a problem because he is surely watching me. If I die before I see Kedrick's killer…

There are no ledges or holds that I can see on this side. I angle the Soar to fly around to the opposite side of the island. The device judders in my hands as the air catches and releases through the twin holes in the fabric. I have seconds to make a choice.

In the next moment I realize there *is* no choice. I have to jump for the rock face now, or perish. Heart in my throat, I pull my legs from the loops, fumbling to unstrap the leather band across my chest. The band across my hips is stuck! I rip at the strap in panic, and watch as my life slips between my fingers. I nearly sob as the band pulls free. My body falls onto the bar beneath me and the Soar is thrown into the cliff face. My limbs scrape across rock as I blindly search for a hold. Any hold! A rod smashes me in the face and my head whips backward. There can't be much time left.

My hip bumps against stone and it orientates me. I kick out at the Soar, throwing it from me with one last scream. Then, arching back, I grab at whatever I can.

The stone of the Oscala is known for being razor sharp. As the surface tears at the skin of my hands, I dig in my boots in a last attempt to save myself.

I hang.

My forearms resting on the ledge, supporting my body. My legs in empty space.

It could all end so easily, this whole war. Which is no doubt why I've been targeted.

Or maybe the assassin is finishing off the job he botched when he shot the prince of Glacium.

But I'm not dead yet. The ledge is a curved groove in the island's side. Almost like the makings of a tiny hole, or cave.

I lay panting when a whooshing noise stops my breath in its tracks. Pulling myself up with bloody hands, I roll onto the ledge. If the assassin sees me I have no chance of surviving. He'll land on an island close by and shoot his arrows until I am dead. This ledge is barely large enough to hold me, let alone dodge arrows on.

I clamber to my hands and knees and crawl into the curved space, pressing myself as deeply into the shallow alcove as I can.

There's no way I can resist looking; if my death is coming, I want to see it.

I freeze when the black wings of a Soar glide silently into view. The assassin circles in front of me, just beneath my hiding spot. Could he be watching as my Soar falls into emptiness, trying to glean if I am attached?

He must have lost sight of me when I rounded the island.

I hold my breath and fervently hope this is true.

The man directs his Soar upward and circles back. I tighten into the smallest ball I can, hoping the slight shadow of the rock is enough to mask my presence. If he looks directly here, there's no way I'll be missed.

In this instance, seconds before I could die, will I finally see Kedrick's killer?

I peek over my arms, between the curtains of my hair, riveted on the scene before me.

…And I set eyes upon the assassin's face.

The murderer's skin is a deep olive, typical of my people. His dark hair is cut short and covers small brown eyes. He is lean, obviously fit; a fighter. The muscles in his arms bunch as he swings the soar in loops. He's one of the six Ire traders.

The Ire's traders were rarely at home, and it was only by chance I'd met them.

I'd noticed immediately that their arrows were made of Seedyr wood. The same wood as the arrow that shot Kedrick.

I'd taken particular pains upon seeing the matching arrows to memorize the family and connections of each of the six men. I thought the details might hold a clue, but they hadn't. I was still glad I'd interrogated Hamish so thoroughly, because my assumption one of the traders murdered my friend was correct.

And he's trying to kill me again—except this time there is no prince to save me.

Recognition tickles the corners of my mind as I study the flat plains of the assassin's cheekbones and brow. I can't help feeling I've seen him somewhere. But that's impossible; we've never met. I don't even know his name. Still, the sensation is unshakeable. Have I wronged this man? Is that why he tore my world apart?

Now that I know *who* the killer is, the burning question is, why?

Hamish's information streams back to me and I realize, of the six traders, my connection to this man *is* the most personal.

I saved his daughter, Cara, when she fell off Nursery Rock. And yet he wants to kill me…

I don't dare move a single muscle as he glides silently past my spot. The only thing that saves me is that he glances down as he floats past my ledge.

He circles twice more, lower down.

And then I lose sight of him.

It's a long time before I unfold from my curled position and dare to peek out of my hiding spot. Blood rushes to my legs and pain shoots through my hands as I remember the damage caused by my desperate scramble to find a hold on the razor-sharp rock. Just another wound to add to my ever-growing tally.

At least it's not a broken bone. Or a sword through the gut. And at least I have my life. There is no sight of the black-winged Soar. The assassin isn't in sight. Will he be sticking around somewhere to see if I crawl out from hiding?

Cold terror spills over me as I make another realization. Why would the assassin stay? His job is done either way. I have no Soar. He must know that if I hadn't fallen to my death already, I'd be killed in a matter of hours.

I only have until the smoke unfurls on the Oscala to be found!

I have no water; I drank it all after my earlier training, thinking I would get more at the cave. There's no way to make a smoke covering. Standing, I search the vast space before me. It's a repeated series of the same thing: rock, cliffs, caves, and nothing. No life. No plants. No food. No water.

It's early afternoon. The smoke will start to gather soon enough.

I cautiously turn to study the wall behind me and it becomes obvious I won't be climbing my way out of trouble. The surface above me and to the sides is vertical and sharp. No wonder I had difficulty slowing my descent.

It takes me twenty minutes to acknowledge I cannot extract myself from this situation. I sit on the ledge and drag my legs into my chest to wait, in a doomed sort of agony.

For the first time since the Dome, I must rely on someone else to save my life.

CHAPTER NINE

*A*FTER SITTING FOR an hour, I begin to call out at intervals.

After two hours, I shout every minute.

After two and a half hours, I scream until I'm hoarse.

And after three hours I search the wall behind me again, desperate for some way to get to the top. No one is going to find me at the bottom of an island in some obscure area of the Oscala.

Is this it? Have I survived the pits, the Dome, the Ire, and the Elite, just to die here? The cruelness of it would appeal to my mother. I cough three times before I understand the smoke has begun to unfold.

It will slowly suffocate me until I am dead. Jovan will never know what befell me. It's possible they'll never even find my body. I curse my actions of this morning when I pretended to crash.

I cover my mouth with my tunic, knowing it will do little to help. It doesn't stop the coughing, which gradually grows more frequent and longer-lasting. I'm inhaling smoke. Soon it will be too late.

My throat burns and my eyes sting as I start to see the physical evidence of the change in the Oscala's air.

The smoke is affecting my mind; I swear I can almost hear the rush of air as the tendrils gather.

My eyes begin to droop. It won't be long now. This death will be painless. I shake myself upright, trying to resist the smoke's effect. With the last of my energy, I scream as loudly as my raw throat will allow. I lay on my back, exhausted, and continue screaming, each cry growing weaker.

This time when my eyes begin to droop, I let them.

"Olina!"

I roll my head to the noise.

"Olina! Willow!"

My eyelids crack open and tears stream out from the smoke.

"Olina!"

Someone is here. Someone has found me!

I scream. At least that's what I intend to do. It comes out as a horrible, wordless groan. Even though I hate the Oscala with every part of me in this moment, I've always appreciated the way sound echoes through the islands.

I make the noise again.

Then the beating wings of a Soar are above me. There's not enough room for whoever it is to land.

"Shit. Olina. Where are you hurt?"

Hamish?

I crack open my eyes. Another bout of coughing hits me. Hamish, balancing the Soar, rips off the smoke cover from his own mouth. The sopping cover hits me in the face. The next breath I take through the wet fabric is hard to draw in, but blissfully lacking in smoke.

"I need to go to the top and figure out how to get you," Hamish hurries, coughing himself. "Don't move. I'll be back."

I might doubt Hamish's ability to handle all my baggage. But I've never doubted him in any other way. As I breathe through the cloth for the next several minutes I begin to feel my wits sharpen. Enough to realize how difficult it will be to save me from this position. Tying the material around the back of my head, I force myself to kneel.

I can no longer see more than a couple of meters through the smoke.

The telltale sound of wings alerts me to Hamish's return. He's fashioned another smoke cover. Water drips from it. He expertly moves the Soar back and forward to maintain his position. He surveys the tiny ledge and shakes his head. There's no way Hamish can land here with the Soar.

"I don't think there's any other way we can do this, except for you to hold onto me." His words are muffled through the cloth.

I nod and use the cliff face to stand on shaky legs. Dizziness assaults me as I rise and I sag against the wall begging my body not to lose consciousness. For once it listens.

Eyes closed, I wait for the black to recede.

Hamish sees I am ready. "I'll try to bring myself to you as straight as possible. Hold on to me. It's around fifty meters to the top. Can you do that? How injured are you?"

I smile wearily and feel water trickle into my mouth from the cover. I'd held onto Sole with a broken wrist and dislocated shoulder. Perhaps because the rope was wrapped around my arm, but I still did it.

I can do this. I set my mind on the goal: fifty meters.

Hamish very slowly guides the Soar closer, and I approach the edge. His green eyes show fierce determination, and a distant part of me is in awe at the skill he displays.

"This is it," he huffs through gritted teeth. "I can't come any closer."

He's close enough that I can reach out and grab him. My turn.

I lean out and clasp my bloody hands around his neck, my feet still on the ledge behind me.

"You ready?" I hardly recognize the raspy sound leaving my mouth.

I'm familiar enough with the Soar to understand he'll need to counteract my weight when I leave the ledge and pull him forward. He jerks his head in a nod, eyebrows furrowed.

I count. "On three. One, two." As I say "three" I push off the ledge and throw myself at him. My arms strain as I lift my legs to wrap around his waist.

The Soar tips forward, despite his movements to draw back. I squeeze my eyes tight, expecting to smash into the cliff.

With a yell, Hamish twists us sideways. His legs kick and I hear the scraping sound of his boots connecting with the island, catapulting us away. My arms tremble as I cling to him.

I won't let myself believe this is over until we reach the top.

Fifty meters seems an age when your salvation rests at the end.

⚔

"Where was she?"

I don't get a chance to undo the straps at my hips and chest before Jovan is in front of me ripping me free of the Soar. His yelling is muffled by the cover over his mouth. It speaks of how scared Hamish was that he doesn't become angry at Jovan's actions. As it is, I am too tired and sore to complain at the treatment.

I blink into Jovan's furious and... desperate eyes as he turns over my hands and swears. He half carries me to the cave, pushing through the material at its entrance. I barely have a chance to smile weakly at the nostalgic thud of the cave's fans before I'm laid on blankets, the material pushed down from my mouth. A dozen heads gather to peer down at me.

But Jovan's is the face I see.

He searches for Hamish. "Where did you find her?" His voice cracks and my mouth dries as a tear tracks down the side of his face.

Losing me would destroy him. Just as losing him would destroy me.

Hamish's voice trembles. "She was right at the bottom of the Oscala. I heard her scream as I was turning around to return."

Jovan stiffens and turns over my hands again. His jaw clenches. "Get water and cloths."

Ashawn and Olandon leave the tight circle.

Jovan brings his face close. I feel his exhale on my cheeks. "You are *never* flying on that thing again."

His words make me remember why I needed saving in the first place.

"Didn't crash," I try. It comes out as, "D-sh," with a squeak halfway through.

Shard props me up as Olandon returns with water and dribbles some down my throat. It is like skidding over ice on bare skin. But I silently ask for more.

And try again. "Didn't crash," I repeat. This time enough of the word is present for the king to understand. "Was shot down."

"What!" Hamish explodes.

"With arrows," I add, unnecessarily.

But Jovan understands what I mean straightaway.

"But how?" Hamish asks, shaking his head. "If you were shot there, it means..." He swallows and lifts his brilliant green eyes to the group. "That it was someone from the Ire."

He's right on that account. But I won't allow rumors to fester. The man had to be working outside Adox's commands. Somehow, I doubt the old Ire leader ordered my assassination.

A wordless communication passes between Jovan and myself.

"You saw him," he says tightly.

There is a buzz of whispers around us. The men are noticeably confused.

I reach my hand up to Jovan's face as his form becomes blurry from my tears. Because it has been so long since Kedrick's death. And just as it stabbed me in the heart, it stabbed the man I love, too.

This means everything to us both.

I nod. "I know who killed Kedrick."

CHAPTER TEN

*W*E CANNOT WAIT a day for me to recover. Another fifty men will arrive at this cave by nightfall. We can't be here when they do.

I could soar to the next cave, but no matter how Shard, Hamish, and Ashawn attempt to reason with their king, Jovan will not be swayed. I will not be transported to the next cave on a Soar. I will be staying with him.

His grip on my wrist is like iron as I stumble over a wooden bridge after him. This is the compromise I made after he tried tying a rope around my waist in case I fell. Aside from refusing that demand, I yield to his need to hold on to me in some way as we pick our way along the path. I'd terrified him yesterday. I sigh, wondering how long it will take for him to trust me enough to let me out of his sight again.

"You are lucky the king pushed us so hard to reach the cave yesterday," Olandon says with a sniff.

Jovan gets clingy-angry. Olandon just gets angry.

The king's party had arrived at the cave early to find I hadn't arrived. Jovan sent out all the Ire folk at his disposal straightaway.

Jovan glares at me.

He grows steadily angrier over the next few hours, his fear taking second place. His grip becomes borderline painful. I've known him for nearly half a revolution, and have been the subject of his anger many times. I know the signs. Jovan is going to explode.

We arrive at the cave and Jovan dispatches me onto a rock in the far corner. He's breathing far too heavily to be calm. I'm breathing far too heavily to be at optimal fighting fitness.

Ashawn edges toward me, down the side of the wall. "The scouts say there's another cave on this island. No fans, though…"

I throw him a grateful look. I didn't want Glacium's leader to lose it in front of his men.

I approach Jovan, who shoots me a withering glance. This is one of those times he is completely transparent. He's angry because he nearly lost me and doesn't like the vulnerability of it. It brings up old scars. I arch an eyebrow. "There is another cave. We can talk," I say into his ear. I move to lead the way, but he stops me with a hand on my shoulder. I let him pass with a roll of my eyes, and follow him outside.

The second cave is around half the size of the one we'll sleep in, but it's oddly beautiful, shallow enough that the firelight from the Oscala reaches all the way into its depths. Because of our proximity to Osolis, the walls of the cave are painted in a soft orange light.

I don't wait for Jovan to explode. This whole day I've craved closeness with him and I know he has, too. He just doesn't know it yet. I wrap my arms around his waist and rest my head on his chest.

"I was scared," I admit.

His breath stutters in his chest before he encloses me in his strong arms and holds me tightly. "So was I." The reply is so quiet I can only just hear the words.

"How did you know to send the men to look for me?" I ask. It's been irking me all day.

He's inhaling the scent of my hair. I imagine it smells like smoke, myself, but whatever calms him down, I suppose.

"Because you weren't there," he says. Helpful.

He continues before I can deliver some kind of sarcastic reply.

"I pushed the men to hurry all day so I could see you. I knew you'd be waiting for me when I got there."

"That's…" Overconfident, bordering on arrogant.

"Accurate?" he provides.

Humor is returning to him and I heave a sigh of relief.

I could stay here like this throughout the night if the smoke would let us. But as I think the words, something warm stirs in my belly. "Hmm," I reply. I tilt my head for a kiss. Jovan kisses my forehead and tucks me back into his chest, not taking the hint. And why would he? He's always been the one to initiate further intimacy. I had a month to linger on that bath we took together where nothing happened. It's like the closer we get to Osolis, the smaller the window that Jovan and I have to be as we are now becomes. Together, uncomplicated. And I want every part of that. Not just the hugs and kisses, as breathtaking as they are.

"So who is our assassin?" he asks.

I frown. "One of the traders, as I suspected. It's strange, but I got a sense I know him somehow. Does that sound crazy?"

A moment passes. "You think this is more personal?"

I shrug. "I have no idea."

His arms squeeze me hard. The muscles in them catch my eye and I run my fingers up and down the bare skin. Flashes of our intoxicated night together after the ball come to the fore.

"There's another point we must talk on." It's not the question so much as the tone he asks me in that makes me tense.

"We need to discuss what our plan is when we get to Osolis."

I begin to run both hands up his arms to his shoulders. "Get there, defeat Mother, save my people."

He watches my hands with confusion. "No, I… I don't mean that. I mean what happens to *us*?"

My insides freeze, though I keep it from my face. "We could talk about that, I guess. Or you could realize that we have this cave to ourselves for two hours." My cheeks are warm, but I hold his gaze as his blue eyes read me.

"Do you…?" He swallows. "What do you mean?"

I smile and lift my face to kiss the base of his throat. "I mean that I want to take advantage of you again."

"Oh?"

I nearly laugh at the hope in his voice. He stays stone-still as I take a breath and draw his shirt slowly upward, revealing his sculpted torso. I avoid his gaze, but from the corner of my eye I see him smile as he bends his head forward so I can remove the tunic completely. I pause, unsure what to do next. I mean, logically, I'd remove the rest of his clothing. But taking off his trousers seems like an insurmountable hurdle.

He takes over, closing the gap between us to lift my own tunic. My eyes must display my uncertainty because he stops, still gripping the material.

"If it makes it better, I've seen you naked six times now."

"What?"

Jovan chuckles at my appalled response. "When you were stabbed, I saw you naked twice."

I narrow my eyes. "That leaves four other times."

"Remember when you were behind that screen and I frightened you?"

I'd been changing out of my harness into my normal clothes. "You never came around the screen! I was watching."

A mischievous glint enters his eye. "I was there for a minute or two before I revealed my presence."

My mouth falls open. Though, I should have expected nothing less of a Bruma man. "And the other times?" I ask weakly.

"There was that bath before I left," he adds. "You have no idea how that memory has tortured me."

I drop my gaze to a point on his shoulder. "I think I have a pretty good idea."

His lips are on mine before I have time to process he has moved. Our teeth clash briefly from the ferocity of our meeting. His groan is one of longing and I greet it with my own hungry moan. I've waited forever for this moment. Yes, we slept together after the ball. And there was the beginning of something present at the time, something desperate, perhaps. The first time was uncontrolled, spontaneous. But this…

This feels like the first time.

Neither of us has a mask on. Everything we've been through together has burned away the need for artifice. He's everything I never thought I could have. His eyes drink me in as my clothes are removed. There's no doubt in my mind that he wants me, and that he thinks I'm beautiful. I take the plunge, eager to explore him, touching only what I'm comfortable with. My hesitancy probably amuses him, but he doesn't say anything.

There is only love in his eyes when I reach up to kiss him again.

He moves his fingers and mouth across me and my skin grows uncomfortably hot. I move against him in an attempt to extinguish the frustration building within. When he looks up from where he kneels, his blue eyes are dilated. They catch me and I can't move.

In a fluid motion, Jovan picks me up and wraps my legs around his hips. He carries me to a smooth wall of the cave and gently places my back against the surface. I shiver at the cool rock.

"This isn't good enough for you," he whispers across my skin.

I arch into his mouth. "I want you, Jovan."

He positions himself and a thrill of yearning so intense I could explode sprints through me. He is watching my face closely, inching. Always so careful with me. But that's not what I want.

"More," I whisper.

Grateful relief breaks across his forehead as he gives me what I ask for.

This has been so long coming, and I need something more.

I beseech him with my eyes to give me whatever this is. The fire is consuming me.

Jovan's breath comes out in a rasp. "You've got it, baby."

I hold my breath as a wondrous sensation takes hold. An odd languidness is spreading through my body and I'm not entirely sure if I'm in control anymore.

A low, tight growling sounds in my ear. "I want it all."

We move together and my voice cracks on a scream, still hoarse from yesterday. Jovan tenses a moment later, groaning my name into my neck.

It takes a while before either of us moves. I'm utterly spent. Jovan lifts his head and stares at me with a smile that's almost shy. I can't help the answering smile from spreading over my own face. He lifts a hand from beneath me and pushes a strand of hair back from my damp skin.

"I love you, Lina."

I trace his jaw and kiss the corner of his mouth. "And I, you."

It's hard to tell how much time passes while we are in our own little bubble.

We finally drag ourselves upright, dressing quickly to return to our duties.

His earlier question hangs over me as we pick our way to the front of the glorious cave. If all goes to plan in the coming months, who knows what will happen to us. *That* is why I cannot talk of what happens next between us: I don't want him to say something that cannot be. But I don't want him to break my heart, either.

A thought strikes me. "The other two times."

He stops and throws me a puzzled glance.

"The other two times you've seen me naked. When were they?"

A smirk crosses his face as he grabs my hand. "You know that argument we had about Blaine? How I left the baths, and you stayed?"

I gasp. "You came back and watched?"

"It wasn't to spy on you… at first. It was to make sure you got back to the castle all right."

"I can't believe you!" I whack him on the shoulder.

He shrugs. "There's something wrong with me. You'll have to show me the error of my ways."

I squeal as he grips my bottom. "And the sixth time?"

Jovan throws me a haughty glance. "Just now."

His words stop me in my tracks.

"You…"

He arches an eyebrow.

"You counted the sixth time *before* you'd seen me naked?"

Jovan leans in and pulls at my lower lip with his teeth. I moan and he lets go.

"Was I wrong?"

An outraged snort leaves me. "You give overconfidence a new meaning."

He pushes me ahead of him, maintaining a grip on my hips at all times. "You were taking advantage of me," he reasons. "It only seems fair that I take advantage of you in return."

We duck through the cave and I walk to the back where my pack lies next to Jovan's. I'm glad I hadn't taken it with me yesterday. I would've hated to lose Kedrick's arrow and my swords. As an afterthought, I tuck the arrow into my boot. It hasn't rested there in months. If the assassin is from the Ire, I'll need the fletching as proof. It cannot be lost.

A few sniggers catch my attention and I survey the cave.

Ashawn is talking in a low voice to Olandon, whose face is bright red. "Yeah, but it's different. My brother was banging your sister. I'm proud of my brother, while you have to be feeling almost *violated* in a way. Your sister, Landon. Having sex."

Olandon shoves Ashawn aside and stomps past me without meeting my eyes.

Ashawn saunters closer, watching my brother. "Just a word of advice, Tatuma."

"What's that?" I ask warily.

He gestures to the surrounding space. "Caves echo."

My face flames. I can't think of any retort as Ashawn walks away, chuckling.

CHAPTER ELEVEN

*I*REVEL IN THE warmth, breathing in the hot air as we trek closer to Osolis. Has Osolis changed? Will the ground still be hard and the grass that same straw-yellow?

The night before we arrive, I toss and turn next to Jovan until he pins me down with an arm and leg. The Ire folk scouting ahead have told us the Tatum hasn't yet reached the first rotation. It must be the presence of Glacium's archers that has her hanging back. Whatever it is, it's a massive advantage to us. It gives us time to assemble our forces at her doorstep. We're the third group of fifty to filter through the smoke barrier. The Ire should have transported over three times that number. Plus, with the Ire folk themselves, we could have close to one thousand soldiers present.

As soon as the light filters through the cave's entrance I'm up, kissing Jovan gently on the ear. He scratches the spot and rolls over, fast asleep. I grin and scoop up a water skin. I pick my way up the crumbling roughly carved steps until I'm at the top of the island and select a seat facing Osolis.

I unwrap my hands and survey the healing. Some of the smaller wounds have a soft scab over them; the rest are still wide open. I dampen my tunic and attempt to clean the injuries before re-wrapping them and pulling the knot tight with my teeth. I can't say I'd relish holding a sword right now, but otherwise I'm recovered enough to engage in a fight.

Inhaling deeply, I gaze across at Osolis and my heart squeezes tight in my chest. The nearness of my world fills me with impatience and disquiet.

Through the smoke haze await the last of the people I love.

Olandon sits beside me and passes me my robes. I take them with trembling hands and look at my brother. I really *look*. "Thank you, Landon," I say. "For loving me enough to risk death. Thank you for treating the Bruma well. For everything."

He dips his head in acknowledgement, but I catch the glisten of his eyes before he turns toward Osolis.

"What will it be like, do you think?" he asks.

My voice is hollow. "No idea."

He whispers. "You were born for this, Lina. Don't ever doubt that. This is your destiny. You will be the greatest Tatum ever to live."

My stomach somersaults at the reminder of what happens next.

Jovan screens me from view as I change into my robes. The silky black material slithers over my frame and feels entirely foreign from the fur and leather I just removed. Brown and gray robes were my norm on Osolis, but I had been wearing black robes on my last night in Osolis. I finger the sleeves gently. This is what I wore when Kedrick died.

I keep the boots on, checking to make sure Kedrick's arrow is still there. My sandals are long gone, hacked to pieces by Sanjay. I automatically raise my arms to braid my hair back as I used to, but I stop. I don't want to be what I was before.

I braid the top half into a ring circling my head, leaving the rest down. When I turn, Jovan is regarding me with a blank expression. He's only garbed in light pants, not fur-lined like his usual clothing, and he doesn't wear a shirt.

Can different clothes make things awkward? I fidget. "This is... strange."

He steps forward and tilts my chin up, kissing me firmly. "No," he says. "It's not. But I prefer when I can see down your top."

I snort and push him out of the way.

As we wind around the remaining few islands of the Oscala, Osolis underneath us, I watch the robes kicking around my feet. I'm not the only one. Men I've laughed and joked with stare at me from a distance, unsure how to talk to the Tatuma version of myself. Olandon is in his own green robes, the least tattered set of those he'd hauled through the Oscala on his journey. A bright color, more typical of my mother's flamboyant court. Then again, my brother hadn't needed to blend in during childhood.

Tensions in the group rise as we continue on our trek. Jovan walks at the front of the procession, safe in the knowledge that the first two groups would have sprung any traps set by Cassius. He turns frequently, and I know he wants me there beside him, but I can't. I need to do this alone, with my brother on my right.

It is hard to keep my eyes on the crumbling stone under my feet when I know what is coming. My heart beats in my ears as we round the last island.

"We're here." Olandon's voice is reverent.

With dreadful excitement I lift my eyes from my robes and gaze upon Osolis. Tears prick my eyes at the beauty of my world: vast, smoky, and familiar. My eyes reach farther. Before me is a tapestry of black trees with purple-red leaves. Long grass extends as far as the eye can see, patches still green where the heat has not completely dried it for harvest. The image warps in the heat. I cover my mouth, completely taken with the sight. My world. My home.

The Tatum's army is nowhere in sight and I'm grateful to bask in the untainted view.

I look around for Jovan, eager to point a few things out. He's never been here before.

A few meters from where I've drawn to a halt on the last flat rocky island, a rope is looped around an exposed boulder. The loose end dangles over the edge, down to my world; it signals the end of the maze-like Oscala.

With a small frown I see Jovan is no longer here… he's already at the bottom of the rope.

Shrugging it off, I make my own way down the rope toward the hundreds of Bruma tents arranged in neat rows. The wraps on my hands go some way toward helping, but the torn skin protests the task and blood is seeping through by the bottom.

...Can the ground be familiar? The firmness of it is. The tiny fissures in the bone-dry ground I know so well. The rolling hills of endless dried meadow. The lattice of vines visible in the tree line. My feet are moving of their own accord. I nearly run through the tents of Bruma soldiers. I break through the last line of them, and my feet fumble, threatening to trip me, until I slow to a shuffle.

Tears threaten to fall as I step into the grass, close my eyes, and push away the sound of the hundreds of soldiers behind me. And I *feel*.

The slight breeze caresses my face, rustling the meadow. I brush the stalks with my fingertips, lost in the impossibility that I am actually here. A grin breaks through.

I made it. My grin falls as the triumph drains away and determination takes its place.

I make for camp, but pause; Jovan is there, watching me. I was so absorbed, I hadn't noticed. I smile at him, but this, too, slides away as he turns without acknowledging me.

I don't chase after him. I don't know what stops me from calling out to him.

And I don't ask him why he looks so sad. Because I know.

We are the biggest impossibility of all.

CHAPTER TWELVE

*T*HERE IS NO rest after our journey. Olandon pushes aside the tent flap for me to enter. Most of the attending advisors are present, carried from farther back in the procession.

"We don't know why they haven't attacked. Even with the archers I can't make an end of it," Malir says.

I settle into a position opposite Jovan. It is where I'd usually sit, but the action holds more significance after our awkward exchange earlier.

Rhone points at the huge map spread over the table beneath us. "We've sent scouts to these locations. They all reported the same thing: The Tatum's army is nowhere in sight."

"Tatuma?" Shard asks me.

Why would Mother and Cassius be waiting to attack? The difficulty in attempting to guess Mother's strategy lay in that there had never been a battle like this in our history. Last time, when Olandon and I worked out Cassius's plan, it was based on my memory and what I knew of my cruel uncle.

What did I know of my mother?

I turn to Olandon. "Mother likes to play with her food." I ignore the disgruntled mutters from the Bruma as I refer to them as a meal.

"She plans to draw us in. I cannot see the benefit," he replies.

There wasn't any benefit that I could see. If your enemy outnumbered you, you funneled them into a small space... but it made more sense to pick us off as we arrived in small numbers. As twisted and depraved as my mother is, she isn't stupid. "She wants us to enter Osolis," I agree.

"Then we meet her with our swords!" Drummond bellows.

The tent erupts into roars of approval while those who have any sense are staring at the map wondering what we've missed.

The next morning, I head to the food line to grab dried meat and stale bread. Bruma soldiers lower themselves down the Oscala's rope in a steady trickle.

"Miss me, princess?" a husky voice asks.

The sultry words could only come from one man: Sin. Devastatingly handsome, and devastatingly aware of it.

"I can't say I have."

He saunters in front of me with false casualness. The only reason I never fall for his games is that he loves himself more than he could ever love another. There is a keen intelligence underneath his outward facade, however, and I secretly enjoy that he is always despicable. Even in the worst of situations.

I frown. I understand why most of the Outer Rings Bruma have come, food being the biggest reason. But I can't fathom why Sin is here.

Before I can ask him, someone shouts my name.

Ice approaches at a fast clip. "Girly, you're wanted by the big man."

"Is anything the matter?"

He shrugs. "King Boss sent out scouts a bit farther, and they found somethin'. Don't know what, but your fancy brother said you'd wanna see."

Forgetting Sin, I jog after Ice, curious as to what the scouts have found. We run through the bustle of the Bruma army, toward the outer edge of Osolis and around in the direction of the Sixth until we reach a small group. There are two from Glacium, Jovan and Ashawn; two from Osolis, Olandon and Rian; and two unknown scouts from the Ire.

Olandon's face is grim.

"Who is it?" I ask, dread already rooted within me.

"You remember I told you about the man and his family..."

I breathe through my nose and push past. Mother was always fond of hanging her minions from the Oscala for everyone to see. Those who broke her rule, usually protecting their family, ended up here. As Osolis's rulers always maintained, punishment extended to your whole family. That is why Mother didn't just kill the toddler who attempted to lift my veil half a revolution ago. Blankly, I stare down at the smallest skeleton. The sight isn't uncommon here, but it disturbs me more because I can picture the child in my mind, and because I caused the annihilation of this family by getting too close when I should have known better.

Slightly larger bones sit beside the toddler's. They belong to his sister, the girl who attempted to offer me food.

I continue to my right and swallow at the remains of Turin and what I assume used to be his wife. What I don't expect is the fifth body. While Turin's family are just bones now, the fifth is a mostly decayed body. I recognize the person nevertheless.

Clearly my friend has not been dead more than a few weeks.

"Lina," Jovan says.

I turn to him to rid myself of the sight of the orphanage matron and he takes me in his arms. The woman who helped me in the limited capacity she could. A person who always helped the families of Osolis and aided me with my small rebellion—distributing apples to the orphanages. Just one more person who is dead because of me.

"There have been many others," a calm voice states.

I separate myself from Jovan, squeezing his hand before I do. Rian stands before the five dead Solati, gazing impassively at the sticky remains.

"Not all from conspiracy. Most from starvation. A few during the day's work," he says.

Olandon strides away, unable to mask his reaction and embarrassed because of it. I don't care about hiding emotion anymore. Tears stream down both cheeks.

"I will make it better," I say.

Rian raises his head and looks through me with blank eyes. "You are our only hope."

<hr />

There still hasn't been any sighting of the Solati force.

Yesterday, Jovan sent more scouts to travel to each rotation. Mother is hiding somewhere, and he wants to know where. I want to know *why*. Foreboding hangs over me like smoke.

We gather in the large tent for another day of useless mutterings. These talks have no point until we know the location of the Tatum. The tent space is stuffy. Everyone is sweating aside from Olandon, myself, and the attending Ire folk. The king sprawls in his chair, listening intently to Adox, who arrived, to our surprise, this morning. Clearly the old leader didn't trust anyone in his stead. Or couldn't relinquish control to someone of limited experience.

Jovan's tunic is soaked through. It's clinging to him. If I thought his hug yesterday had meant a bridging of the distance between us, I was sadly mistaken. We'd resumed our standoffish behavior immediately after.

I wonder if he craves my touch as much as I crave his.

The room is riveted on Roscoe as he lays out plans to rally the surrounding villages to our cause. Personally, I think this could go either way. But revealing my blue eyes *would* cause greater disgust toward my mother than myself. It could help in the short term. The long term was another matter. I'd convinced two races. Could I convince the third and most difficult to accept my mixed heritage?

The voices drone on and I settle back into my chair, closing my eyes. The warmth of my world makes me sleepy. Or maybe it's this ineffective use of our time.

The noise in the tent space blurs into a humming buzz, and I focus on the spurts of sound outside the fabric wall. There's a regular clanging, the grind of a sword, and the laughter and shouts of Bruma letting off steam. A different sound catches my attention. A thin, weak disturbance in the otherwise boisterous clamor.

I strain my ears to hear it again. For some reason it makes my heart pound.

My eyes fly open as I hear it again. I jump to my feet, causing the men closest to me to yelp in surprise.

"Everyone shut up."

I pace across the tent and then stop, holding my breath and closing my eyes once more.

"Lina." The thin wail travels to me from afar and I nearly fall to my

knees right then and there. As it is, I cannot prevent a whimper from leaving my lips. And then I am running out of the tent, ignoring the shouts behind me. I am running as hard as I can toward the sound, pumping my legs, my hair whipping out behind me. Through the camp I race, the cries of my name growing louder.

I break free of the last row.

And then I cannot go any farther.

My chest heaves in sobs at the sight in front of me.

My boys. My brothers, either side of Aquin, my old trainer. They cannot really be here. Footsteps thud behind me as, gasping through my tears, I stagger to my brothers, desirous that no more time passes between now and the moment they are in my arms once more.

"Chave, B-beron?" I choke as I near them. My heart is going to shatter inside of me. They are so grown, nearly seven years old now. Ochave has lost his chubbiness. Oberon's eyes are as intelligent as ever.

The twins exchange a look, and Ochave, my brave Ochave, steps forward. "Lina?" he says haltingly.

I nod at them, wiping at my tears. My veil is off. They are seeing my face for the first time. "It's me," I say, smiling tremulously.

Oberon shuffles forward beside his brother. I ignore Aquin for the time being. I see nothing but my kin. I stop a pace from where they linger and fall to my knees.

This time when I smile, it's stronger. "I've missed you, my boys. I have missed you so much." My voice cracks again.

Oberon believes me first, breaking past Ochave to close the distance between us. He throws himself into my arms and I encircle him with shaking hands, pulling him close. Ochave is next. His addition to my hug sends us toppling to the ground.

I cry unabashedly, too full of gratitude and love to be ashamed of our audience. I stroke their hair. I touch their faces through my blurry vision.

"I love you," I whisper for only them to hear. "I love you both so much." I wipe the wet tracks from Oberon's face with my robes as Ochave frantically sniffles to prevent the threatening tears.

Olandon steps to my side and takes them into his arms. They go willingly, familiar with his face.

I turn my attention to Aquin. There is no smile on his face. I strike the tears from my eyes and stand tall under the regard of the only father figure I have ever known. His intent brown eyes are set on my face, more particularly on the blue color that shouldn't be there.

I have no idea how he will react, and I am only just realizing his opinion on my eyes matters dearly to me.

Oberon and Ochave accept me because they are young and have not been taught to hate. If my old trainer accepts me, it is with the knowledge of what this might mean, and what I intend to do.

He steps forward, only a slight limp marring the grace with which he moves. He is beyond old, much older than the age I suspect Adox to be. But he has always stayed in shape, and always will until the day he dies.

"Tatuma Olina." He dips his head.

"Aquin," I reply.

His mouth twitches and his eyes shine. He has always known what I need—whether a stern word, a kind ear, or a hard training session with absolute silence. I see his throat work as he swallows. Then he opens his arms wide and I run into them, squeezing him around the middle. He hushes me, rocking slightly side to side, resting his chin atop my head.

A minute passes before he is pulling away. A firmness has returned to his expression. "That is enough of that," he grumbles.

I purse my lips to contain my laughter. Where to start? There is so much to say. "Thank you for bringing them to me, Aquin."

"It was not safe for them anymore. Hasn't been for some time."

My gaze lands on all three of my brothers. And I face Aquin once more, a question in my eyes. His returning glance is grave and weary. I cannot imagine what the last half a revolution has been like for my old trainer.

"We must convene with the king of Glacium," he says. "You must be wondering where Tatum Avanna is hiding."

CHAPTER THIRTEEN

"*M*Y EYES ARE blue."

They are the first words I say once we've reconvened in the tent. And they are leaden with guilt.

Aquin and Adox are the only ones seated. I think the others are like me—too deep in shock to say much.

Aquin's eyes widen in mock surprise. "You think I trained you from five years old and never saw them?"

My jaw drops to the floor. "You *knew*?" I ask in a high-pitched voice.

Whack!

I wince and rub the spot where his cane had connected with my head, not missing the growl from across the tent.

"Mind your manners," he barks.

Olandon sniggers from Aquin's other side.

Whack!

Blood pours from Olandon's nose and I meet my brother's glare with amusement, which swiftly disappears when Aquin turns back to me.

I bow slightly. "My apologies, trainer. I have long been away from this world."

Aquin observes those around him. His gaze rests upon the king and flickers back to me.

"You were aware of my mother's affair," I amend.

He gives an almost imperceptible nod.

"I never suspected." How could he not tell me?

"I feared your reaction would mean your death."

I mull over his response. Aquin does not say these words lightly. How would I have responded to the news if I'd learned sooner? More likely than not, the information would have crushed any remaining spirit I had.

I accept his explanation with a nod.

"Tell us what you know of the Tatum's plans," Jovan orders.

Aquin fails to be impressed and I share a fleeting glance with Olandon. He's just the same, grumpy old coot.

I glance to where the twins huddle in a corner, cowed by the present company. They can't take their eyes off of Jovan. He's probably the largest man they've ever seen. Wait until they see Avalanche. Aquin is waiting for me to give my permission.

I lift my hand and he begins. "The Tatum and all of her forces await you in the Third Rotation."

"Why?" Jovan asks.

Aquin jerks.

"You must remember questions are normal on Glacium," I reprimand in a low voice.

The trainer doesn't acknowledge the comment other than to continue. "I imagine Tatum Avanna means to draw you in and cut you off from the Oscala."

"She boxes her army in against the Fourth," Olandon muses.

He's right. She has backed herself into a corner. Why? "The villagers," I ask Aquin.

"Left in their villages to die at the hands of the savage Bruma king." He watches Jovan for a reaction. A flicker of respect sparks when the king doesn't give one. "The First is largely empty," Aquin says. "Those who are able have moved to the Fifth or Sixth Rotations in the hopes they'll avoid the carnage."

"Their condition." I don't want to know, but I have to ask. What kind of Tatum will I make if I cannot handle the horrible truth?

Aquin does not immediately answer, which speaks volumes. "Not good."

The king rises and circles the space, frowning in thought.

I rise as well, addressing him. "We can leave the villagers alone for now and take Osolis without their help."

He stops and meets my gaze. "Can they last that long? The battle could take weeks. How many more would die?" Jovan continues. "And waiting could weaken the strength of your rule in its infancy. If you wait, once you defeat your mother, you will still need to win the favor of your people. That means you'll need to leave the court and palace during a time when it is crucial to uphold a steady presence."

He's right. I just didn't want to involve anyone in the battle that I didn't have to. The decayed face of the orphanage matron flares before my eyes. "I do not want to cause unnecessary loss of life."

He gives me a ghost of a sad smile and I return as much of it as I can. It's the most communication we've had in days.

I turn away with a sigh. "So we rally the villagers to fight for us. We are in agreement?" I survey those in the tent and clear my throat after they show their assent. "I believe our first move should be to open the stores and distribute food."

"This is wise," Drummond adds. "It will endear you to the people."

"And prevent further starving," Roscoe says, brows raised.

Drummond flushes.

"Yes, for both of these reasons," I interject. "Specifically, I want Bruma to hand it out. Only those who can be trusted to behave while they do it." I glance at Shard.

"I can gather a force," he replies.

"Of fifty or so."

"Done." He gets up to leave.

"Not Sin!" I call after him.

A large, warm hand rests on my shoulder. "We'll need the villagers to gather in large groups so their Tatuma can address them," Jovan says.

That was a polite way of saying I am meant to whip them into a frenzy. I snort.

Jovan's arm blurs, stopping Aquin's cane an inch from my face.

…Guess I shouldn't snort anymore either. The king wrenches the stick from the old trainer's grip. Aquin watches him with interest.

"You will stop hitting your future Tatum." Jovan lowers his arm from where it protected me.

I swallow nervously.

"I will stop when she stops me herself," Aquin remarks cryptically.

Snap. I look down at Jovan's hands to see Aquin's stick snapped in two.

"Jovan," I say in annoyance. "He needs that."

He ignores me, engaged in a battle of wills with the seated man.

Aquin looks at the two pieces. "Now I shall be able to hit them both at once. I thank you."

Jovan grows deadly still. Then he holds out the pieces to the old man. "And I shall find a stick twice as big to beat you with if you touch her."

Aquin remains still, but I can see the slight movement of his eyebrows as he takes the sticks. "You would hit the elderly."

Jovan's teeth gleam. "This savage Bruma king would relish it."

Ashawn pipes up. "What about not hitting Landon, brother? You only mentioned Olina."

The king shrugs. "The boy still needs it."

An ugly red creeps up my brother's neck.

I narrow my eyes at Aquin, who has his lips pressed together. Now he decides this situation is funny? Olandon begins to rise.

I clap my hands to draw attention my way. "Malir, please ready a guard for Jovan and I. They should be light on their feet. The majority of the army will stay here."

"And if we should be caught unawares?" Rhone inquires quietly.

I grin. "Then a small force will be a lesser loss to our cause, and we will have greater speed in escaping. Olandon and Ashawn will remain here to lead if the worst should occur." Both Olandon and Ashawn decide they have something to say about that.

Jovan speaks. "It will be as the Tatuma says."

He holds up a hand as Ashawn opens his mouth to argue again. "I need you to remain here and lead our people if I should fall, Ash." It is not a request.

Ashawn lowers his head, jaw clenched.

Aquin rises in a fluid motion. "That was not as difficult as I feared it would be, talking to a bunch of babbling Bruma." He pats me on the cheek as he passes. "It must be your influence, Lina."

CHAPTER FOURTEEN

"TELL ME OF it," Aquin speaks. The old man swats a vine out of the way with his new cane. The *thwack* echoes through the bush and Jovan glares over his shoulder. His blue eyes flicker when they meet mine, before he turns away.

"You can start with that," Aquin grumbles.

I smile. Starting by explaining my relationship with Jovan is like building a castle from the top. It doesn't make sense. "No. I will start at the beginning."

As we duck and clamber through the hanging Kaur forest separating the First Rotation from the Sixth, I talk. I talk and I talk. About Kedrick, about the delegates, about the pits.

Aquin puffs his chest out. "Of course you won."

I peek a look at him from the corner of my eye, concealing my grin.

Hours pass as I recount everything that has happened to me, or happened *because* of me, in the last three rotations. I didn't realize how much I had to tell my trainer. "I've seen the assassin's face, so it is simply a matter of killing him once this war is done. And I still don't know who my father is, but I've narrowed it down to four men."

Aquin's feet stumble and I whip my arm across his shoulders to steady him and glimpse his face.

"You know who my father is." I aim for calm, but accusation creeps into my words.

His eyes dart to my face and stay there. He opens his mouth. Twice. I gape at him. Aquin never told me who my father was, and he knew the whole time? The quiet murmur of talking Bruma hushes. Aquin glances around us at the men who are now watching us with interest.

He clears his throat. "I do."

"Who—"

He raises a hand. "And I will not tell you who he is. Only that he came to Osolis with your army. He has personally approached me and said he wants to tell you himself."

Really. Whoever he was, he hadn't hesitated to pull Aquin aside— only a few hours had passed since the meeting in the tent. "Well, he's had half a revolution to do it," I snap.

My trainer's eyes narrow. "Maybe his choice to tell you affects more than just yourself."

"Poor him," I mutter.

We continue on in silence. A part of me is stunned Aquin won't tell me who my father is. But I've learned something useful: My father is here. I'll be watching my old trainer to see who he interacts with. It is obviously someone he respects, or he wouldn't even entertain the man's request. Unfortunately, I know that if Aquin decides he won't speak on a subject, nothing will convince him. I don't waste my breath.

Aquin takes the lead as we continue on, directing us to who knows where.

I roll the square of fabric in my pocket absently. The veil. I have to put the cursed thing on for the next step. My stomach rolls as I think of what that step involves. How crucial it is that this works. How crucial it is to *me*. I'm about to show an entire village of people my greatest fear. I would rather stand in front of them naked.

"They just need to react, though, right?" Ice scratches his chin. "They get angry and rampage, win. They love you, win. Either way it's a win if they react. The worst that could happen is they don't do anything."

Shard and I share an amused look. Ice is firing on all bows today.

Blizzard snorts. "Frost wants them to like her, idiot. It'll be more mess to clean up if they don't."

"Don't call me an idiot!"

Shard sighs as the two men bicker behind us. "You all right?"

I swallow down some bile. "Yep."

He wraps an arm around my shoulders as we walk. I can see the top of a thatch house over the next rolling hill. That must be where Aquin is leading us.

"They'll love you," he whispers. "And if they don't, fuck them."

I frown. "What? All of them?"

Shard stops in his tracks and stares down at me. "Did you just—?"

I snigger loudly, unable to hold it in.

"You did," Shard says. His eyes are wide in wonder. He turns to the rest of the barracks, and Sin.

"Olina just made a dirty joke," he exclaims proudly.

Blizzard and Ice break off their argument. There's a small silence before what he's said sinks in.

The barracks erupt into whoops. I'm flung into a Kaur tree as Avalanche slaps me on the back in congratulations. Ice wrenches me back and pumps my hand up and down in a handshake. Blizzard is wiping an actual tear of pride from his eye.

"All right," I roll my eyes. "Get over it or I won't make another one."

That shuts them up. Sin saunters up to me. "So…"

"No, Sin."

I turn to Shard. "I thought I told you not to bring him."

He shrugs. "Sorry."

I jog up to join Jovan and Aquin, ignoring Sin's outraged comments behind me.

"What was that about?" Jovan asks.

I avoid his gaze. Things between us are changing, and a deep anger simmers under the surface because I thought what lay between us was stronger than that. Honestly, I'm angry he's treating me so strangely. What is it? Now that he sees me on Osolis, he can't ignore who I am anymore? Did I do something to annoy him? Or is it just that we haven't spoken about… well, anything?

"Shard found a shiny rock," I mutter.

He looks back at the still laughing group. "Really?"

I ignore him and scan the thatch house in front of us. Most of the Solati villages are filled with houses such as this. Houses made of the straw harvested from the Second. The homes burn down every revolution in the Fourth fires, meaning the villagers have to rebuild their shelters over and over again. The richer you are, the more permanent your housing. Some villagers—tradespeople—have houses with a couple of Kaur walls. The Satums, who are the equivalent of ministers on Glacium, have homes entirely made of the fire-resistant Kaur wood, signifying their wealth.

It's fair to say I'll be having a very long discussion with the Satums when I am in power. Though, to be fair, there was only so much they could do against someone like my mother.

"Lina, put on your veil."

I nod to my trainer and take the material, supplied by Willow back on Glacium, from my pocket. I grit my teeth and float it over my head, jamming the circle band on top. I hate it. After this is done, I'm going to burn the stupid thing.

Aquin shakes the straw door with his new stick. The occupants are aware of our proximity, I'm sure, with the raucous barracks in the background. I hear the brushing of the door pulling back, in complete darkness for the moment. It has been a long time since I've worn the veil. It will take getting used to.

"Tatuma Olina, well met. Master Aquin," the voice states.

I frown at the fragility of the voice, but dip my head. Jovan has tensed beside me and I wonder why.

"They are around the back. Please, follow me."

I grab Jovan's sweating arm as he makes to move, blinking rapidly to clear my vision. Jovan guides me slowly after Aquin and the villager. By the time we've rounded the house, my eyes have adjusted and the villager is gone.

A snort reaches my ears and I turn to see five dromeda stabled there. Leaving Jovan's side, I approach in quick steps.

The beautiful creatures stamp and toss their manes at my approach.

"You are gorgeous," I murmur to one. It has been an age since I last rode a dromeda. It used to be one of my favorite things to do. I wonder how it will feel after riding in a sled.

"The fuck is that?" Ice shouts.

"Tell that fool of a boy to be quiet," Aquin says.

"Come and tell me yourself, old man."

Aquin hobbles over to him and I grimace. He's playing on his age the way I play on the fact that I'm small. Shard and Blizzard realize this and distance themselves from Ice immediately. Ice stands there with a cocky grin and my heart pangs for him. Aquin is about to bring the pain.

My trainer doesn't say anything. He just springs onto one leg and catches the barracks man under the jaw. Ice crumples to the ground in a heap. I shake my head. It was bound to happen sooner or later.

"Do you mean for us to get on top of these things?" Sin asks. He wipes away the sweat dripping from his brow. Even drenched in perspiration, the shirtless Bruma is the most beautiful man I've ever seen.

"No." The king moves between Sin and myself. "You will walk."

There are only five beasts. Sin holds up his hands and gives me a seductive wink before he saunters away. Hairs raise on the back of my neck where Jovan is staring at me.

Grabbing hold of the dromeda's mane, I swing up onto the dark creature's back. My robes gather around my knees and I push them down as close to my new sandals as possible. Its powerful shoulder muscles move underneath me and sheer delight courses through me.

I shift atop the dromeda as it shuffles side to side.

Jovan rests a hand on my thigh. The movement is casual, but his palm feels like it burns a hole in my robes. I have blue robes on today. Aquin thought it best, as blue has always been the color of peace. Maybe he hopes the association with my eye color will help my cause.

"Am I supposed to get on one of these things?"

I shrug. I don't know what Aquin's plan is. "You are afraid, mighty Bruma king." My tone is teasing and light.

"Of being trampled to death? Yes." Jovan's tone is curt and I know why. His father was killed while dogsledding.

I squeeze his hand, listening to the catch of Aquin's breath at the king's honest reply.

"You can ride with me," I say.

"No," Aquin says. "You need to be seen as independent. King Jovan, two of his men, and myself will ride behind you. Followed by the others."

"King Jovan," I say. "Get up behind me. You can get the feel of the movement before riding your own." Aquin might have orchestrated this, but I am the Tatuma.

Jovan swings behind me without another word. Even this, he does with the graceful movements of a warrior. Jovan's warm thighs rest behind mine, and his grip around my waist tightens. I cluck and the dromeda strides forward.

I circle the thatch house as Aquin instructs Shard and Roscoe onto the remaining dromeda. The unconscious Ice is slung over the dromeda in front of Shard. Avalanche is guffawing in the background.

"I could get used to this."

I shiver as Jovan's breath tickles my neck. It is interesting riding with someone else, or maybe just because it's Jovan. I can feel him moving behind me. His fingers spread low on my stomach.

He nuzzles the side of my neck. "I think I should ride behind you the whole way. For safety."

My eyebrows lift under the veil. "I wouldn't think you'd want to," I say, thinking of the way we've been avoiding each other.

He holds me tight. "I'll always want to."

I remain silent and he sighs.

"We need to talk," he says.

His tone makes me smile. "We're good at talking," I say.

Jovan chuckles. "That's the exaggeration of the revolution."

Aquin is calling us back.

"Are you particularly attached to that old-timer?" Jovan asks.

"Yes." I press my lips in a flat line.

I rein the dromeda in and Jovan swings from the mount, landing with soft feet.

"That's a shame," he says.

I watch as the king swings up onto his own dromeda. The Bruma look too muscular for the mounts—Jovan most of all—but the dromeda don't seem to notice the extra weight.

We start off once more. Forty-five soldiers trail behind us. It's unfortunate that I'm riding. At least when I was walking I could distract myself by talking to those around me. Up here, the conversation is stilted.

Aquin sits to my right. "When we enter the village, it will be best to—"

"Secure the food stores." Each village had one, but it would be guarded. "And then address the people."

Jovan rides on my other side. "She knows what she's doing, old man."

There's a pause. "I see that she does."

Aquin had heard my recount of life on Glacium, but he hasn't had time to see how I've changed. I hope we have a long time to get to know each other again.

"Perhaps the girl who left is not the woman who has come back," Jovan is saying.

"How do you think we are best to contain the force protecting the food stores?" I ask Aquin. I don't want him to feel like I don't need him. And I want Jovan and Aquin to get on. Though I can't imagine Aquin ever liking a man I'm interested in—I remember how he used to glare at Kedrick.

He takes a few moments to answer. "The villagers are aware you are coming."

"They are?"

Aquin's cane whacks across my thigh at the question. I make no movement to show it affects me. Mainly because I can feel Jovan simmering on my other side.

"Rian has told you there is dissent," Aquin says.

"Well, yes," I admit. "But I haven't had much time to talk with him, with being stabbed and all."

"No excuse."

I roll my eyes. Of course not. "The situation," I ask.

"Tatum Avanna obliterated the first rebellion. Since then she has kept them weak so they have no energy to rise against her. There are those in each village who have kept in contact with myself and a select few others."

"Satum Jerrin," I ask.

"Correct."

"And…"

"The matron was one other. She was caught relaying a message on my behalf."

I close my eyes against the image of her decaying corpse. "So the villages expect me."

"They expect you. However, I was not certain of the Bruma's involvement. You will need to contain any panic. Not only do you need to convince your people you are a worthy choice, you must convince them to reserve judgment on a people who have always been considered their enemy."

"Veni," I curse.

The cane whacks down on my thigh again.

Jovan is off his mount and at Aquin's side. There's a snapping sound followed by the clatter of what I assume are the pieces of Aquin's newest cane, landing on the forest floor.

Aquin doesn't say a word. Jovan doesn't either as he swings back onto the dromeda to my left.

I look between them, but neither seems inclined to talk. "So," I begin hesitantly, "we have the villagers' ears already. Thank you, Aquin. I didn't realize the work you have done in my absence."

"I have done it since you were born," he says simply.

I turn my head to him.

"The Tatum has been losing her sanity for a long time. I knew this day would come," he clarifies.

Jovan speaks. His voice is tight, but he otherwise shows no sign of what just happened. "The villagers must see you, myself, and my men defeating the Tatum's force."

"And then your men will disperse the food," I add.

"When everyone has food, address them."

"It will be less threatening if your men are dispersed through the crowd, rather than standing in a bunch. We'll introduce them slowly."

Jovan wipes his forehead. "You're right. Shard?"

"Got it," Shard replies. He and Roscoe have been quietly plodding behind us.

"And make sure each of them knows if they harm the villagers in any way, they will meet the edge of my sword."

"Yes, my King."

"Roscoe?" I ask. "You have knowledge of my world. What is your opinion on how the villagers will react to Glacium's presence?"

He clears his throat. "I believe the villagers will be afraid of us no matter what you say, Tatuma Olina."

My heart sinks. I don't want to overthrow my mother for the sake of it. I want *peace* between our peoples.

"But," he says, "you must make them see that you, and an alliance with Glacium, is their best choice. They know what life with the Tatum is. They know what it is like to have Glacium as their enemy. You must offer them better and then deliver on your promises. Trust must be your goal. In time, trust will lead to love."

I twist atop the dromeda to look back. I can only see Roscoe's outline. "Thank you. That is sound advice."

It hasn't stopped my stomach from churning, but it has put an impossible task into possible lines.

My ears pick up the sound of people ahead of us.

My nausea soars to new levels. "Wait!" I gasp. "Stop!"

I slide down the side of the dromeda and race to the forest edge, hearing Jovan call after me. Hopefully out of sight, my veil pushed up, I systematically empty the contents of my stomach onto the ground. Every time I think of what I'm about to do, I'm attacked by another bout of gagging.

I groan and rest my head against the black trunk.

A warm hand rubs my back. "Lina, your people will accept you. It will be okay."

I spit out a mouthful of bile. A part of me wonders whether I should refrain from this in front of Jovan, but I figure he's seen me beaten to a pulp, so this won't rankle him. "If they don't?"

"Then I'll kill them."

I laugh shortly. "That's always your answer."

"It always will be where you're concerned. Feel better?"

My stomach has settled. I sigh. "This is one of those things that will feel horrible until it's over."

A large palm appears to my right. I grip the hand, pushing my veil down with the other hand. Jovan grabs at the material. "I want a kiss."

I lean away and pry his fingers off my veil. "I just vomited. We are *not* kissing." I have limits.

"You think I care?"

"I think *I* care," I retort.

He groans. "Fine. Then let's do this damn thing."

I walk back to our mounts in the king's wake, echoing him softly.

"Let's do this damn thing."

CHAPTER FIFTEEN

"THERE ARE FOUR," whispers Ice.

"Two guards at either end of the village," Blizzard says.

"Twenty in total," I mutter. The rest of the guards were stationed around the food stores. We had fifty. It shouldn't be a problem. The skill of our small force is high. That's not what has me stalling. My hands and chest wound are healed, but...

Sin whacks me on the back. "A good fight will get rid of those nerves. What are you worried about? The village men will back you just because you're hot."

Avalanche rumbles with suppressed laughter.

"It's possible that you've missed the fundamental differences between Bruma and Solati," I retort.

Ice sniggers. "Don't know what no fund'metals are, but Solati men don't go for the hot ones. The uglier a woman is, the more likely they'll want her! That's why no one wanted Frost."

It's my turn to muffle my laughter. "Where the hell did you hear that?" Bloody Bruma rumors.

"Sanjay told me," he replies indignantly.

A scuffle in the leaves behind us has me tensing. I'm worried about how I'll fight. I've become sorely unused to the limitations of the veil.

"King Jovan said to tell you he's in place," the watchman says.

I nod to the man and he disappears back into the vined trees.

The village is nestled in the midst of surrounding hills. Like all Osolis villages, a pathway winds through the middle. The thatched village houses are set farther apart than Glacium shelters. This is a fire control; a purposeful design so there's a small chance at containing any spot fires that might start. The clanging of a hammer beats rhythmically over the other side of the hill. A baby wails for its mother. The sounds of my people. But there is a difference. I sense it.

In my memory, villages were the unattainable happy place of my dreams. There is no laughter here. No playing children. No bustling mothers.

I can sense the despair as though it is a bad smell. The suffering is tangible in the air, choking me, and squeezing my throat in a tight grip.

The watchman should have reached the others by now.

"It's time."

The barracks men around me tense in anticipation. The thrill only the promise of a fight can bring. I'm going to protect what is mine. Finally, I will show my people what I've always wanted to show them.

That I would do anything for them.

We creep down the hill. I take the fore.

The stores are a tight black Kaur shed, designed to withstand the fires of the Fourth. Once inside, the space extends down into the ground. Not for a decrease in temperature as on Glacium; the underground springs prevent that. It's built this way to minimize the amount of Kaur trees needed to build the structure. If we cut down too many trees, it upsets the delicate balance of smoke. Kaur trees keep the air clear enough to breath.

I push everything from my mind as I near. The firelight from the Fourth, two rotations to our right, is at its brightest right now.

The outline of the storage is clear. Four men will be standing guard on each side, according to Rian and Olandon.

I stop attempting to see the guards and force my attention to what I can hear.

A shout goes up from Jovan.

"Charge!" I shout.

We sprint. The surrounding men yell their battle cries. The ringing of metal leaving the sheath sounds ahead of me and I draw my own twin swords in readiness. I rid myself of thoughts that I'm about to hurt my own Solati people. Sword meets sword as the two forces clash together in a rattling mess. I spin at the whistle of a blade. Shouts reach me from the other side. Aquin and Jovan will be there. Aquin, the Solati presence on the other side.

I slice behind a soldier's calves and hit them with the hilt of one sword. "Disarm only!" I scream. Solis knows I understand what it's like in the midst of battle. You forget yourself—and it's not always possible to disarm.

"I am your Tatuma," I shout. "Lay down your arms if you wish to live."

It's cruel, really. I've put them in an impossible position. They can fight me and probably die. Or they can lay down their weapons and die at the hands of the Tatum. Which by her reputation alone would be a much worse fate.

I get my answer when a punch catches me in the jaw.

Someone deals to my attacker as I roll to the side, cursing the veil for my throbbing face. *Heavy footsteps.* I leap to my feet and engage with another guard—a woman by the subtle curves of her. I kick her in the side of the head, but the air is forced from me as she crushes her fist into my side. My scar rips in protest. Distracted, I feel my uppercut miss its target. Shard gets between us and I give him space to fight the woman, rubbing my chest.

Yells echo to my left.

Two of the Solati who were guarding the village entrance bear down on us. Avalanche grabs both and smashes their heads together.

The barracks are burning for a fight; the Tatum's force hardly lays a finger on them. Even the fifteen other watchmen with me are throwing themselves at the guards. A tedious trip through the Oscala has added to their eagerness for action.

Recognizing there are more capable fighters than myself right now, I survey the area while the others incapacitate the guards. There is still clanging from the other side.

"Report," I pant as the fight dies down.

Blizzard answers, panting. "Two of ours, injured. One of theirs, dead. Ten Solati soldiers accounted for."

That's our half of the job done.

"Restrain the living soldiers," I instruct.

I approach the storage unit just as Jovan comes running around the corner. He slows when he sees me.

"You're all right?" He circles me.

I'm doing my own stock take of him. He doesn't limp or stagger. His voice is strong. He's unharmed. "Yes, the chest wound gave me a little trouble. And fighting with the veil on is much stranger than it used to be." I frown. "But my hands held up okay. I just need to build my stamina."

He gives a terse nod. I want to touch him, but anyone could be watching. That's all we need—for my people to guess the king of Glacium and their Tatuma are involved. Jovan knows this and, for once, keeps his distance.

I wonder if what we share will survive this secrecy, or if our relationship will dwindle and die. I've always known the risk. That giving him my heart could merely result in more ache, and bitter hurt. I can't bring myself to regret it.

"We need a key," the king says, tracing a hold on the shed.

A jingle and limping footsteps. I hold out my hand to Aquin and he places the key on my palm.

"Get everyone back from the doors. If any villagers are watching, I want them to see," I murmur to my trainer.

We place the food on tables in the middle of the village. The dry area is devoid of any life aside from the stream of Bruma watchmen passing food out from the deep storage shed.

My people are watching. Deciding. I wait outside by the filling tables before realizing they won't come out while the Bruma are here. Instead, I enter the stores and bask anew at the smoked meat, preserved fruits, and barrels of vegetables crammed into the space. There's enough in here to feed Jovan's entire army for months.

"What was the point of this?" Shard asks.

I stare at the barrels of potatoes around me. "It's the careful planning of insanity. There is no point, no logic."

Three tables groaning with the stores are laid out when I exit the building. The watchmen mill around the tables, eyes bulging at the sight before them. It is mainly vegetables and fruit—we're not big meat eaters, though I ordered meat to be brought out. Meat helped Olandon regain strength after the Oscala. I know it will be good for my people. Still, regardless of the greenery on the table, the men stare. They've been on army rations for weeks. And Jovan has issued strict orders that none of the Bruma are to touch the food.

"They won't come out while the Bruma are here." Aquin hobbles toward me.

I give a short nod. "Malir, I will need you to draw the men back. Far back. Only myself, Aquin, and King Jovan will remain."

He hesitates, then sighs. "Yes, Tatuma." Poor Malir. The stress of trying to protect Jovan and I must be exhausting.

I listen to the sound of my order spreading through the clearing. What if my people don't come? What if they've already decided not to give me a chance? If I was starved for months and saw a table full of food, I wouldn't trust it either. This isn't going to work.

"They will come, my Lina," Aquin soothes, sensing my turmoil.

Barely-there footsteps approach.

"The barbarian wears a shirt for the first time," Aquin mutters.

I strain to see Jovan through the veil. A giggle bursts out of me when I do. "Doesn't help much," I answer. The shirt is pulled tight over the muscles of his chest. He stands towering above both of us and it calls to the fore my memory of when we first met. Jovan was the most terrifying man I'd ever seen. The king's menace lay in the air surrounding him. Putting on a shirt did nothing to help.

I approach the table and select an apple. My mouth waters, but my stomach rolls. I'm too nervous to eat. I quickly put it back down.

Jovan rests his hand on the hilt of his sword. I frown at the weapon.

"Your mother has quite the food stores," he growls.

I remain silent. There's nothing to say on the matter. My mother wants Glacium. We suspected before, and now we've seen the evidence of her careful rationing. I'd be pissed off, too.

The veil flutters with a small breeze and panic rises in my throat. "They're not coming," I choke.

"Then they won't eat," Jovan says simply. "I know what choice I'd make."

"I don't think your weapon is helping. You should take it off."

"The weapon stays," he replies calmly.

"But—"

A cooing noise grabs my attention.

What on Solis? "Is that a—"

"A baby," Aquin finishes, sounding just as confused as I do.

The baby's gurgling draws closer and the tension in the air grows to palpable levels. Who does this baby belong to? They must be terrified.

"It's going to fall over," Jovan says.

I take a step forward, but Jovan lunges and swoops the child up.

"Is it hurt?" I ask.

Jovan grunts. "No, but I'm not sure how it is still alive."

"What do you mean?" I hold out my hands for the child.

He places the baby in my arms, and I take the too-light weight from him. This cannot be a child. The baby's face is so gaunt it looks more skull than face. She must only be a year old, though it is hard to tell with how malnourished her life has likely been. I could be looking at a much older child. I stroke the squirming girl's head and watch, numb, as a clump of her hair falls to the ground. The angles of the child's bones are so sharp that if I pressed down on the skin, I'm sure the bone would pierce through. Horror wracks through me as I see just how much my people have suffered.

The child needs food.

"You didn't see how starved the villager was? The one who provided the mounts?" Jovan asks softly.

I hold out the baby to him, which he takes with awkward hands. "No," I reply.

Without waiting for him to say more, I turn to the table and select some dried fruit. I can't talk about it. How is this child still alive? I should have come sooner.

Wailing comes from the emaciated form in Jovan's huge arms. It is a terror that will haunt my sleep forever.

"You should take it." Jovan foists the crying child my way.

I take the baby carefully. I've handled children hundreds of times and yet never held a child so breakable. Bringing a small piece of dried fruit to my mouth, I force my mouth to chew until it is a pulpy mess and spit it into my hand.

"I'm going to feed you, little one." I coo over her tears, rocking gently. "Jovan, dab a bit on her lips."

"How can you tell it's a girl?"

"The usual way. Do it now, please." I need to feed her. The sound of her cry tugs at something primal within me.

He takes some of the pulpy chewed food and ever so gently dips his finger on the tiny mouth.

The wailing stops. And suddenly the starved baby finds energy. Her face contorts as she sucks at Jovan's finger. He hurriedly returns with more. The baby arches towards him and Jovan chuckles, but there's no room for laughter in me, only heartbreak. And fury.

You can torture me, you can kill my friends, but to hurt a child is the most depraved act of two worlds. I am going to stab my mother in the heart. Over and over again.

"Lina, they're coming." The king's hushed whisper rouses me.

I spin slowly. Unlike earlier, my eyes are adjusted to the veil's limitations. My chest tightens in agony as I see their frames. They creep from the trees and homes in dragging steps. They don't trust that I am here to help them, but it is almost as though they don't have the energy to care.

I cannot spot a single posture in the exhausted skeletons of my people that suggests anything other than desolation.

They've given up on everything but breathing.

A burning lump rises in my throat and though I can't force it back, I do not let it rise to a sob. And the reason is simple: my people are not crying, and they are starving. I have not earned the right to cry on their behalf.

Aquin squeezes my arm. "You must speak, my child."

I cradle the child in my arms and collect myself. The dry area is utterly quiet, and though they are hardly alive, the Solati do not touch the food.

"I'm sorry," I say. The mournful sound echoes and I don't hide the emotion from my voice, though it will never be enough. Words cannot describe this. It can only be felt. It can only haunt.

"I'm here now. To put a stop to your... suffering. I want you to eat now. Please do not eat too much." My voice gains in strength. "It will make you sick after so long without proper nourishment." I blink down at the tiny girl once more. "I want you to take all the food, to distribute it among yourselves. If more is needed, you will have it."

They don't make a sound.

"Please eat," I beg. My voice cracks. I stare at the ground, hands gripping the now sleeping babe.

A shuffling begins. I don't look up as the villagers drag forward, some moaning with the effort. I see their bare feet from the corner of my eye, but still do not lift my head. I keep it down. In shame for what my mother has done.

CHAPTER SIXTEEN

I DO NOT ADDRESS them that day. I wouldn't have addressed them for two weeks if possible. But the other villages are suffering.

This morning, I'd called five Bruma from our party back to the village to assist those in the homes too weak to get food. By the afternoon, I'd called in ten more. Now, around thirty Bruma stand throughout the assembled villagers. There's almost an equal number of Bruma and Solati. Something never before seen in a peaceful setting. And my people are simply unresponsive to them, too tired to fear them. It's a cruel advantage for us. It allows the watchmen to care for the villagers without protest. It allows them to be painted favorably. And I almost wish my people would show some fight. Anything but this despondency. I have to remind myself of the weeks it took Olandon to recover after crossing the Oscala. The villagers have starved for much longer.

I stand partway up a hill to allow my voice to travel over the gathered people. Adox's words come back to me—about trusting that I am the best hope for my people. My mouth sets. And I realize, I do trust this. I am their hope. I am their salvation. I will be the one to restore their happiness. It falls on me alone.

Some of my people are near collapse. This isn't a time for an elaborate speech.

"I have come back to Osolis to end Tatum Avanna's tyranny." My voice cuts through the morning smoke. I picture my mother's face: the cruel twist of her lips, the blackness of her soul. "She has put you through unspeakable hardships, ones I can only begin to imagine."

The veil wavers with the breeze. "I have been at the mercy of her depravity my whole life. You are all aware of this. And now I will tell you why." I grip the end of the veil and the crowd makes their first movement. It is not toward me in eagerness to see. My people rear back in panic, away from me and certain death. I revel in the sign because it shows there is some form of self-preservation left in them.

I raise my voice. "You will see that the Tatum's hate of Glacium is built on hypocrisy and lies."

This is the heaviest the veil has ever felt. But I am the strongest I have ever been. The veil is nothing.

It floats to the ground.

I gaze up at my people. Face-to-face for the first time.

And I watch, clear-sighted, as their eyes widen. As confusion vibrates through them. As a shock so deep runs through them that they expend what energy they have on turning to their neighbor and sharing their bewilderment. They whisper; they stare.

In this way they are very similar to the Bruma—just quieter. In Glacium terms, they are screaming and pointing.

I hold up my hands, palms up. "I have blue eyes. Tatuma Avanna has kept a grave secret from you all. This, along with her insanity and greed, is why she starves you. Because she wants this secret to *remain* a secret. She wants to continue this *lie*." I twist my face. "To punish you all for her mistakes. To starve your children."

I walk down the hill. "I won't let her," I shout. "The Tatum will pay for her heinous crimes. I promise I will see it done. I will restore Osolis to greatness. You will no longer need to live in fear!"

I reach Jovan and take his hand, turning around to show the villagers. "See here! The Tatum tells us the Bruma are our enemy. But who is here now? Caring for you, feeding a baby with his own hands?" The Fourth fire burns within me. "I want true peace! Between *all* races in both worlds. I want harmony, and an end to the madness."

I climb the hill. "It is time that the Solati people stop paying for the Tatum's greed with the skin off their backs! Rise with me!" A tingling shivers over my body. "Rise with me! And I will offer you your salvation on both knees."

And so I, the only blue-eyed Tatuma in history, become the first royal Solati to lower onto both knees, head bowed, prostrate in front of her people.

And there is no sound for a long time. Until there is a small commotion.

I raise my head and see that one man is struggling downward. Blizzard rushes to aid the man who, panting, pushes up onto his knees. I doubt my barracks friend has spared a thought for how he currently looks: a Glacium man fallen on his knees to help a Solati.

Aquin lowers gracefully to his knees, hand over his heart. "I will lay down my life for you, Tatum Olina." *Tatum Olina*. The name shocks me. Hardly different from Tatuma, but so different in meaning.

Others are falling to their knees, Solati and Bruma alike. They murmur "Tatum Olina" and the sound disturbs me because it is not true, yet—not until I've fulfilled my promises. Only then will I lay claim to the title.

The king of Glacium holds out his hand. I meet his eyes and am consumed with the pride, the respect, and the intensity of his love for me. He has helped me become who I am, though he doesn't see it. Loving him has led to this moment and given me strength.

He pulls me up gently, and in front of all, he bows low over my hand and lays a whisper of a kiss on the back of my hand. Then he rises, and rises, until he is straightened to his full height. The people below us watch him with wary eyes.

"Tatum Olina has earned my unwavering loyalty during her time on Glacium. I am honored to align my kingdom with hers. And I pledge that no harm shall come to you from the hands of my people. I want as your Tatum does—as *you* do. To live in peace; for ourselves, our children, and for our children's children!" He dips his head. "You have my solemn word as king."

I squeeze the hand he still holds. "Please help my people to their feet," I direct the Bruma. "They need food and rest. All village duties are postponed until further notice. You must focus on recovering your strength. A small force of King Jovan's men will be left at your disposal. You will have access to all the food you need."

Hands linked, we watch our people help each other. And it is the most beautiful thing I will ever be privileged enough to see.

At our lowest moments we recover the essence of who we are.

CHAPTER SEVENTEEN

"*B*UT HOW GOOD was that baby crawling out?" Sin drawls.

Ice shakes his head. "I know! We were screwed seven ways with a whore before that."

Sin inspects his fingers. "Some might say, it was perfect timing."

I narrow my eyes at the handsome man resting against the trunk of a Kaur. Shard beats me to it.

"You didn't," he says.

Sin blinks in innocence.

Shard glances at me with uncertainty. "He couldn't have… could he?"

The man from Tricks's barracks stands with a yawn in the thatch home. His abdominal muscles leap into action. "I never have liked words like 'couldn't' and 'didn't.' They imply lines. I'm not overly fond of lines."

"You put the baby there," I say flatly.

Blizzard spits his food over Avalanche, who punches him in the face. Blizzard keels over against the wall. I see Aquin watch the exchange with interest.

"I wouldn't say I *put* the baby there. I just helped it to the food."

A dagger flies passed Sin's cheek and embeds in the straw behind him.

He holds out his hands to the threatening gleam in Shard's hand. Another five or so daggers dangle from the advisor's belt.

"I took her from her sleeping mother and gave her a shove in the right direction." He glares at me. "And I saved your ass." His gaze flickers down. "Which, can I just say, is very distracting under your robes."

I stop myself from bursting out with laughter. Just. Does he think of nothing else? And he's right. He did save my ass. In the pits, I learned from the best showman. And that showman was Sin. His instincts are infallible—but he doesn't need to know that. A head can only get so big before it explodes. I don't break my stare with Sin as I tilt my head. "What do you guys reckon?"

The handsome man preens under the attention of the men in the room, but noticeably gulps as the grim expressions surrounding him sink in.

"You aren't serious?" He backs up as Avalanche stands.

Wrath, turned Warren, also rises with an evil grin.

"About what?" I say, matching his earlier innocence.

Sin disappears from sight underneath a tangle of limbs.

The Fifth Rotation is next.

Jovan pushes us hard to reach the next village. With the state of the last village, every hour we wait another person will die. We left ten watchmen back in the Sixth Rotation for protection. I just hope it's enough. I hate to think we might have given the villagers hope, just for my mother to rip it away.

Securing the Fifth is just as heartbreaking and stirring as the Sixth. Mother's men are locked in the storage shed, and Bruma fill the tables with food.

I feed them, and show my face.

Breaking the news of what I am has been easier than I expected. It is Aquin I should thank. He's paved the way for me to overthrow Mother with his numerous contacts spreading the word. Gaining the support of the villagers never would've been so straightforward without Aquin's groundwork. He said he'd been doing so since my birth.

I slide down beside the king of Glacium where he lays sprawled out under a tree. The shade offers no respite from the heat. Most of the Bruma are strewn around, finding themselves overwhelmed by the intensity of the temperature this close to the Fourth fires.

I steel myself. "I'm going to get Aunty Jain."

The king rolls to his side and I watch the power in his limbs with longing… and, my heart tells me, the same distance present since I first set eyes on Osolis. Though we joked about talking, neither of us has made a move to do so. It seems pointless now. If I ever entertained for a second that I could forgo saving my people, the notion disappeared when I saw their emaciated forms and the lack of hope in their eyes.

I am the future Tatum, and Jovan is king of his own people. I will always do whatever he asks of me. And he will do the same for me. And maybe that is all we can be. Though a part of me yearns for more, the same part also wishes he cared about the gulf between us.

Does he experience the same fear as our love slips through our hands like water?

"Lead the way," he says. He stretches out a hand to my lower back. Something he would've done without thought before. Jovan stops the movement, just before we touch.

The moment grows heavy. I swallow thickly. "Olandon told me where. This way."

The vines are yet to grow back from the recent passing through the Fourth fires, so we walk with ease. My aunt lives not far from the village, in the tree line. From what Olandon could glean, a villager is paid to bring her food, cook, and clean the house. I don't know what to expect. My aunt is damaged. But how much? Will she recognize me? Would she recognize my father? I want to see her. But, I frown at the ground under my feet. It is more that I wish for an answer. I'd given up wanting this answer when my mother had the young girl's throat slit before my eyes… but I dearly wish to know.

Why did my mother choose not to love me? She did not have to hate me. She could have sacrificed all to love me. But she did not.

Why?

"Are you prepared?" Jovan asked as we approach the Kaur building.

It's ironic they've housed their prisoner in the most expensive resource. Did Cassius care for his wife? Doubt it.

I stand in front of the door, my kin on the other side—someone who could love me—and I realize I'm not ready. I push aside the strange distance between us and turn around, into Jovan's arms, begging without words for him to comfort me.

"My Lina," he breathes into my hair.

The wind is squeezed from me as I'm crushed to his chest. And I squeeze back, as hard as I can, with my arms around him. And slowly, the world is righted again.

I step back and take a heavy breath. And I knock on the Kaur wood door.

It's early evening. She should not be asleep. But then, my expectations of the elderly stem from watching Aquin. Maybe this isn't a good average to judge by.

Gathering my courage, I push through the door.

She is sitting at a table, sipping from a cup.

She's as startled as I am for a moment. Then her face breaks into a smile. "Lina, how nice to see you."

Jovan grunts behind me and I want to do the same thing.

"Uh, hello, Jain. A-aunty Jain."

She claps her hands in glee as I shuffle closer. Jovan hovers in the doorway. He turns to leave and I throw him a panicked glance. No way is he leaving me here.

"The last time I saw you, you only said ba-ba-ba." Tears spark in her eyes and her mood sobers in seconds. She stares down at her hands and I follow her gaze to the scars there. Olandon has told me he believes she was tortured until her mind broke.

I crouch beside her and take her hand. "Aunty Jain, I do not remember it. I was too young. But I hope you can tell me more. I have come to take you away. If you will come with me."

She lifts her arms and throws them around my neck. The woman is surprisingly strong. I gasp and shift into a position where I can get air. She pulls back and I startle at the fierceness on her face.

"You are taking the throne, just as you always should have." She brushes my hair back. "My girl, how you have suffered. And I'm sorry I wasn't there to protect you."

My mouth goes dry. "You did more for me than my mother ever did," I croak.

She smiles sadly. "Yes, my spark. And that is not how life should be."

Tears flood my eyes.

"I will need my teapot," she says. I wrench back as Cassius's wife jerks away.

Jovan, still silent, crosses the room and helps me to my feet. We watch in amazed perplexity as my aunt busies herself collecting various random and large, impractical objects.

Jovan's eyes are often on me as I lead Jain back through the forest. I cannot take my eyes from my aunt. She displays more than a dozen different emotions on the dawdling walk, but in all of them she loves me. She consoles me and sings my praises.

This woman no longer has a mind. And yet I wish she was my mother.

The Ire and Glacium back me. Now two villages have listened to what I have to say. I have found acceptance and love in the unlikeliest places. As I guide my aunt into the thatched home where I will also sleep, something clicks into place—a way of thinking and a belief that had been missing up until now. When I dreamed of ruling Osolis as a child, I always pictured myself ruling alone, simply because that is how my life was. For months my new goal has been to rule without secrecy. It was my first step toward happiness.

It's as though now that the villagers appear to be on my side, and I have friends and my aunt, I'm able to contemplate happiness as more than a dream and a wish.

For the first time, I consider the possibility of a life where I'm not alone.

I know how to be happy and what it will take.

I just have to find the courage to permit myself to have it.

CHAPTER EIGHTEEN

"*O*UR VULNERABILITY LIES in the food stores being spread over five sectors. We need to allocate time to move the stores to one area. To protect them."

Roscoe nods at Jovan's comment. "Drummond has reported that they were able to secure the food shed in this rotation, but the shed is empty."

Olandon speaks from the entrance to the tent. What is left of our party arrived back at the First Rotation camp this morning. "The Tatum wouldn't have left food within easy grasp."

"The Second Rotation will have been emptied of food also?" Jovan asks my brother.

Olandon arches a brow at Rian.

Rian answers. "This is likely, King Jovan of Glacium. Our strategists will be prepared for a siege in the worst-case scenario."

"But why didn't they empty all the stores?" I wonder.

"There wasn't time," Shard answers. "Not long passed between their presence on Glacium and our presence here. Not when you are looking at shifting hundreds of people and the resources needed for survival."

I hum noncommittally. "It's almost like she's giving the food to us. Was it meant to lure us into false security? And why would she want us to drop our guard?"

"You believe there is more to this?" Roscoe asks.

"Avanna is involved, so it's safe to assume Olina is right," Jovan replies.

I smile at him and he doesn't return the gesture.

He taps a finger on the map before him. "We also need to shift the villagers to safety."

"The Sixth should do," Olandon says. "That way, if we are chased back to the First, the villagers will not come to harm."

Aquin peers sideways at me and I dip my head. He sees the changes in Olandon. Such a sentence would never have been uttered by my brother before he left Osolis.

"Roscoe, Drummond," Jovan barks. "See that it is done."

"My King," they murmur before leaving.

Jovan looks over his hand at me. His fist is in front of his mouth. How I long to press my lips to his. I glance up from the softness and see a glint of humor in his blue eyes. It's been a while since I've seen it.

"There will be little choice but to march on Rotation Three once the food is secured. The longer we wait, the more we cut into our supplies," he says.

"The Ire can provide more," I say.

He rubs a hand over his bottom lip and I watch. "Not for fifteen hundred men." His mouth quirks into a smile.

My eyes fly to his... Is he doing that on purpose?

He arches an eyebrow. He is!

I catch an irritated eyebrow twitch from Aquin and clear my throat. "You're right." I lean forward and trace my finger around Osolis's perimeter on the map. "This will be the best way to go. Around the outer edge, fanning inward. If we go to the center first, there is a risk they could cut us off by moving through the bush. Landon?"

"Agreed," my brother states.

"Rian," I call.

"Tatum," he answers. I try not to show my surprise.

"What is your guess as to the strength of Avanna's army?" I ask. I listen as he gives me his closest guess, berating myself for asking a question. Maybe I *should* give Aquin another cane. I've fallen into bad habits. Habits I love. But bad habits, nevertheless. I have enough going against me without offending every Solati I encounter with misplaced questions.

"There are those in the palace we can rely upon," I say.

Rian's eyes shift. "If they are still alive, Tatum Olina, then yes. But I have no way of knowing if they are."

"Very well. Thank you."

He bows and exits with Olandon. I raise a finger to Aquin and he nods once before leaving as well. Now *that*, I have missed.

"We're really doing it," I say to fill the silence.

Jovan watches me, his eyes running over my frame. Is that allowed while we aren't talking about all the stuff we should be talking about?

I stretch and push back my hair. It's dirty, and full of smoke. There's a reason I bathed every day. Eyes wide, I straighten.

Alarmed, Jovan does the same. "What is it?"

"The springs," I say with glee.

He frowns. "The underground ones?"

Not put off by his lack of enthusiasm, I race forward and grab his hand. "You haven't seen them yet."

"Probably because of the thing called *war* going on."

I snort. "But now we will have at least a week until our next move. Trust me, you need to see them."

He pulls his hand from mine. I glance up in confusion as he turns away from me. "Do not ask me to do that. I have seen enough. I cannot watch how happy this world makes you. And how I have no place in it."

His back is tense. Neck rigid. My mouth opens and shuts as I stare at him.

I should take the steps toward him. I should talk to him, now that he has opened the discussion.

But anything I could say would be a false reassurance, and just because I am brave in most things, doesn't mean I can be brave now.

I choose the coward's path, running from him and leaving the man I love alone.

I walk as quickly as I can without alarming the men that something is amiss. Even now, when everything with Jovan is in turmoil, part of my mind is still on what our problems could symbolize to the rest of his army. Bruma and Solati need to be seen working together. Jovan and I should be acting like we are more in love than ever. But Jovan would never agree to such a subterfuge while things between us are… whatever they are.

Oberon and Ochave sit outside their tent watching the watchmen work with wide eyes. Their tent is nestled next to mine and Olandon's. The twins will provide the perfect distraction from the pain in my chest.

"Ochave, Oberon," I call. My heart swells as both of their heads whip towards my voice. I sink to my knees and gather them in my arms. Oberon relaxes into my embrace, but is pulled back by Ochave.

I blink at the more boisterous of the twins. What was that for?

Ochave's jaw is set, and some unspoken communication passes between the twins before the inquisitive twin in my arms pulls back, too, avoiding my gaze.

What is happening? I wrack my brain and can only guess they have been told I'm half-Bruma and what it means. Why else would they be acting strangely? I decide to ignore the moment. The way Ochave is scowling at me, he won't be able to keep his silence for long.

"I have blue eyes," I say.

Oberon will leap at the chance to ask me a million things about them. Sure enough, his brown eyes alight and he opens his mouth, but in the next instant stark terror flashes on his young face and his mouth snaps closed with a click.

Ochave's hand is clamped down on Oberon's forearm. In warning? What has happened to them? For the first time, I scan them from head to toe. I push aside my memories of how they *should* appear, and I truly look. I creep closer, scanning Oberon with precision.

By the time I see the scars, I'm almost nose-to-nose with my young brother.

Little dots are arranged systematically, outside his top lip. In horror, I trace the dots around his mouth, seeing that they continue underneath the bottom lip, too. I sit back on my heels. What instrument could have caused this?

From the way both boys are sitting frozen in terror—I can see the erratic leaping of the pulse in Oberon's neck—and Ochave is so protective of his twin, it's obvious. Someone has hurt them. With a shaking hand, I reach out and stroke the scars. Oberon doesn't flinch, but large tears build in his wide, brown eyes.

"What happened to you?" I croak.

His eyes shift to Ochave, who shakes his head emphatically. "Don't answer it. It's a trick."

The tears track down Oberon's face. "But it's *Lina*."

Ochave regards me with crossed arms and a scowl. "Yeah. And she left us."

Hurt rocks through my chest. They think I left them? I draw closer, shaking my head. "I never left you. I love you both. I was taken. And—"

"You didn't take us with you," Oberon says to the ground.

My throat tightens so much that I have to force out the words. "I didn't have a choice." I probably wouldn't have, anyway. At the time I'd believed I was traveling to my death. Mother hated *me*. They should have been safe here.

Ochave's hand creeps out to Oberon and I watch, heart sinking, as the boys console each other wordlessly.

"I will not hurt you for talking. I will never hurt either of you. I am your sister. I've only ever loved you. I will always love you both." I swallow. "If you will share it with me, I would like to know what happened."

Ochave still shakes his head, but Oberon gazes straight at me, ignoring the persistent shaking of his hand from his twin. "I asked too many questions."

I allow my bafflement to show.

Ochave leans across, blocking me from Oberon. "No one but us. We said, no one but us," he whispers.

His words break me into a thousand pieces. My playful Ochave has learned to shut others out to survive. It's a lesson I protected Olandon from my whole life, yet I could not save the youngest of my siblings.

"Chave, it's okay. She has an army here to kill Mother."

I saw nothing wrong with the words, but knew they displayed how twisted our childhoods had been.

Ochave hovers, not convinced. He sighs and turns to me. The sound is foreign coming out of a seven-year-old's mouth. "Uncle Cassius must die, too," he says.

A dangerous calm settles over me, subtle and promising. I understand in that moment that no matter how long it takes, that even if I lost all of my limbs, I would somehow drag myself back from death, across two worlds to kill my uncle because he has hurt my boys.

"He will die. Painfully," I promise.

Ochave nods and sits back, giving me a view of my smaller-framed brother once more.

His brown eyes are flat. "I asked too many questions, so Uncle sewed my lips shut."

I've had many moments when I've struggled to keep a reaction from my face. This is the hardest of them all. My face muscles work to remain smooth, and the simple fact that they're doing this will show I'm trying not to react. The calm anger within me does not change. I will obliterate Cassius from the face of Osolis.

It appears that this is all Oberon has to say; however, words burst from Ochave's lips like a dam has broken.

"For an entire week," he cries. "And I couldn't see him. He couldn't eat, or drink. And when they took the string out, he screamed and screamed." Ochave covers his ears, drawn back to the horrific memory.

I can't speak. I don't speak. I just crawl to my brothers and draw them into my arms. Oberon comes willingly, melted into my embrace. But Ochave throws off my grip and dashes from the tent space. He disappears into the crowds of Jovan's army.

That makes two people disappointed in me today.

I suppress a sigh and hold my more forgiving brother tight. "Oberon, I'm so sorry I wasn't here for you." *I should have come back sooner.*

He pulls back. "You don't call me Beron anymore."

I stroke his black curls back. "I wasn't sure if you wanted me to."

He smiles gently. "You can call me Beron."

I look at the faint, hardly there scars around his mouth. "And you can call me Lina." I kiss his cheek.

"I better go check on Chave," he says.

I nod without words and let him free of my arms. He looks at me once more, still expecting everything to be ripped from him, and turns to follow his twin.

And when he has moved out of sight, I push wearily to my knees, determined to make it to my tent before I cry my heart out.

CHAPTER NINETEEN

"**W**E CAN ONLY allow one hundred of our men to stay behind and protect the villagers, my King," Drummond says. "It is my recommendation the Ire force also remain here for the time being. They will be able to catch up once the main force reaches the Third Rotation. We won't have to carry as many supplies, and it will provide extra security to the villagers in the meanwhile."

This last week has seen the Bruma shift all stores to the First Rotation, alongside the trickling evacuation of the villagers from the Fifth and Sixth Rotations. In my first plans to gain control of Osolis, I counted on the villagers joining the battle on my side. But they are far too weak.

They arrive empty-handed, without a spark of hope on their faces.

Time will tell them if I am worthy.

"Any further reports from the scouts?" Jovan gestures to Malir.

Instead of my usual seat, I sit to one side, between Adox and Aquin. Thinking of Aquin reminds me of my sore muscles. He's been quick to show me my Glacium training was lacking, conveniently forgetting about my brush with death months before. Every time I rub the scar on my chest, he makes me do fifty agonizing push-ups; however, I can't deny I feel better than I have in months. Aquin's methods are mean, but they work.

Malir stands tall and stares straight ahead. "No, my King. Scouts report zero disturbances from the Second. Though half of the scouts who ventured over the river to the Third did not return."

Aquin shakes his head.

I agree. It was a waste of men. My mother is in the Third. There's no need to send more men to die to confirm the fact.

"I still cannot decide if Avanna simply wishes to cut us off from retreat, or she has some other plan," Adox muses beside me.

His words are lost amongst the multiple conversations in the tent. But his question is the most pertinent of them all. I share a dark look with the Ire leader. Bruised circles discolor the wrinkled skin under the older man's tired eyes. His eyes flicker past me to Aquin and Adox narrows them before glancing away.

My eyebrows furrow as I send Aquin a searching glance.

Adox doesn't like Aquin? They have not met before now. Solis knows Aquin didn't welcome everyone, but I would've imagined he and the Ire leader would get on well.

Identical curly black heads duck into the tent, the yells of their pursuers close behind. The twins pull at my hands, both talking at once.

I close my eyes against their combined—and unintelligible—protests. "Shh, Beron, Ochave. I cannot hear a word you say. Tell me what is wrong."

Two panting watchmen hover at the entrance of the tent. The twins both try to speak at once, stopping when I hold up a hand. I give Oberon a pointed look.

"We're going to the Sixth." His words are accusing.

The twins will be staying in the Sixth with Jain and the villagers during the battle. I shift uncomfortably and glare at the two watchmen.

"Aunty Jain told them," one grunts. My aunt has quickly endeared herself to the entire camp.

Aunty Jain is a constant source of confusion to me. My hair has never been stroked so much, my forehead never kissed so often. Rather than find it consoling, I find myself uncomfortable with the loving touches. They pick at some deep wound only a mother could affect. It makes me angry I never had this woman's love, and saddened she was so badly mistreated because of what I am.

I crouch in front of the twins. "You'll be safe there. You cannot come into battle with me. I can't protect you there."

"You can't protect us if you're not there, either!" Ochave shouts.

I sit back on my feet and study the boy. "You wanted me to kill Uncle Cassius. That is no longer true."

Hamish gasps on the other side of Adox.

Ochave kicks his feet. "No, I want you to kill him."

"If you want me to do that, I cannot also be worrying about your safety."

"We want you to stay, Lina," Oberon chokes.

My eyes burn and I blink rapidly. I dart a look at Olandon, who shrugs. "You can't have both. And I have a promise to keep." I stare at Ochave until he meets my eyes. "Cassius must pay for what he did to Beron, remember?"

His chin wobbles. "Will you hurt him bad?"

"He will never take another breath once I am done with him. And that is not nearly enough for his crimes."

Ochave curls his fingers into tight fists. His face hardens as he looks at his brother. "He sewed Beron's mouth shut." There are further gasps. Ochave approaches me, drawn to his full height. "I want him to feel *pain*."

I don't break away from Ochave's gaze.

But it is Olandon who answers. "He will regret what he has done before his death. I swear this to you, brother. I also have a score to settle with our uncle."

Ochave dips his head toward his elder brother. "And we will come with you," he tries.

I sigh just as Aunty Jain slides into the tent. She smiles brightly at the boys. "There you are! Bothering your sister." She sidles over to me. "Well met, my love." She lands a warm kiss on my temple before stroking my long hair.

I stir in my chair, determined not to flinch away from her ministrations. A snigger breaks out and I glare at Shard across the room. He doesn't stop.

"We're coming," the twins declare.

I untangle myself from Jain and lead the twins outside. The warm breeze brushes over me and I crouch down to their level. "Aunty Jain needs you."

My brothers stare back.

I try to make them understand. "Cassius treated our aunt badly. He hurt her like he hurt Beron, but he treated her much, much worse. He broke her," I say sadly. "I need some people I trust to care for her while I'm away."

They share a curious look. A silent exchange only the twins could understand.

"I need you both to do this. Can I depend on you?" I press.

Ochave purses his lips, and Oberon raises a brow. Whatever happens in that moment, they both turn to me a second later with determined expressions.

I squeeze their shoulders. "Thank you, brothers."

"You will be back." Oberon's voice wobbles.

I gather them both and wish with my entire being that what I say will prove true. "I will be back for you both."

I re-enter the tent and cross to my seat. I'm bothered after the discussion with the twins and don't immediately pick up that an odd silence has fallen over the tent.

"You are just as handsome as you were all those years ago," Jain is giggling. "I hope you still sing."

My entire being freezes. Not just inside, but outside too. And I cannot shift my eyes her way.

I stare, wide-eyed, at Aquin. Watching him for a sign. A giveaway. Does this mean what I think it means?

Then Aquin nods. And I understand that I wasn't waiting for a clue; I was waiting for his acceptance. His permission to see who my father is. For reassurance that I'm ready and that the time is right.

I also understand that it doesn't matter that Drummond might be my father. Because my real father sits in front of me. The man who taught me everything and made me strong at the risk of losing his life.

Aquin will always be my father.

So I turn.

And my world comes to a standstill when I see who Aunty Jain is speaking to.

CHAPTER TWENTY

I'D ALWAYS THOUGHT his voice had a harmonious timbre to it. I'd even discussed it with him long ago.

But the suspicion that Roscoe was my father had never occurred to me. He had a family.

I stare across the room at Adnan's father. And he stares back at me, though Jain continues to fuss over him and chatter.

He has a family.

Several things click into place. His fatherly attitude toward me; his interest in seeing my face; the odd moment in the cave before Adnan left.

Adnan hadn't known before that moment!

"Adnan," I say hoarsely. It is the only word I can say.

Roscoe appears to be having similar difficulty. "Is your brother," he stutters.

"You had a family." I cannot help the accusatory tone I adopt. That's why Olandon hadn't added Roscoe's name to the list, after all. He hadn't added any delegates who were married.

"My wife died shortly before the delegation," he whispers.

I can see the memory pains him still. At least it removes the black mark against his character I was so quick to put there. Unanswered questions rise, but I cannot voice them. I am staring into his blue eyes. *My* blue eyes, I realize. My father.

I want to sob, or scream, or run and run until I cannot breathe any longer.

He steps forward and I take a trembling step back. "I did not know," he said. "Until you were in front of me, and I heard your supposed age, and then connected it to the reason you were veiled. I swear."

That happened that second day I entered the Glacium castle! When I first met him, *he* asked my age, but I never connected the question to my heritage because I discovered my blue eyes months later. Roscoe took pains to make sure I was taken care of early on in my stay. He'd softened the blow of Jovan's temper; he'd never pressured me to attend the ball, pulling Sanjay and his son, Adnan, into line when they'd hassled me. I gasp. This whole time I'd thought he was kind, but knowing he is my blood father turns the motives for these kindnesses to self-serving. "You knew the Tatuma was veiled—did you never wonder why?" I whisper. Now I tremble for a very different reason.

It can't be true. What about Adnan?

"I, along with most others, assumed it was because you were deformed. Your mother is vain; I could understand her trying to preserve her own image by concealing yours."

How could he say such a thing about someone he slept with? Even hating the Tatum as I do, his words display traits that make me sorry for the younger version of my mother.

He cannot tell me he never once wondered if the child—conveniently born after his delegation year—was his. I don't buy it. He had to have some suspicion.

Why did he never come for me?

I waited for him for ten years in that tower.

I want him to *understand* my pain. The tears balancing on the rims of his eyes are not enough for what I went through. Nothing will ever be enough for the loneliness and torture. It was too much for a child to bear! Can't he see that? He should have taken care of me!

A far part of my mind knows I'm not using reason. I'm letting emotion rule my head.

"Roscoe," Jovan says. "Leave us."

I close my eyes as my... *father* passes close to me. He doesn't touch me, and of this I am glad. My hands are clawed into a murderous hold. Aunty Jain squeezes my hand and bends close as she follows him out.

"You deserved to know, my sweet," she whispers.

I wrench my eyes open and am taken aback by the lucidity in her gaze. It is gone again the next moment as she twirls to the door.

The occupants of the tent stare at me. Roscoe's secret daughter. The Tatum's unwanted daughter. Mixed. Abandoned. Abused. I blink. I have another brother. It's the best part of the shit-heap that just got dumped on my head.

The thought of having a stronger tie to Adnan is welcome. And nerve-wracking. I wonder what he thinks of me, now that he knows of his father's long-kept secret.

A throat clears. I startle as Jovan begins to speak.

"Send out the order that the army leaves at first firelight," he says. There's a frantic scurry as everyone present tries to escape the awkwardness in the space.

I'm jostled as they leave. Aquin rests a hand on my shoulder briefly and I catch sympathetic looks from a few of my friends. Olandon approaches and gives me a tight hug, which I don't return.

Shock. I'm in shock.

And then Jovan guides me to his large chair and pulls me down onto his lap, holding me close.

"Did you know?" My voice is hollow.

"I suspected," he said. "Roscoe has acted strangely since you arrived."

"You didn't tell me."

He rests his chin atop my head. "If it were me, I would want to tell my daughter at the right time. And I was not completely certain. He did not confide in me."

I wonder if I should be angry that Jovan has kept this from me. But that would require the energy to fight, which I don't currently seem to have.

"Roscoe had so many chances to tell me and he didn't. He never told me. Not when he stood beside me at the first ball for a full half-hour telling me about the musical instruments. Not when I nearly vomited before revealing my face to the council. Not when I was obviously distressed about Drummond being my father."

"He's made a mistake. As we all do."

I squeeze my eyes shut. "I know I'm not being… rational about this. Do you think I'm overreacting?"

Jovan sighs and kisses the top of my head. "Olina, you have always been told to push your emotions to the side. Your whole life you've been told it is a weakness to feel. This is the first time I've seen you react the way most people would. Who cares if you're overreacting, or being irrational? No matter if Roscoe knew you were his or not before you came to Glacium, he sure as hell knew after. He can simmer in guilt for a while; bastard deserves it for being a coward. You can only feel the way you feel. If you need to blame Roscoe, or be disappointed, or bitter, or furious, then do it. Don't feel beholden to anyone because your mind wants to process this shit-heap a certain way."

Tears trickle down my cheeks as I register his words. I do want to scream and shout. And I am feeling guilty about it. What happened today has picked at a festering wound that isn't entirely Roscoe's fault. But maybe I need to do as Jovan has said and not try to rationalize how I feel. Honestly, this is one issue I don't think I can reason my way through. It's a new and uncomfortable feeling for me.

He doesn't press me to talk, and I don't. My mind is a flurry and I'm incapable of settling on one thread of thought.

My attention is stolen by Jovan's chest, which rests underneath my cheek. Then I notice his thighs underneath me. He clears his throat in an absent kind of way, not having noticed my turn of thought. The sound is low, and for some reason it reminds me just how much I need him. I lift my head and press my mouth against his in a fierce, all-consuming kiss. He's surprised at first, but catches on—he's always been quick, my Jovan. The kiss is breathless, frenzied, and leaves us both gasping.

"I want you," I say.

It's in his eyes. He wants me, too.

I wake up, bleary-eyed, to find a naked Jovan slumbering over the top of me. This is going to be the best part of my day, so I take my time memorizing the taut lines of his legs, torso, and arms, allowing myself to be lulled by the restful rise and fall of his chest. I trace his jaw with my eyes and remember last night.

Today we march.

I sit astride my mount, hours later, surrounded by the barracks and a few of the delegate members.

Adnan is not here. And I have not seen Roscoe. For now, I'm quite content to exist in denial. In fact, I cannot foresee a time where I will want to talk with Roscoe, or even scream at him, let alone try to understand and forgive him.

Luckily, I'm at the head of an army. It's nearly as good a distraction as the king of Glacium. He smiles at me today. Jovan isn't atop a dromeda, preferring to walk. But he turns often and I'm quick to return his looks with a shy smile of my own.

The meadow of the First stretches out before me, and I long to put my mount through her paces.

I trot up to Malir, who rides just behind his king. "Malir, have the scouts seen any sign of my mother's force?" I ask.

"Why?" he asks with narrowed eyes.

I grin. "I would like to gallop my mount through the meadow." I've named the dromeda Otari.

"Will she be safe?" Jovan asks.

Malir looks over the area. "I haven't been informed of any sightings."

It's the best answer I'll get from the over-cautious commander. I don't wait for Jovan's reply before I circle my steed and dig my heels into her sides. With a leap, she dances away from the army.

It is like something from a dream.

My hair fans behind me and I want to move faster. I flatten myself against the dromeda's back. And she pushes her neck forward as her hooves thunder at the cracked ground. I straighten and close my eyes—the irony doesn't escape me—to fully experience the moment. I throw my arms wide.

It isn't enough. Jovan's going to kill me.

Gathering my robes so they don't trip me, I push onto my knees, and then to a standing position, placing my feet below Otari's shoulders. The beast rocks side-to-side underneath me as the powerful muscles careen us through the tall grass at eye-watering speeds.

Freedom.

This is it. Fleeting as it always has been and ever will be. And it is for this reason these moments are precious beyond measure.

"Got that out of your system?" Sanjay asks wryly as I return.

The grin on my face is all the answer he needs.

He nods toward Jovan. "You gave your boyfriend over there a heart attack."

Sure enough, Jovan's back is tense. He worries too much. Standing on a mount's back is nothing I haven't done before. "He's not my boyfriend," I say instead.

"Oh?" Ice feigns casualness on my other side, but I can see he is dying to hear the gossip.

"The term 'boyfriend' just doesn't suit him," I explain.

Ice ponders this. "True."

"Manfriend?" Sanjay offers.

"Kingfriend?" Ice counters.

"There's a river ahead," Shard interrupts.

I throw him a grateful look. I'm sure Jovan overheard some of that. As well as anyone in a five-meter radius of my dromeda.

An alliance between Sanjay and Ice is something to be feared. But I can only blame myself for introducing them. Blizzard appears a little disgruntled as he glances between the two men. Now that Flurry is gone, Ice is the pit-fighter-turned-minister-of-the-people's closest friend. Sanjay's eyes twinkle as he watches Blizzard's jealousy.

The suspicion occurs to me that my orange-haired friend might be toying with the barrack member. Again.

…Not for much longer.

I twist to face the river ahead.

My brother catches my eye and we share a secret exchange, before hurrying to smooth our grins.

We've been waiting for this moment.

Poor Sanjay should have quit while he was ahead.

Each rotation on Osolis is separated by a river. The waterways were dug by my ancestors and extend from the edge of Osolis to the world's center: Lake Aveni. They are the only reason Solati have survived across hundreds of revolutions. The rivers enable us to live in greater security, knowing that if a fire breaks out, it will be contained to one rotation.

The rivers are wide. Wide enough to prevent most of the traveling embers of the Fourth from traversing the gap and starting spot fires on the other side. Stretched over each river are two bridges. Funneling across them will put our army at a temporary disadvantage.

I survey the smoke layer thickening far above me. "King Jovan," I call. "It is darkening."

I almost kick myself for not saying, "Do you think we should make camp," the Solati words sound so stupid. Sanjay sniggers behind me and I itch to put a dromeda rump in his face, but resist, because I don't wish to awaken his suspicions for later.

"We camp on this side of the water and cross the bridge in full daylight," Jovan says.

It will take a couple of hours for the entire army to filter across. It won't be this river that proves difficult, but the one separating the Second and Third Rotations. That was where we would have to move with haste.

With Rhone's help, I quickly set up my tent. Then, pulling Malir aside, I whisper a request in his ear. I watch the smile on Olandon's face a few minutes later when Malir instructs Sanjay to gather some water.

"I need to wash my pits anyway," Sanjay replies.

I laugh along with the others, perhaps a little too loudly. Olandon and I follow him, watching from the edge of camp as the orange-haired man strolls to the river's edge, whistling and joking with the men he passes.

He's much more relaxed than I was when he told me the falling snow was the frozen tears of children. Or when he told me all of my friends could die from inhaling sage fog.

"It is time," Olandon asks.

We exchange a small smile as Sanjay disappears behind the trees to wash.

"Grab the bucket," I say.

CHAPTER TWENTY-ONE

"THIS STEW IS delicious!" Hamish exclaims.

Avalanche grunts, even as his cheeks turn a ruddy red. He's always happiest when people are eating his food. I don't know how he does it. Every person received the same rations, but the watchmen around us stare with longing as the smell from the pot permeates through the camp.

I'm glad to be sitting where I am, though I should probably be eating with the other leaders—*and my father*. The thought elicits a shudder.

"*What the f—?*" Ice mouths.

Someone is running into camp at a furious clip.

In bliss, I listen as the steps slow. As the person realizes there's no need to run, no panic around him.

Sanjay stands in the middle of camp. a bucket in his hand. But this isn't what everyone gawks at. Sanjay is covered from head to toe in dromeda dung.

I know that's what the green goop is, because I stood there as he rubbed it into his skin. Even if I hadn't been standing next to him at the time, I would've ascertained what it was from the smell. Solatis were born immune to the bite of the venomous insects, we'd told him. The swarm headed our way could destroy the army in seconds. This kind of swarm was only seen once in a lifetime.

You'd think a previous delegate would know better.

There was some hesitation when Olandon held out the bucket of dung. But a frantic reminder about his unborn child had him scooping the runny green slop and hurriedly rubbing it into his pale skin.

The smell of shit eradicates the aroma of Avalanche's stew. A Bruma close to Sanjay covers his mouth and shies away, gagging. Who knows how long Sanjay collected manure for? He looks exhausted and ready to drop.

The army needed as much as he could carry, after all. We'd been sure to emphasize that point. Those already covered in manure had been sent far and wide in the hopes our army could survive the night.

The bucket Sanjay holds is filled to the top with the substance from a dromeda's back end. And he stares around the camp—at the shit-free and un-panicked Bruma scrambling away from him—until his eyes land on me, and on Olandon beside me.

I do okay until Avalanche grunts, "Why are you covered in poo?"

Then I lose the battle to stay quiet. I laugh with abandon, tears streaming down my face as Sanjay throws the bucket on the ground and stomps back toward the river.

Olandon relays the story to the crowds drawn to the ruckus as I roll on the ground. The surrounding Bruma begin to stamp with laughter. I howl along with them.

No wonder Sanjay and Ashawn are so fond of playing pranks.

It's nice to hear laughter; it's warming—for everyone but Sanjay. I listen, still giggling as the story is passed from tent to tent and laughter trickles through the men.

"Well," Ashawn says, collecting our bowls. "I can't say he didn't deserve that. Though it's a cruel thing, playing pranks on people."

I raise my brow. "Indeed."

Ashawn glances at my brother, who jokes with Shard. He turns back with a cheeky grin. "Indeed."

We began the river crossing at first firelight, and now, more than half of the army has made it over.

The voice is so soft, I nearly don't hear the comment over the echoing march of the army. "I heard you gave Sanjay a taste of his own medicine."

I tense as Adnan comes to stand by my side.

He continues. "I was lucky enough to see him leaving camp."

I smile. "You'll treasure the memory."

"That I will." He grins, but the humor quickly drains from his face.

The unassuming inventor next to me, my *brother*, hasn't got a violent bone in his body. It's a little absurd for him to even be here. But every assembly male had to fight—aside from the few left to run Glacium in Jovan's stead.

"I'm sorry," I say.

"Why? It's not your fault." His voice is rough. Angry. Though not at me. "He was in your mother's arms as soon as my mother was in the ground."

"Yes," I agree softly. "Our... Roscoe has lied to both of us. But you most of all."

Adnan tries to speak, but the sound cuts off. I can see the emotion on his face. I can see how much this has affected him. I can't decide if I'm angrier Roscoe didn't tell me, or that he never confessed the truth to his son.

"What I mean to say," I try again, "is I'm sorry you weren't told."

"He lied to me for most of my life. My own father! Why?" Adnan asks hopelessly.

I shrug, not wanting to call Roscoe a dirty coward in front of his son. "I guess only he can tell us that."

Adnan looks toward the king. Sure enough, his father is close by. "I'm not sure I'm ready to ask."

A short, bitter laugh leaves me. "Why do you think I'm over here?"

His expression lightens infinitesimally. His face scrunches. "Sister." He rolls the word around in his mouth like it tastes slightly bitter.

"We don't have to be, uh, siblings. If you don't want," I hurriedly say. "But if you do, that's fine, too."

His blue eyes sparkle and I snap my mouth shut. He scratches his chin. "I've never had a sister before."

"I've never had a Bruma brother before."

He laughs. "I guess that settles it."

We both glance Roscoe's way once more. Adnan tenses and I see he is far from forgiving his father. It's easy for Adnan to accept me because I haven't lied to him—and because I've only known him for a revolution, where he has known his father his whole life. Roscoe has an uphill battle to earn back Adnan's trust and I simply have no desire to help defend his actions. Even as we walk toward battle, I'm surprised to feel no stirring to confront him. I feel so misled by Roscoe.

...Perhaps I know I cannot make one parent understand and intend to punish the other. I pull my thoughts away from the matter, remembering Jovan's advice.

Adnan turns to leave. "Oh, and I would watch Sanjay like a hawk. He'll be cooking up something extra special for you and Olandon."

"I wouldn't expect any less of him," I return.

I continue watching the soldiers cross the bridge. Maybe it's because I'm expecting my mother to jump out from behind every bush, but I cannot rid myself of the uneasy tension that has plagued me since our arrival on Osolis. Things are going our way, I remind myself. The villagers are supportive and safe for now. We have food. And we managed to get the entirety of the Glacium force to Osolis before meeting the Solati army. Yes, it would be nice if the villagers could boost our numbers, but all in all, we are in an advantageous spot.

I shove my unease to the side and swing atop my dromeda.

Rian was right, as we find out while we wait for the rest of the army.

Mother made sure to empty the Second of its food stores before she retreated to the Third. The doors of the Kaur shed are wide open, the insides ransacked, and not a single grain is left in sight.

By mid-morning our army is in the Second Rotation and we begin the slow push towards the Third. We continue all day, eating as we march. I listen as the surrounding men discuss the inevitable battle ahead. It passes in one ear and out the other. If there's one thing I understand by now, it's that no matter how much you prepare, all you can do when faced with your worst nightmare is use whatever is at your disposal.

War is raw. It is like love in this way. You think you're prepared for both, but you cannot predict what either will do.

CHAPTER TWENTY-TWO

*M*Y FIRST THOUGHT as I struggle to awaken is that Slay has strung up another whore outside Alzona's barracks.

It's the screaming.

My second disorientated thought is of Crystal cutting off Slay's head with a sword.

That is when I understand the screams are coming from something else. I'm awake and scrambling for my possessions in the next second. Olandon is not in the tent. But he was on sentry duty.

The flap of my tent is pushed aside and I rip free my dagger, sagging as I see it is Sin.

"Fire." It's all he says before disappearing.

My mouth forms an endless "no." Here, fire only means one thing.

I grab my weapons and snatch up Kedrick's arrow, tucking it into my boot.

Abandoning the tent, I run through the anarchy of the camp in search of one person. Bruma scramble over each other in a half-stampede, furiously rolling their tents. Some are stumbling out, mostly asleep, as they check what the yelling is about. I run toward the Third Rotation. But there is a sight ahead of me that slows my feet before I reach the edge of camp.

The flames lick high into the air. Every hue from blazing orange to molten red streaks the sky. Smoke pours into the already thick smoke layer high above. The air is heavy with it. If we don't move, this will be the thing to kill us.

I spot my brother shouting at the Bruma.

"Leave it all!" he screams at them.

And he's right. I spur into action. Jovan stands watching the fire, too. What are they doing? Why aren't they moving? *Because they've never seen a wildfire.*

"Jovan," I shout. "Jovan!"

He turns my way. Smoke streaks his face.

"We have to go. Now!"

"Our supplies. We need them to lay siege."

I nearly stamp my foot. "You need living soldiers more. Do you have any idea how quickly that fire will reach us? It might already be too late!"

He whips his head back toward the growing inferno.

With a nod, he signals his men. He might not believe the fire will do as I say, yet, but he trusts me.

"We need to leave everything. We need to retreat to the First. We can't be caught at the river on the bridge or we won't have enough time to cross."

Jovan's face grows grim. He shouts to Malir and Rhone, "Give the order—only take weapons and shields!"

I watch as the message spreads. But there's not enough urgency. They walk when they need to *run* as though hell was snapping at their heels.

Jovan and I sprint through the camp, dragging men up and push-ing them toward the First. I scream at Bruma to run until finally, I can see the panic spread. Panic is good like that. I'd take pride in the stam-pede we create if the heat behind me wasn't growing to unbearable levels already. Sweat pours from me, soaking my robes. I spot Aquin pulling the older members of the council and Adox onto the backs of dromeda. Hamish runs ahead, Soar slung across his back. There's no way he'd sur-vive up there in the smoke. Thank Solis we decided to leave the rest of the Ire in the Sixth. That's two hundred less lives at risk.

My mind races with the logistics of crossing the river.

"We split the army in two. One group heads for the second bridge," Jovan says, reading my mind as we run side by side.

I work furiously to keep up with his long stride.

I have no idea where any of my friends are. They could be passed out from smoke inhalation far behind us for all I know. But I need to worry about how fourteen hundred men are going to cross two bridges without drowning, or burning alive.

As it turns out, I don't get to make that choice.

The repeated shout of "Fire!" reaches us from the front.

In horror, I watch as a wall of flame rises before us, separating us from the bridges.

It is a neat trap sprung by an insane mind.

It goes against everything that Solati value, to unleash an uncontrollable fire. Never in our history have we used fire in this way. To burn an entire rotation to the ground. To consume an army in flame. It is the coward's way; the torturer's way. My mother's way. She ordered her soldiers to surround us; it would only take a handful of people to spread out along each side of the rotation and start a fire. This whole time, she'd intended to burn us alive, *knowing* Olandon was in here, too.

Jovan and I had walked right into the mouth of her madness.

I twist toward the center of Osolis, toward Lake Aveni, knowing what I will see before I see it. Another wall of orange is beginning to rise there, too. We are trapped. Coughs wrack me as I face Jovan with hopeless eyes.

"There must be something," he says hoarsely.

I'm about to tear his hope to shreds. This is how it is to end. In fire. A fitting conclusion to my life.

I should never have brought him here.

"Jovan... I—"

"Lina," someone shouts.

I whip around, eyes watering, and spot my brother waving to me. Relief pours through me before I recall we're doomed anyway.

He stands with a village man. And as I approach, I see the man is dripping wet and frail like all the other emancipated villagers I've come across. That he remains upright in his sodden garments with how weak he appears is amazing in itself.

"Tatum Olina." The man drops to his knees before I can stop him.

If my brother was waving to me, it must be important. The flickers of hope stir within me.

"Tatum Olina. If you wish to survive, you must follow me with haste. There is a way out." The man gasps, breathing as though every expansion of his lungs is a colossal effort.

"How?" I ask in shock.

"The underground springs," Olandon answers. "He says there's a way through."

My gaze meets Jovan's. I've never heard of this secret pathway, but the underground system is connected. Every Solati child is taught this. I crouch next to the man. "You understand that if this goes wrong, everyone will burn?"

"They will not, if we can get there in time," he replies wearily. Too tired to be afraid, I think.

"Better to drown than burn," Olandon says solemnly.

He's right. "Jovan, we need to follow this man. Quickly."

I grip the man's elbows and lift him as the king barks orders behind me.

"I would know your name," I say gently.

The man shakes in my grip. "It is Aguan, Tatum Olina."

"Aguan. Please lead the way."

I help the villager onto Olandon's back and we reverse our direction once more, angling toward the center of Osolis, to the lake. A sinking feeling in me guesses that following him will end in the same result. We are probably following Aguan on a fool's errand. But it gives the army focus. It stops them from erupting into chaos and turning on each other. We have purpose. And that is to follow Aguan.

The smoke is making me dizzy when Aquin finally points to a gently rolling hill. A glance behind tells me some of the Bruma are near collapse.

We round the hill and Aguan frees himself of his position on Olandon's back and stumbles forward to an opening in the ground.

"Pass the word back," I scream. "Stay low. Cover your mouth with whatever you can." If they can survive the smoke, we might just make it.

Jovan appears to my left and drags me toward the small gap. My heart races as I enter complete darkness.

"Hold on to my shirt," Jovan instructs. I obey and pass the order back.

We wander through the dark tunnel for a time, stumbling blindly in the confines. The only thing allowing me to control the feeling of being trapped is that Jovan walks ahead of me. If he can get through, I will fit without a problem. I don't know how he moves with such confidence in the cramped space.

Within ten minutes, the warmth of a few puddles soaks through my boots. Soon water is lapping at my ankles. It's on the hotter side of warm. Entirely bearable. Behind us a swarm of Bruma wait in the smoke and flame to enter the tunnel. And who knows what awaits us at the other end. The thought that this is another trap enters my mind.

My barracks friends are nowhere in sight. Or Sanjay. My heart sinks as I remember my promise to Fiona.

"There's a rope," a voice echoes back.

Sure enough, as the water rises to my waist, a rope is thrust into my hands. How long has this been here for?

"Lina?" Jovan's voice reaches me.

"I'm okay." I'm not really. I dislike confined spaces. The degree of my dislike I'm only just realizing. I focus on my breathing as I splash behind Jovan, feeling the sliding of the water around me as it rises to my neck. There's barely any echo. I could reach up and touch the roof right now, but I don't dare, happier to pretend the ceiling is cavernous, that I couldn't even touch it if I stood on Jovan's shoulders. Or Avalanche's.

It works well enough for me to continue. There really isn't another option. Or so I think.

I hear the man in front of Jovan whisper something to him, inaudible to me over the splashing sounds.

And then I hear the words for myself, from Jovan's lips.

"We need to go underwater. For about five seconds."

I don't say anything. Water surrounding me. No space to move. "I can't do that," I croak. "No."

Jovan turns as well as he can in the space, realizing I'm not okay at all. "Lina, I'm afraid you need to get your shit together."

I gape at him. Does he think I want to panic?

He must sense my irritation. "I'm serious. You're going through there. We have a queue of exhausted men behind us. Don't waste their time, or their lives by freaking out. Roll a bit of fabric—that thing you do when you're panicking, and get it together."

My mouth drops open in shock. But I find myself reaching for my robes. I shudder at the thought of the material winding around my legs when I submerge. Instead of rolling them, I rip the ends, tearing the robes off at the knees.

"I'm going first," he continues. "If I can fit through, you'll go through with no problem."

"But you're huge!" I say in a high voice. "What if you cork the hole?" The thought takes root in my mind. "What if I can't get free of you and we both drown?"

A hand covers my mouth and I bite without thinking. I already feel as though I can't breathe without a hand there.

I hear a muffled "ouch" followed by, "I'm going now. If I count to twenty and you're not there, I'm coming back to drag you through."

There's a splash.

I stumble forward, reaching blindly for Jovan. True to his word, he's gone. My fingers brush a rock, I reach down, and then down. Clearly we have to go underneath this. I kick out with my foot and it doesn't connect with anything. There's clear space beneath it. My stomach is in my sodden boots. Olina, you can do this. There are men waiting behind me. Men who will die in the smoke and flames. Much more than twenty seconds passes as I stand there. I reel into the person behind me. Who I clearly don't know or they'd be shoving me into the hole. What if my friends are back there?

I need to move, but my legs stay frozen.

Jovan emerges in front of me and I squeak.

"Take a deep breath," he growls.

I barely do as he asks before he shoves me downward underneath the rock. I thrash, kicking. My skin scratches against the rock of the tunnel. Then a hand grips my foot and pushes me and I remember I must go forward.

They said it would take five seconds. I think I do it in two. I push myself upward furiously, hoping there's air at the top to relieve my burning chest.

I burst from the water, eyes wide in terror. The only reason I don't scream is because I'm catching my breath. And then he is there, simultaneously holding me close and shifting me out of the way of the next person.

"You pushed me in the hole." I think I'm in shock.

It's the most horrific thing he has ever done to me. Worse than putting me in the Dome.

"You can be angry at me later." He cuts me off, taking us uphill in awkward steps.

"I want to be angry at you now!" I snap.

"Or you could be happy the end of the tunnel is ahead."

It is? It is! I untangle myself from his awkward shuffling gait and find my own legs, scrambling for the exit.

Olandon pulls me from the nightmare tunnel and I see where Aguan has led us.

The light from the roaring fire at our backs flickers across it's dark surface.

I blink out at the wide expanse of Lake Aveni.

CHAPTER TWENTY-THREE

*T*HE MEN THAT entered ahead of us are spread out on the beach, tensed for signs of attack. I don't blame them; killing your enemy one by one as they exit a small hole has great tactical value. However, my mother can't have been planning on Aguan leading us to safety. If she had, or if Aguan had been a ploy, we would all be dead.

Watchmen stumble out of the underground tunnel, wet, shaken, but alive. As for how many made it, only time will tell.

"Sister," Olandon calls. "Aguan." He points down to the water, where a dark form lies on the ground.

The terror of the tunnel hasn't entirely left me. I look at Jovan and grip his hand, pulling him down to the shore.

Aguan appears unconscious as we approach. He is skin over bones. Dragging himself to warn us, and then forcing himself back through the tunnel has been too much.

"How does he fare?" I ask.

A man crouching by his head replies, "He's fading, Tatum."

I share a shocked glance with the king. "Dying?" I ask the man. "Are you sure?"

The Bruma—a medic—nods. "His pulse has weakened considerably over the last ten minutes, I'm afraid. He will not last much longer."

My mouth is dry as I peer through the dark at the man who just saved hundreds of men. One of my people.

The medic speaks again. "I'm not sure how he made it all that way, my King."

Jovan rests a hand on the watchman's shoulder. "Do all you can to make him comfortable."

The noise of those arriving is growing behind me. It's a moment where, as a leader, you need to be in several places at once. "I will stay here," I say.

The king nods, dropping a kiss on my head. "And I will organize the survivors." His throat works strongly. Here I am mourning over one man when Jovan might have lost who knows how many men. With a decision *we* made.

"Jovan, we don't know how many managed to get through."

His chin lifts, though it is a façade I see through. "There is no point in guessing," he agrees. He looks down at Aguan's unmoving form. "But not one of us would be alive without this man. He displayed a selflessness of the like I've never seen."

A lump rises in my throat. I nod, unable to speak.

I remain with Aguan alone as the warmth drains from his hand. Listening as his breath labors and rattles. Watching as his chest stops rising. Until he is dead.

Aguan was a hero.

As I move back and allow two men to remove his body, staring at the starved Solati hanging between them, I decide that Aguan will be remembered, forever.

I trek up the sandy shore to Jovan. Men pour from the tunnel and I can see Jovan's gaze is fixated on the hole, afraid the line will stop. I stand shoulder-to-shoulder with him and look around for my friends. Sanjay, Adnan... Roscoe. Aquin and Adox.

Olandon is safe, and in the distance I spot the smoky form of Shard. Well, really I spot Avalanche first. But where are the others? Malir, Rhone, Ice, Blizzard, Sin. The advisors.

It's agony to watch the trickle from the hidden spring, not knowing whether your loved ones will appear. Everyone watches the hole, though Jovan has ordered them into defensive lines.

"Around nine hundred so far."

I don't reply to Jovan's remark. Because my first callous thought is, *that's not enough*. Not enough to defeat my mother; not enough men to return to their families on Glacium. It is simply not enough.

Another hour goes by.

Malir and Rhone stumble from the tunnel. Malir bleeds profusely from a head wound.

"What happened?" I make way for the medic.

Rhone grunts. "He didn't want to get in the tunnel."

Malir glares at the larger, previously Outer Rings, Bruma. My stomach lurches. It would be just like Malir to stay until the last of the men had entered the passage. It didn't even enter my head. I was convinced a trap would lie at the other end of the tunnel. I'm glad Rhone was there to convince him otherwise—peacefully, or not.

"Malir," I say seriously. "I understand, but don't you see, you've now lived to save many more lives. Rhone was right to force you."

I don't wait to see if he agrees or not. Rhone follows me back to where Jovan watches the entrance. The numbers are dwindling now. The intervals between each survivor staggering out are longer. And three of my friends have yet to exit the cave.

"How many, my King?" Rhone asks.

"One thousand."

Not enough.

We'd left one hundred watchmen to guard the villagers, Aunty Jain, and the twins. There should still be four hundred Bruma to come through.

We wait for twenty minutes after the last Bruma has staggered through, to no avail. If there are any more, they are far behind.

Four hundred.

The king's fists are clenched beside me. He's doing everything to hold it in. His fury, his heartbreak, his desolation. Four hundred lives. Four hundred men *burned* alive. Their flesh melted from their bodies as they screamed until death. My imagination summons horrible visions against my will. Of Blizzard, and Ice, and Sin choking in a chaos of smoke and desperate men.

"A large group split off early," Rhone says. Jovan and I both stare at the hulking, muscled man. The dog-sledder never speaks unless he has something of import to convey.

The good thing about Rhone is he doesn't need to be prompted. He knows what his king wishes to know. "Not sure how many. More than fifty. Led by your barracks friends." He nods to me.

"Blizzard, Ice, Sin?" Their names rush from my lips.

Rhone dips his head. "They realized not everyone would get through and took their chance at finding another way."

I'm numb thinking of the possibilities, even though the likeliest probability is still that they are dead.

"Do you think they've made it?" Jovan's voice is curt with his obvious stress.

Rhone bows slightly. "There's no way to tell."

It is one of the hardest things for any ruler—to rule when you feel like weeping. Jovan has failed at this in the past—after his parents' death and after Kedrick. And Solis knows *I* have, running away time and again.

This time we do not do either of these things. My head is tilted back, eyes burning into Jovan's. And we share the gut-wrenching despair of the situation—without words—before hardening our faces and turning to our people.

By the time we take stock, tend the wounded, and count the survivors, the firelight is beginning to streak the sky. It is darker than any morning so far because of the excess smoke in the air. It casts added heaviness over our exhausted and grieving battalion.

I scoop a handful of water from the lake into my mouth. The lukewarm water eases my throat. Whatever we *don't* have, at least there is the lake to quench our thirst.

"Hamish has been dispatched to the Sixth. They'll bring food." Olandon sits on the sand, robes torn, face streaked with dirt and fatigue.

"We're lucky they're here, or this war would be over before it began." I stare behind us at the angry red flames in the distance. The fire will most likely burn for the next year. Until it comes out of the Fourth.

"It was a desperate move." What my mother must have been thinking to do something so dangerous.

Olandon contemplates my words. "Or a clever one."

I skim my hand over the water's surface. "I don't know if we have enough men."

"You wonder if it is best to retreat."

I stare across the lake and say nothing.

Olandon stands beside me in a burst of movement. I shoot him a startled look, but he stares off to the right, face screwed in concentration. "What *is* that?" he muses.

I follow his gaze—stupidly—because if my brother cannot see it, I have no chance.

He makes a gasping sound. "People," he says. "Coming out of the river!"

What! I turn away from the lake to stare at where the closest river spills into Lake Aveni. Those between where we stand and the river have also sighted the people. There are whooping shouts.

Olandon and I push through the sand, waving aside the growing horde of people. Hope squeezes me in its false grip, and I am too weak to tell it no. What if my friends made it alive?

Jovan is already helping a few sopping Bruma from the water. How did they even get to the river through the flames? I wade into the depths and grip the hand of a man clinging to a Kaur branch. There are dozens of people. Is everyone else here? All four hundred of the missing?

The rivers of Osolis are tumultuous, though calmer in this spot where they empty into the lake. Surely, not everyone who went into the water will come out.

"Don't worry about us, girly! We'll just go right out into the middle of the lake!" The words are screamed my way.

Heart leaping, I follow the sound, eyes searching frantically, until they land on three drenched forms.

Blizzard is slumped, unconscious, over the log, while Sin and Ice kick either side. Sin looks as unfazed as ever, though a large section of his hair appears to be gone. Ice's face only shows rage.

He's the one screaming at me. I take it he doesn't like water.

"In your own time, Frost," he bellows again.

I sprint down the river's edge to the narrowest crossing, my robes torn short from earlier, before I dive into the water. The water of the river is crisp and I briefly revel in the rushing sensation before surfacing.

In a few strokes I am by their side.

Ice scowls at my approach. I almost laugh. I never thought I'd see them again! Ice doesn't realize how lucky we are. Did all four hundred of the missing Bruma make it to the water?

"All right," I say, swimming to the other side of the log. "We kick for the shore."

It's hard work, with Blizzard acting as a dragging weight. The three of us kick and kick some more toward Shard and Avalanche, who wait for us on the bank. As we near, Sin—the closest—reaches up and clasps Avalanche's massive paw.

In a slippery tangle, we work to haul Blizzard up the side.

"What happened to him?" Shard pants.

Ice collapses on the ground by Blizzard's side. "He got into a fight with Sin on the way down."

My eyebrows shoot up. An incredulous silence meets his words. We look at Sin, who sits whistling. My eyes dip down to his hand. Sure enough, two of his knuckles are split.

I rise to my full height. It isn't that effective, so I also place both hands on my hips. "You got into a fight in a river, after escaping a fire and trying to survive," I clarify.

Ice thinks hard, muttering through his memories, before saying, "That sounds about right, girly."

I round on Sin.

But then I see his hair... or what's left of it. A startled laugh is pulled from my lips as I process that Sin's glorious silken blond locks have been scorched away with fire. Half of his hair remains untouched, while the rest is a patchy, singed mess.

"You find something funny?" Sin snaps.

A laugh rumbles within Avalanche's belly. "Your hair."

Ice cranes his head to stare. "Huh, didn't see that. I was on the other side." He snorts. "You look fucking ridiculous."

Sin scowls. It must be hard for the beautiful man to be a little less beautiful. I wonder what he and Blizzard fought about. I don't think I've ever seen Sin take anything seriously. Even in the Dome.

Blizzard stirs. He groans, and the four of us lean over him, heads together.

One eye cracks open, showing bloodshot blue. "What happened?"

I peer around us while Ice refreshes our friend's memory. Many are still being helped to the shore. "How did you guys get to the river?"

Ice's eyes sober. "Piled into a tight group. Shields on the outside."

"Most on the outside died," Blizzard says, hollowly. He weaves slightly as he sits up.

"Some were trampled, some burned. But some made it to the river." Ice shudders.

I notice an angry burn on his forearm. I cannot imagine the terror. "How many left with you?"

They glance at each other, nonplussed.

Blizzard answers around a cough. "Around one hundred and fifty left with us."

My heart sinks. Two hundred and fifty men still unaccounted for. I'd hoped all those left had made it to the river.

"Not everyone made it through the fire," Blizzard continues. "And then the river was…" He swallows, thickly. "Powerful. We only made it because we dragged a Kaur log in with us. I have no idea how many have survived."

Many, I hope. No doubt Malir will organize men to count the survivors. It's impossible to tell in the splashing chaos.

Avalanche helps Blizzard along as we return to the other Bruma.

"What's the situation?" Shard asks.

I haven't had a chance to speak to him yet. Sighing, I say, "Likely a couple of hundred men dead; no supplies to feed the rest of them; we've lost the equipment we were going to use to lay siege to the castle—our battering ram, and the ladders. And I have no idea if another trap lies ahead, no inkling whether there are enough men to continue on, and there is now zero morale amongst the army."

Shard swings an arm around my shoulders. His twinkling eyes stare down at me over his nose. "Then we've certainly faced much worse."

I smile, grateful for his unerring support. His loyalty knows no bounds.

"You serious?" Ice blurts. "There's nothin' good about that! What're we gonna do?"

I roll my eyes, even as Shard sighs. For a spy, Ice has a poor time deciphering sarcasm. But his question reminds me just how precarious this position is.

And the devastating answer to his question is: I have no clue.

CHAPTER TWENTY-FOUR

SCOUTS ARE SENT out early the next day.

Hamish and the Ire folk have yet to return. We each expended everything we had last night and there are some very hungry men around us. But as happens in the wake of disaster, people pull together. There are no complaints—except for Sin mourning the loss of his hair.

We lost 273 Bruma last night. In my mind, I multiply Olandon by that number and my stomach churns. Each of these men who burned, or drowned, or inhaled too much smoke had a family and loved ones. Someone to go home to.

I watch Sanjay splashing water over his face.

Each of these men could have a baby on the way, or young boys and girls waiting for their father to come home. How would Glacium survive without their fathers, and brothers, and protectors? Am I asking too much of Jovan's people? Is the right path to turn around and return them to their children and wives?

A presence sits beside me, drawing an arm around my shoulders.

I lay my head on his shoulder, drawing in his tangy-wooden scent. It grounds me, just like its owner.

"The scouts haven't discovered anything amiss." Jovan breaks the silence in a soft voice.

He knows this doesn't mean anything. My mother won't advertise her next move. That is not the Solati way.

"What's our next move?" he says next.

"Shouldn't we discuss that with the advisors?"

"I want to hear what you're thinking first."

I chew on my lip. "I'm unsure if we should retreat or keep going."

"And if we keep going, what way do we head?"

A Kaur forest sits in the distance. Beyond it is the Third Rotation. I point in that direction. "Hug Lake Aveni until we can turn inland to the Third. The Tatum cannot repeat the same trick without killing herself, too. And she will be trapped. A fire on each side of her, and an army in front. One way or another, the battle will be over."

The king tilts my chin up with a finger. I stare at the hard planes of his tired face. I don't understand how he's acting so strong. I feel like I've been beaten.

He kisses my lips—a whisper. Not enough, but everything I need. "Then that is where we go," he says.

He presses another lingering kiss there to cut off my reply. "What do you think happens in war, Lina?"

"One side wins, and the other loses."

"No." He shakes his head. There's so much sorrow in the movement I forget to breathe. "Both sides lose. But one side loses a little less." His blue eyes burn into mine. "I came here knowing many of these men would die. That I might die. That is a fact of war. There is no glory in it. No victory. All there is, is relief when it is finally done."

"Two hundred and seventy-three men," I whisper.

He does not speak, *cannot* speak for a few minutes. His voice is choked with emotion when he does. "Those men did not die in vain. We *will* not dishonor their memory, nor their families by cowering away. You haven't come this far to have doubts."

I blink at him, our noses nearly touching. I process what he's said and realize I've been a soft fool with glorious notions of battle. Jovan is right: no one wins. Our focus needs to be on the future our actions could bring.

"All right then."

He raises a brow. "You're actually agreeing with me?" he asks.

I mock frown. "Don't act so surprised. You occasionally have a passable idea."

He pulls me upward. "Now we need to convince the others."

It's not hard. It seems most are set on vengeance. Olandon and I are quick to lay the blame on our mother and uncle. The last thing I want is for bitterness against the Solati people to set in. I'm glad when I see no signs of dissent. I imagine the watchmen remember the starving villagers from the previous weeks. They know who is behind this. And for that I'm immensely thankful.

The lake water keeps us going until the Ire are spotted the next day. Hundreds of wings dot the sky. As they land, I see each of them carries a large pack of food. They've stopped at the storage sheds. The food boosts the army's morale more than anything else so far. Especially Avalanche's.

A council session is held on the riverbank. A large portion of the Ire are sent to bring supplies to replace the ladders we lost in the fire. Despite Olandon's caution against my decision, I send Rian and twenty-five Bruma into the Kaur forest ahead of us. Aquin is not happy to give up the giant Kaur log in his training shed as a battering ram, but he yields after a stern look. The training shed is not far from our current location, and I hope against hope that I haven't sent twenty-six men to their death. It's a risk I have to take. Without a battering ram, we'll be picked off like lint once at the palace wall.

If we'd used the Ire to scout ahead previously, instead of foot soldiers, it might have averted disaster. It was a grievous error. But we will not be caught by fire a second time. With the Ire circling above us, Mother's forces will not sneak up on us again.

Two days later, I stare into the black mass of the Kaur forest. This forest separates two armies.

The vines between the black trees have dried and dropped, which will make the march a little easier. I don't like the lack of visibility, but the Ire will help us there. And Malir will send out ground scouts.

Like the Bruma, I'm reluctant to leave the safety of the water. My mother couldn't be stupid enough to set fire to the Third, but then, I didn't expect she would set fire to the Second, either.

I hear Aquin's uneven step. "It will not be an easy battle."

I hum in agreement. The loss of so many will have a large impact on how many more men die. My people are skilled soldiers. Solati always have been. I'd be proud if it didn't mean hundreds more Bruma would perish.

"Your mother wasn't always this way," he says, catching me off-guard.

He glances at my, no doubt, wide-eyed expression.

"I remember her when she was young and carefree. I wouldn't say she was as selfless as you are. But then she was raised as a Tatuma should be, spoiled and arrogant—like Olandon. Her happiness could light up a room, though, and there was nothing she would not do for those whom she loved."

My mouth is dry as I hang on to every word Aquin says.

"Giving birth changed your mother. Broke her in some way, as birth sometimes can. No one knew of her pregnancy at the time, except your grandparents, and your Uncle Cassius and Aunty Jain. But everyone in the court noted the shift in Avanna—Ovanna at the time. Or Vanna, as she let me call her."

I jerk. I hadn't realized they were that close.

"The Tatum, your grandfather, forced Ovanna to remain hidden during the pregnancy. And even when she had you, she was taken from you immediately and married to Olandon's father. She was impregnated again almost immediately."

He says "impregnated" like she didn't have a choice. I frown, not used to feeling sorry for my mother.

"Her body was not healed, her mind fractured, and then the light was gone from her eyes. And as happens when we cannot cope, her love turned to anger. A deep-rooted and bitter form of it. The second pregnancy, with Olandon, sealed her downward spiral into bitterness and darkness. After which there was no return for her."

"And you know all of this," I ask.

He stares into the tree line. "I was a confidant of your grandfather in the end, as he lay dying, poisoned by your mother."

"She poisoned her own father," I say. I was aware he'd been poisoned, but not by who.

Aquin nods gravely, tears sparkling in his eyes. "He knew she did it. But he did not understand why. He thought it was because she was broken."

I take a half step forward.

Aquin's eyes shine from the weathered lines of his face. "Your grandfather could have raised the alarm. In his final hour, he held the power to reveal Avanna's treachery and demand her execution with his last breath."

"Why didn't he?" I frown.

Pain flitters through his expression. "Because that is the sacrifice you make for your child. You would rather die than cause them pain."

"Then how do you explain my mother?" My voice cracks at the question.

"Your mother poisoned your grandfather because he planned to kill you. Though just, he was ruthless where he believed himself to be right. And he did not foresee a future for Ovanna while you were alive. He saw what your birth had done to her and despised you for it. He believed your mixed blood had caused Ovanna to lose her mind; that it had infected his beloved daughter somehow. He spoke his intentions to end your life in Ovanna's presence a single time. And the next day he was dead."

"My mother protected me." My mind balks at the information. I can't collate this with the ordeals she has put me through during my life.

"She did," he says simply. "Though I do not believe it was your blood that made her snap, it was clear Ovanna was changed." He clasps his hands in front of him. "Oh, she hid it well, behind layers of smoke and ash. She covered any lapses with the sharp intelligence she'd always possessed. But to those who knew her before and who were close enough after, the gradual slip was clear."

"And that is why she hurt me?"

Aquin shakes his head. "As to that, I cannot say. I guess her paranoia eventually overrode her love of you. Who can guess the logic of someone who has severed ties with reason."

A new thought occurs to me. "You are telling me a lot about my mother. I would know why."

He takes a long moment. "I want you to understand."

I wait for the rest, but it doesn't come. My old trainer faces me and raises a hand to clasp my shoulder. Reading his expression is fruitless. Aquin is an expert at veiling his feelings.

As he repeats his last words, "I want you to understand," once more before leaving, a rock lands in my stomach.

He wants me to… feel sorry for my mother? To see that she was once a person? That once she loved me enough to protect me against all evils, as a parent should. To see that *I* destroyed any good in her.

What use is any of that to me now?

I quickly lose sight of the soaring Ire folk above as the trees close in on us. Jovan's army spreads wide to march through the Kaur forest. The black trees slow our progression to a crawl. It's funny; I used to run through these forests. It used to be one of the only moments when I felt free. But now the mood of the forest is oppressive and foreboding. I shiver.

It doesn't take long for the light to disappear completely as the day wanes into night.

On Glacium, this would be accompanied by freezing temperatures. Here, people are removing their packs—and clothing—in relief. The Third is one of the hottest rotations. Though we walk through the forest, the ground is a hard, cracked brown surface, littered with fallen branches and the occasional dying shrub. Dust kicks up with every step, coating your nose and drying your mouth until the only thing you can taste is ash. And then there's the ever-present smoke. It is akin to standing close to a small fire. The tendrils stick to your clothing and hair, until all you can smell is its tanginess. Even with the water we took from Lake Aveni, I see medics are hurrying about treating signs of heat sickness. I can't imagine how unbearable it is for the Bruma—even I'm uncomfortable. And as hard as it is to walk in the heat, harder still is sleeping in it. Hundreds of men toss and turn, overriding any sounds of the night that may have been. Olandon and I are as far apart as our small tent will allow, avoiding any extra body heat.

These sweltering temperatures will be a major disadvantage in battle, as we realized long before the army left for Osolis.

In the early hours of morning, I give up on sleep. Pushing aside the tent flap, I crawl out, nodding to the sentry close by.

"I was asked to fetch you when you woke," he says with a bow.

I tense, gathering something bad has happened. But the camp doesn't seem to be in a state of alarm; everyone is slumbering.

I follow the large sentry through the camp to where the medics' quarters are set up. The thin man who pronounced Aguan's imminent death leans over a man. A very still man. As the senior medic straightens, I start. The man is dead, face contorted in agony.

I turn to the exhausted doctor, blinking away my shock.

"I cannot find that a weapon has been used to kill him, or any of them," he starts.

"How many?" I croak.

He sighs, and rubs at his eyes. "Ten overnight. They all possess these small indents. Do you recognize them?"

I step to the deceased soldier's side and peer down at the side of his ankle. There, in a curved row, are a number of small pin-pricks. A familiar row of pin-pricks, though I've never seen the body of someone who has died from the poison.

"Tellio lizard bite," I say aloud. The medic's face tells me he has no idea what this is. "Small lizards that possess extremely fatal poison. There must be a nest here."

The medic nods somberly. "There's no cure?"

"Not that I know of." I clasp a hand to his shoulder. "You need rest. We march tomorrow." I turn to the sentry who still lurks, curious. "Soldier, I need you to move all those sleeping in the same areas as the ten dead comrades here. Immediately."

"Tatum," he salutes, before exiting the tent.

I wish the sentry had woken me as soon as the men began to die.

Fifteen more pass overnight, twenty-five men in total. The further dent in our already depleted forces is one thing; the punch to the army's morale is worse. It was badly damaged after the fires. To face another obstacle so soon after escaping death is cruel and disheartening for all. Without effort, my mother has embedded herself into the Bruma's minds, psyching them out before the battle has even begun.

All twenty-five of the men were from the Outer Rings, and I can hear conspiracies flying about as we march. But they were not targeted. The simple matter is, the poor don't have tents; they had no protection from the scuttling lizards.

This is rectified the second night.

All three rings cram into the tents of the Inner, Middle, and Outer Rings. Somehow Olandon and I land Avalanche in our tent. Sin was the first volunteer, but Jovan quickly vetoed that. I was glad at the time. Who knows where Sin's hands would roam, and where my brother's knife would end up, or what appendage Sin would lose—possibly his favorite. Then we got Avalanche instead. He doesn't even *fit* in the tent; he just lies in the middle with our jackets wrapped tightly around his overhanging legs.

"If I die because our tent flap is open for the giant, I won't be happy," Olandon says.

"No," grunts Avalanche. "You'll be dead."

I giggle sleepily and lift my hand for a high-five. His goliath hand gently pats my own.

That night I learn something. Not only is Avalanche an apt description of the barrack man's fighting style, it's a fairly accurate word for the sound that pours from his mouth when he sleeps too. Olandon sits up halfway through the night and leaves, who knows where to. I'm comfortable and persevere for another hour or so, but even I give up. It's that loud.

The very first streams of firelight shoot through the branches above me. A couple of Ire folk are swirling high above.

"Any deaths overnight?" I ask a sentry.

He shakes his head. "None, Tatum." Relief pours through me. Let's hope our luck continues. Then maybe we can rebuild the army's strength.

Eager for silence after having my ears blown off by Avalanche, I circle the outer edge of the tents. Sweat drips down my temples, and a slight dizziness assaults me for a few seconds. I need to drink more water. The lack of sleep the last two nights can't be helping, either. It's so hot.

I glance around and tie my new robes in a knot high on my right thigh and roll the sleeves to my shoulders. Much better. I'd forgotten how dark my skin could be. My legs have regained some of their olive color. A bright dot of light shines on my legs as I study it.

I look up, squinting through the trees to see what has caused it. It flashes in my eyes. I lift my arm to shield them and move forward to investigate. Someone must have lost a weapon.

The light disappears as I approach. I bob my head up and down trying to find it in the bush. It was close, I'm sure of it, only fifty paces from camp. I duck under a low branch and come up on the other side. It was high, perhaps lodged in a tree.

I inspect the ground around my feet as well as the trees, kicking over branches, readying myself to run if a tellio lizard should appear.

Nothing.

Where on Solis is it?

Is someone playing a trick on me? Sanjay? I glance back, and cannot see camp. My heart sinks in my chest as I realize I've been lured away from the others.

A whirring sounds behind me.

I spin away, the arrow slicing through my upper arm instead of the kill shot intended. I face my attacker.

It's *him*!

The filth who killed Kedrick.

The Ire folk trader who tried to kill me on the Oscala.

I reach a hand down to my boot and feel for the broken fletching I've carried with me for half a revolution.

We stare at each other. Him, in shock because I'm sure he expected his arrow would hit the intended target between my shoulder blades. And me, in dead calm. This is it. I'm going to uphold the vow I made so long ago—or die trying.

The strange thing is, there's no anger. I cannot summon the tiniest flicker of loathing or rage. It's gone, extinguished, numbed by months and months of heartache, and trial, and responsibility. I just want this to be over. I want my friend back. I want Jovan and Ashawn to have their brother. I want to laugh at Kedrick's playfulness.

Killing this man won't achieve this… but I *will* feel better for it.

As an Osolis trader, the assassin is required to look like a Solati. Brown eyes and dark hair on a tall, lean frame ensure no one would spare him a glance—maybe only to double-take at the gleam in his eyes. Or maybe I notice the cruelty there because I know what he has done.

My feet spread into a fighting pose as the Ire man smirks and drops down from the tree branches.

I watch his graceful descent with growing dread. I'm only at three-quarter strength, and this man is a fighter. A very good fighter, judging by his agility and the control of his movements. How did he learn this on the Ire?

"You were going to shoot me in the back," I say.

He shucks his bow and arrows, leaving them at the base of a tree. He turns his back to me as he does so, an insult to what he thinks of my fighting skill. Maybe a cockiness I can exploit.

"I prefer to shoot my targets in the back. Then I don't see their faces at night." He rolls his shoulders, and the movement stirs a memory. "I sleep better that way."

Disgust twists my face. "Coward," I spit.

His lips curl into a taunt. "You play the hand you're dealt."

"You kill people under the guise of being a trader because your life on the Ire is so hard?" I say sarcastically, beginning to circle.

He counters in perfect patterns. I was correct. He has been trained.

"No," he snarls. "I do it because I love it. I love killing you pompous Solati. I enjoy causing misery for you, paid in gold from other Solati. I'll particularly relish the blood pouring from your body. I might even make an exception and watch the life leaving your eyes." His eyes regard me intently. "I'll kill you slowly."

His words sicken me. "Then why did you kill the Bruma prince," I ask, "if you hate Solati so much?"

The question will cater to his vanity, but I need to know.

"I hate you both," he hisses. "You both think you're better than us, throwing us from your worlds, abandoning us out of embarrassment, hiding us away."

He's crazy. "But why Kedrick?"

He laughs softly, but the sound sends a shiver through my bones. He notices and laughs harder. Our movement reverses, our circle becoming a little smaller as we size each other up.

"I was aiming for you."

My stomach drops like a stone in water, though I knew this already. Kedrick pushed me out of the way, after all. But hearing this from the murderer's lips hurts. It takes everything I have to continue moving in sync with the dark-haired assassin.

He continues, drawing closer. "I was aiming for you," he repeats. "But my orders were to kill him."

What? My feet fumble.

And he strikes.

CHAPTER TWENTY-FIVE

I BARELY TWIST IN time to avoid a direct blow to my jaw that would have ended this fight.

I scramble back to the far edge of the small clearing while he waits at the other side, biding his time, knowing he's rattled me.

This is a battle where you cannot be half present, but what did he mean? That he *chose* to kill me instead? Why would he do that? What did I ever do to him? If anything, he should like me because I'm mixed as well.

He begins a languid dance forward and I'm not fooled by the laziness of his step. The man is an expert. I haven't seen someone rival his speed since Slay.

I was in the best shape of my life when I faced Slay.

"You'll die today," he says. "Just as your lover did."

I haven't thought of Kedrick in that way for a long time. It is odd to hear of him as my lover. I only have one lover. So I don't rise to his bait. I still want to know why he changed his mind and decided to shoot me. Or did he just say it to put me off?

"You seem very sure of that," I remark.

"I'm very sure that I'll plant your body in the king's tent, a bloody, pulpy mess, and then go to the Sixth Rotation and spread news of Glacium's betrayal. The two worlds will finally finish each other off. And the Ire can live on land once more."

Now *that* makes me mad. I've worked so hard for peace. Kedrick worked hard for peace. The familiar thrill of the fight stirs deep within me.

"It doesn't sound like Adox's kind of plan." My tone is mild as I try to garner if the Ire leader is involved. I eye the assassin's stance. A little wide. If I can hook my leg around, it will unbalance him.

The man sneers. "He's an idiot."

"And you're crazed and bloodthirsty. Personally, I'd choose Adox."

His brown eyes flash at the insult and his body takes on a new tension, one that tells me the talk is over. I'm within screaming distance of the camp. This will be the assassin's first priority: to shut me up. That means a punch to the throat, direct knockout, or a blow to knock the breath out of me. He'll rush me.

My body will not be left in a pulpy mess in Jovan's tent.

The Ire man rushes me as predicted. I remain still, not dodging this time, and we clash in a bout of blows. Sure enough, the hits are directed at my face. I raise my hands in a vertical wall above me as the blows rain down, his height giving him clear advantage.

Doesn't he know I've never once entered a fight where I was taller, heavier, or stronger? Obviously not.

His advantage is the length of his limbs. Mine is a low center of balance.

We take turns gaining and losing ground. A punch glances off my cheek, blurring my focus. I'm pushed back, but twist and drop, kicking out at his wide stance. It gives me enough time to recover.

We watch each other from opposite sides of the space, panting. I blink away the last dots in my vision from his hit. His jab is lethal. I need to watch it. He'll be ready for me to exploit his stance again. I can't use that trick a second time, yet it's the only weakness I've seen.

This is a fight where there are no guarantees. All I possess is a belief I will survive because I *need* to. Because Kedrick can't have died for nothing. Life cannot be so unfair.

It can't just *be over*.

Heart thundering in my ears, I charge him. His recovery is slower. One thing in my favor. *I need to win.*

I unleash punch after punch, my arms blurring with my fury.

This time it is I who breaks through his guard. A blow to the jaw. If only I were stronger, that hit could have been the end.

I prepare to take advantage of his pain, but to my incredulity he shakes it off. Instead of pressing my attack into *him*, I find myself giving up space. Too much space. The trees aren't far away.

I can't get boxed in. If someone of my size gets trapped, it only ends one way. There's always been a way out.

Before now.

Every way I spin, he's there. Each double-backed dodge and innovative duck, he blocks me. I cock my leg back to kick out and my mouth dries when my foot scrapes on the bark of a Kaur tree.

No.

His dark eyes are wild, the heaviness of his breath just making him appear even more unstable. The assassin thinks he has won.

In this position, the best choice would be to work him around to the side so I can escape. He's too quick for that. I could try to deliver a quick, painful blow and use his distraction to gain space, but his recovery before shows he has been trained to work through high levels of pain.

Then there's the main issue.

It's like he knows what I'm going to do. Like he's studied my movements. He expects me to do these things. And I'm not sure I like doing what's expected of me.

I have one chance. I won't get time for two.

Every fighter I've ever known would scream at me for throwing out the book on basic defense as I step closer to Kedrick's assassin.

I throw my fist up under his chin, and he catches it, giving the wrist a savage twist. My first distraction.

I kick at the inside of his ankle. He lifts his foot and is barely affected. Second distraction.

My knee moves in a blur as I bring it forward to connect with the most sensitive part of the male body. It's not a technique I've used before—I find it a little repulsive.

This man used a bow—a coward's weapon—to kill Kedrick from afar, so I relish the underhanded move. It is exactly what he deserves.

My knee crunches into the murderer's balls and his eyes roll back in his head before he doubles over in agony.

I'll hand it to him—he still tries to crawl away, his mind still on the fight. But it's over.

Just not quite finished.

I approach him slowly, scrunching my nose at the excuse for a man all but crying on the ground. He could have killed thousands with his actions today.

And all for what?

...I mean to find out.

Turning on my side, I line up his jaw and throw my body weight into a cross hit, twisting my upper body as I slam my fist into his face.

I return to camp, dragging the tied and unconscious form of the assassin behind me. My life has been uprooted, yet the camp is exactly as I left it. Slumbering, still.

I kick a sleeping sentry. He scowls until he sees who has woken him. And then he's afraid. Then confused when he sees the bloody man at my feet. Not the nicest way to wake, I have to admit.

"Carry this man," I order. "If you're lucky, I won't mention you were sleeping on duty."

My muscles are aching, though I'm pumped after the fight.

I let the Bruma fret over his fate as I lead the way to Jovan.

Kedrick's brothers deserve to see the killer, for closure. And Jovan is skilled at convincing people to talk—if the assassin won't speak freely. Torture normally bothers me, but I don't think I'll mind his methods this time.

It takes three seconds for Jovan to fully wake after exiting his tent, hair tousled. His eyes fall on the now-groaning form in the sentry's arms.

"Who?"

"Kedrick's assassin," I answer, avoiding his gaze.

His nostrils flare with a glance at the slightly conscious form again. Jovan studies him for some time, eyes narrowed as the man tosses his head around, moaning in pain.

"I might have been a little overzealous with that last punch," I mutter.

Jovan's eyes snap back to mine, his jaw clenched tight. "What happened? Tell me."

I don't think the king needs to hear about me following something shiny. "I saw something in the woods and went to check. It was a trap. We fought; he lost." I step closer to him. "It's him, Jovan. I've seen him several times in the Ire, and again when he attempted to kill me on the Oscala. This is the killer."

"He admitted to it?" Jovan asks.

And I know why he does. We're about to accuse one of the Ire folk—our new allies—of murdering the prince of Glacium and attempting to murder the Tatuma. We need to be sure. "Yes, he confessed. But there's more I need to find out."

Jovan grows quiet for a moment. These moments are his strength.

He takes the assassin from the sentry. "Go wake Adox of the Ire and his men, as well as my advisors, the Tatum's brother, Prince Ashawn, and Rhone."

The sentry's eyes widen at the list, and I can nearly hear his brain scrambling to remember the names. I wonder if the last three people on the list will get the message.

As soon as the sleepy guard scampers off, Jovan drops the man to the ground. Even I wince. Jovan is not short. It's enough to render the man unconscious once more.

The king doesn't seem too bothered. He paces the clearing.

Maintaining a relationship with the Ire is important, but I know the king feels avenging his brother is just as important. Especially to a Bruma. Loyalty is everything. The people judge their king by his strength.

"He doesn't seem big enough to have killed my brother," Jovan says quietly.

I shiver, stepping back as the clearing in front of the king's tent begins to fill. Those entering—Shard, Roscoe, Drummond—gape at the unmoving form. But no questions are asked. Not until Adox pushes through the circle.

He gazes down at his fallen kinsman and then up at the king and myself, eyes sparkling with anger. "What is the meaning of this?"

I feel, more than see, Jovan begin to vibrate. I place a hand on his arm. "Adox, you're aware I've tracked Prince Kedrick's murderer for some time. This man killed the prince."

I stare down at the assassin who ripped away the first happiness I ever knew. "The arrow was not Kaur. It was not of Glacium." I search inside of my boot and draw out the fletching I've possessed for so long. It still draws the memories of that night with ease. I can still feel Kedrick's blood bubbling between my fingers; can still feel the cold stiffness of his hands, and his unblinking gaze. "This was the arrow that ended Kedrick's life."

I hand the fletching to Adox. He examines it closely while I continue.

"It is Seedyr wood. It took me months to find out that much. When I did, it led me to a dead end." I face the old ruler. "Until, quite by accident, I was taken to the Ire."

Adox hands the arrow back, listening carefully, not interrupting. His eyes dart to the man twitching on the ground. His expression is impassive. It's possible Adox doesn't overly like the assassin either.

"Even then, it was weeks until I saw the same arrows in the Ire. It was after we'd sabotaged the Oscala pathway."

"You were asking me questions about them," interrupts Hamish in a low voice. He stands beside Adox.

His green eyes are burning.

I nod. "There were six men. And of those men, Hamish told me only three went to Osolis to trade."

Jovan is impatient. I place my body so it's between him and the assassin. Adox has to hear everything, first.

I say, "I was attacked on the Ire."

Adox dips his head. "I know of this."

My eyes flicker to Hamish. "Two arrows pierced the wings of my Soar. And this man," I say, nudging his side with my foot, "is the person who did it."

"That does not mean he killed Prince Kedrick."

I shrug. "But it will result in the same fate."

"Damn right it will," growls Jovan.

Adox isn't placated. Not yet.

"He admitted to killing Jovan's brother. Ashawn's brother." I gesture to the silent men. Ashawn stands to one side of the assassin, fixated on the killer.

Adox swallows and looks away. It's hard to meet the gaze of someone who has lost a loved one.

"He took someone from them," I say. "And nearly took me from my family, and those who love me. By his own admission he has done this many times. How many lives has he destroyed? I'll be questioning him, Adox. I must know the information he hides."

Adox finally lifts his eyes. His men are already moving back, convinced. Finally, the Ire leader closes his eyes and gives me space.

Water is thrown over the assassin. He's been stirring for the last few minutes, but his eyes fly open at the shock and he gasps, clutching his head in agony.

He's tied. I crouch, grabbing him by the hair. "What is your name?"

He moans, not answering. I can't say I've really tortured anyone before, but I understand the gist of it. I dig my finger into the growing bruise on his jaw. It appears to be fractured. Sure enough, the man's eyes begin to roll back in his head. I shake him roughly. "Your name," I prompt.

"Hayce," he whispers, eyes unfocused.

His brains are addled. This could work to my advantage. I glance over at Adox and raise my eyebrows for him to confirm the murderer's answer. Adox nods silently. The truth. Who would've thought?

"Did you kill Prince Kedrick?"

"Only by accident," he hisses, wincing as the air rushes past his teeth.

Ashawn curses and I shake my head at him, warning him not to make a sound.

"Who was your intended target?"

There's a burst of movement as Hayce arches upward. "You! Bitch." His scream echoes through the campsite.

I sigh, wondering if I should press on his jaw again. "Didn't your mother ever teach you manners?"

He throws his head back. "Mothers?" he shouts, incredulously. "Are you lecturing me about mothers?" His cackle raises the hairs on the back of my neck. "*Your* mother gave me orders to kill your boyfriend!"

And there it is.

I sit back on my heels as Hayce laughs and laughs.

From the time of Kedrick's death I'd changed my mind a dozen times about who could have commissioned the services of this hit man. I'd long since dismissed my mother as the culprit. Because I'd known for a while the murderer came from the Ire, and the Ire was a secret...

Hayce made it sound like he received regular requests to assassinate various Solati. *Something doesn't add up.*

I disregard it for the moment and turn my thoughts to the shocking revelation that my mother did not order *me* killed, but the prince. Either target would have achieved her goal of war, so why did she not choose to end my life and rid herself of fear at the same time?

There's a question I need answered if the guilt and "what ifs" are not to eat me up inside.

I turn my attention back to Hayce, raising my voice over his horrible laughter. "If your orders were to murder Kedrick, why did you decide to kill me?"

It makes no sense! I'm sure I'd never met this man in my life before visiting the Ire.

His laughter cuts off abruptly. "I hate you!" he snarls. I lean back quickly as he attempts to head-butt me.

Jovan steps forward and places a booted foot on the man's throat until he stops fighting.

The crazed man gasps, muttering to himself on the ground. I cannot grasp how his family and children have not glimpsed his madness.

The sound has woken those in the tents around us. They are drawn to the shouting.

A peek at Adox's face shows he's appalled.

"Hayce was always eccentric, Tatum. But we have never seen this side of him." Adox's words are so shocked, I believe him on the spot— especially as Hamish and the other two Ire folk present share similar stunned expressions.

Hayce has hidden his hatred well.

I listen in on his mutterings. "Always in your shadow. It should have been me! Why did he pick you? Even your mother didn't want you. He left me!"

I can't make sense of it. Olandon appears as clueless as I. Jovan is watching me also, but I give a subtle shake of the head. I have no idea.

The Ire leader steps forward. "Tatuma, there is something about Hayce you should—"

At that moment my old trainer Aquin steps through the five-deep crowd. Carrying no cane, he walks upright in slow steps so his limp is negligible.

He does not look at me.

He looks at Hayce.

And Hayce looks back at my trainer.

My friend. The only father I've ever known. The only person my mother allowed me to leave the tower with as I "watched" Olandon train. The man who has guided me, who has reprimanded me, and who has lent me secure, unwavering strength.

"Hayce," Aquin says shortly.

I look between them, confusion sweeping through me.

Hayce's tone is mocking as he replies, "Father."

CHAPTER TWENTY-SIX

"*I*... I DON'T..." I trail off, my eyes darting between the pair.

One sick on revenge. And the other the only safe presence of my childhood.

I'm numb. It can't be true. Aquin cannot be Hayce's father, the father of Kedrick's assassin.

I would have known. Aquin would have told me...

The clearing is as still as a whisper while my world crumbles. I stare at the puzzle and the pieces I've forgotten begin to assemble. Aquin's unusual behavior. I'm taken back to the beginning, where I was sitting beside Aquin, listening to Olandon and Kedrick fight in the training shed. Though it was so long ago, I remember it clearly. Aquin was acting unusually that day... sentimental, or so I'd thought at the time. When I was leaving he made me promise to be careful. He'd acted as though he were saying goodbye.

Hayce didn't learn to fight on the Ire. He was taught by the same trainer as me...

I'm frozen to the spot, unable to approach Aquin. Because if he's done this, I cannot ever look at him again.

"You *knew*?" I breathe.

Jovan is behind me.

"You still don't get it, you stupid little girl. Aquin has a filthy little secret."

The laughter is getting on my nerves. I can't think with the sound screeching in my ears. Aquin...

I close my eyes as a tearing unlike anything I've ever felt rips me apart from the inside, leaving me in two pieces. The only other person I'd trusted wholeheartedly in my childhood to protect me… has destroyed me.

"Nothing to say," I whisper, staring at Aquin.

He lifts his head, clearing his throat. "It is as the boy has said."

"The boy?" I shake my head. "The *boy* is your son. Who are you?" How was I fooled so?

Aquin's eyes blur. "You are like a daughter to me."

I snort. "Do you often ask your son to murder your daughter's friends, at the orders of someone who has tortured your 'daughter' her entire life?"

"Don't give him too much credit." Hayce smirks. "I deal with the Tatum directly. She's the only one hiring me. When I told her exactly who I was related to, she said she had a very special job for me."

"*You fool,*" whispers Adox. "You could have given up the Ire."

"I wouldn't give up my wife and children," Hayce says. He spits in Aquin's direction. "Unlike some."

"I was given a choice by the Tatum," Aquin whispers, head bent. "She asked whether she should kill you, or the prince. I chose to save you."

I turn away. I've heard enough.

Jovan grips my arm. "Lina." He speaks into my ear. "You need to listen to what he has to say. You'll never forgive yourself if you don't."

Even in my shaking hurt, I understand he's right.

Aquin sees I've stopped. "Hayce's orders were to kill the prince," he says hesitantly.

"And you didn't bother to tell me?" I wither.

"You were not ready!"

I've never heard him shout in my life. Olandon jumps back. I'm too angry for that. I take two steps forward.

"You were not ready to take her on and win," he says on a sigh, calming himself with effort. "The prince was the choice I made, when given an impossible choice over which of you to save."

You're telling me my mother allowed *you* to decide."

"There is much you don't understand about my relationship with your mother. I have known her since she was a girl. I have watched as she descended into madness. I do not know if she passed the decision to me, so that I might save your life because she did not trust herself to. Or if she is truly insane and gleaned entertainment from watching how it tortured me."

The unsettling conversation I'd had with him two days ago comes back to me. Aquin's son writhes on the ground, shouting profanities.

"And despite witnessing her descent, you somehow missed the signs of your own son's demise."

A tear falls down my trainer's weathered cheek. "I understood my mistake too late. I did not realize the grudge he held against you. For being, in his eyes, more dear to me than my own blood."

My vision blurs, and I dash away the evidence. Everything has been a lie. My whole life.

Hayce screams, "You left me to die! You killed my mother, cheated on your wife with a villager, and left me to die."

So Hayce is full-blooded Solati.

Aquin's eyes spark. "Your mother died giving birth to you. Bedding her was a mistake I have sorely regretted. And your life here would have been horrible. The bastard son of an Elite soldier. The Tatum would not have accepted the blemish within her guard. Keeping you would have either meant your death, or your exile, or the loss of my post. I had a wife to take care of. I did the only thing I could do: I dropped you at the trading post. The men who traded there disappeared for weeks at a time, and nobody knew where to. Later, when I was reunited with Hayce, I learned of the Ire. Back then, I simply guessed they had somewhere secret where you could be kept. I hoped—"

"You had no guarantee they would take me!"

The Ire leader clears his throat. "He did. I gave it to him. I was a trader at the time, which you well know, Hayce." Adox frowns as Hayce throws him a disdainful glance.

Whatever Hayce has done, he has been wronged by the very person who should have cared for him.

"What kind of person are you?" My voice is laden with judgment.

For the first time Aquin's face hardens. "My wife had not been pregnant, but suddenly I pronounce I have a son. She would be ridiculed. It would bring dishonor to our ancestors."

"Yet you chose to dishonor your sweet wife with unfaithfulness before that moment. You expect me to have sympathy for someone who mistreats their child? Of all people, are you trying to convince *me*?" I'm nearly shouting. I cannot take it anymore. "You should have left with him! You should have cared for your son!"

"Then you would be dead." Aquin bows his head with the quiet words.

I'm not done. "Do not pretend you had noble reasons for making the choice. Simply put, you did not want to be caught—by your wife or by the Tatum. But your biggest mistake was not telling me what you knew before Kedrick was killed. That was your chance to salvage any bond we had." I cannot see for the tears streaming down my face. "But you didn't," I sob. "And so you lose my trust, my friendship, and my love. Because you never deserved it. Because you are not who I thought you were." And I finish with the harshest words I can summon. "Do not call me Lina anymore."

Olandon gasps. Aquin absently clutches at his chest, horrified hurt on his face.

What I've done is rarely enacted. It's why the choice to give permission to use your shortened name is a decision that many take years to give. Once given, it is rarely taken back. Because to take it back is to admit you made the wrong decision. To a Solati, that is an embarrassment like no other.

That is how strongly I feel at my father's betrayal. I do not wipe away the tears as I stride from the clearing. Inside, I'm a heartbroken five-year-old, clutching at her favorite toy and crying for her parents. I don't care where they take Hayce. Or Aquin. I don't care what any of them do. The Bruma make way for me, soaking up the sight of my display.

It just adds to my humiliation.

I leave.

And I run.

And I run.

I run until, exhausted, I trip and curl into a broken ball on the forest floor. And I cannot care that I have people to worry about. My head and heart will not reconcile what happened, and I blame myself for not seeing some sign of Aquin's betrayal long before this.

But to entertain the thought of betrayal, you first must entertain the thought the person *could* betray you.

And such a notion never entered my mind.

———

I rouse, cracking open my swollen eyes as I'm lifted.

"I've been following your tracks for hours," says Olandon.

A traitorous tear leaks from my eye; surely there aren't any left. Aquin doesn't deserve any of them.

"Where are we?" I say after a couple of attempts. The sound is cold and hoarse. A perfect reflection of how I feel inside.

He crouches. "Not far from the forest edge," he whispers. "We need to be careful. You shouldn't have run this way."

I don't say anything. I'm wrung out.

A short silence goes by. "But I understand why you had to. And… I'm so sorry, Lina." His voice cracks.

The news has affected him just as much. Neither of us had a father, after all.

"I'm sorry, too, Landon."

For the first time since we left Osolis, Olandon and I cry without shame on each other's shoulders. His body wracks with emotion, as does mine. If any of my mother's men are near, we're done for, because we are incapable of protecting ourselves, too heartbroken to care.

"Lina, I understand what you're feeling," he says hesitantly. "And I hope you know I'd never do that to you. I never have, and I never will."

I want to say anyone can, but some protected part of me knows that if I give up my faith in people I will truly be beyond repair. It's my faith in people that keeps me from becoming like Hayce. Or like my mother.

I hug my little brother tightly. "And I will never betray you. No matter who uses us, lies to us, and tries to hurt us, we will always have each other. I'll never hurt you, brother. It would go against every part of me."

Fresh tears fall from his eyes. "And I, you."

When we're hurt, we recede to the fundamental truths in our lives. We return to that which we are certain of, to lick our wounds and heal. Olandon is my fundamental truth.

"We must return," I say eventually.

Olandon tips his head back. "We have time. The army will take a day to catch up. We can intercept them tomorrow."

"Thank Solis." I fling myself back, and curl into a different, more content—though no less heartbroken—ball. "I love you, brother. But you're on first watch."

"And it's only because I love you that I will do it," he says softly.

CHAPTER TWENTY-SEVEN

*A*QUIN BETRAYED ME.

The morning brings fresh worries, though fewer tears. Aquin betrayed me, and his son—who murdered Jovan's brother—tried to kill me.

Osolis and Glacium have one thing in common: the laws for dealing with these crimes. And though the methods of execution differ from world to world, the fact that each method ends in death is the same. I have no idea what to do.

We loiter in the forest, listening for the army's approach, taking turns resting. I have no idea how much ground I'd covered yesterday. But as the sky begins to darken, even Olandon is worried.

"They should have passed us by now," he says.

"You are certain."

"I am."

I stand up, brushing the dirt from my black robes. I shouldn't bother. They're torn and covered in dust. The garment is still tied up at one side from the day before. "We need to go back, then. There might be something wrong."

"Maybe they wait for our return."

"No, Jovan would keep pushing forward."

We jog through the forest, Olandon leading the way. Running is the best thing we could have done: the air clears my mind, and rids me of the headache I have from crying.

It turns out the army has made some ground. We find them after an hour; they must have only stopped at midday or so. A cry goes up as we are spotted. We slow, breathing hard.

"Tatuma!" I turn to see Roscoe running toward us. "Olandon." He huffs, out of breath.

"What's the matter, Roscoe?" My tone is colder than it should be, but I've surpassed my quota of caring for the day.

He either doesn't realize I'm pissed, or ignores it. "Hayce got loose an hour ago."

"You let him escape!" I leave for one night and they fuck everything up.

"No, he had a hidden weapon," Roscoe rushes to explain. "We've recovered him."

My patience is wearing thin, in the extreme.

Roscoe swallows. "Tatuma. He wounded Aquin. Badly."

After everything—the betrayal, the hurt, the *everything*—why is it my first thought upon hearing those words to wonder if Aquin will live? It shouldn't be possible I would care after how badly he has broken my trust.

"Nothing less than what he deserves," Olandon says, grabbing my hand.

Roscoe's eyes bore into my own. He waits for my decision. He'll be disappointed if I make the wrong choice. He believes I am better than that.

When did he earn the right to give me advice?

I set my jaw and cross my arms. "When do we resume the march?"

The march doesn't resume that day.

Olandon and I sit apart from the others that night, and the Bruma gather we don't wish to be disturbed. I have no idea where Jovan is. His absence feels significant. Like it means something that he's not here for me, like he has been in the past.

One more chink in my armor. One more break in my heart.

"He doesn't deserve our presence there," Olandon is saying. I wonder who he's trying to convince. It's not me, that's for sure.

Aquin betrayed us. He knew his son was hired to kill Prince Kedrick. And part of him must have sensed Hayce would try to kill me instead, or why warn me? Not that I'd call the warning he gave me anything other than a cryptic *nothing*. This whole time, I'd assumed he hardly knew my mother. *He* led me to believe that.

Now he intends to die, when all I want to do is scream and scream at him for days. I don't want to care that he may be dead already. I don't want to care.

I'm woken partway through the night by someone entering the king's tent. That's where we've been hiding all day.

"Just me," Jovan says softly.

I snort at his words; they are just as ridiculous as ever. Just Jovan. I roll my eyes.

My brother doesn't wake.

Jovan picks his way to me and drops down on the furs in an exhausted heap. He wraps a large arm around my waist and draws me close, snuggling his face into the nook of my neck. "I'm sorry, baby."

I sniff dismissively, except it ends up sounding like I'm trying not to cry. "It is what it is," I say.

He doesn't say anything, just kisses my shoulder. He's silent for so long I think he's fallen asleep.

Until I hear his soft words in my ear. "He's still alive."

We resume a slow march the next day. We should reach the edge of the forest by nightfall. I pick up snatches of conversation throughout the day and it annoys me that I'm intentionally listening in to hear how Aquin is.

I can't deny hearing he is stable gives me relief.

Jovan stays close all day, and when we stop for the night, he doesn't give me an option, drawing me to his tent. I glance over my shoulder at Olandon, but Ashawn has him under his wing. My brother will be fine.

"Do you want to talk about it?" Jovan pulls his shirt over his head.

I discover as I'm staring at him undressing that I do want to talk. "It was him," I say flatly. "This whole time."

"Him that what?"

I blow out my cheeks. "He killed Kedrick!" I explode.

Jovan shakes his head. "No, he didn't. His son killed Kedrick."

"Same thing." I cross my arms.

Jovan rests his arms on the chair I'm perched on, and leans in. "It's not. Tell me the truth. What are you angriest about?"

I'm angry about everything. How am I supposed to pick the one thing that annoys me the most?

"Close your eyes, Lina."

I obey.

"Think back to the moment in the clearing when you first discovered the truth."

A flood of images assaults me.

"Replay the whole thing. Where was it that you lost control?"

I open my eyes to find his face right before me. Neither of us moves. "When I realized he knew Kedrick was going to die and didn't tell me."

He kisses my lips, and then my forehead. "Yes. Now come to bed."

He holds me to his chest, throwing the blankets off. Too hot for that.

"Next question," he says.

I nod into his chest.

"If you could keep the twins from feeling pain… would you?"

"Of course." Then I see where he's going with it. "It is *not* the same thing."

He shrugs a massive shoulder. Jovan's other arm is bent behind his head. He stares at the tent ceiling, not answering.

I sit up, throwing off his arm. "Why are you defending him?"

He draws a finger down my back. "You would come to the same reasoning in time. But you might not have time."

"He's stable."

Jovan shakes his head. "Lina, he's *old*."

I sink back down, lying on my back. A thought occurs to me. "Why aren't you mad at him? He chose to kill your brother instead of me."

Jovan rolls toward me. "If he chose you, I would have both my brothers. Because he chose Kedrick, I have found love and happiness. Either way, I would have lost. And if it were up to me, both Hayce and Aquin would be minus a head by now."

"Then why aren't you stomping around like you usually do?"

"I don't stomp."

A giggle escapes my lips.

He heaves an exaggerated sigh. "That sound." He leans forward and presses kisses to my neck.

"But seriously," I say, trying to remember what we were talking about.

He lets out an actual sigh this time, pulling back. "Because killing Aquin would upset you. That is your choice."

"And Hayce?" I can't help it. The man is insane, but a large part of me empathizes with how he grew up.

"He is connected to Aquin. You need to be there for that decision. And I've promised your trainer the choice will not be made until he has passed."

"Why?" Why would Jovan make such a promise to Aquin?

"He talked, and I listened. As you will do in your own time."

I sigh. "I'm not sure I can, Jovan."

Jovan presses another kiss to the side of my neck. "Then that is also your choice."

I can only just make out his face. "Thank you."

He grinds his hips into me. "Don't thank me just yet."

He swallows my laughter as our mouths meet.

CHAPTER TWENTY-EIGHT

*W*E MAKE IT to the edge of the Kaur forest the next day. The moment feels like a hundred emotions rolled into one.

There are things I took for absolutes that are no longer absolutes.

Tomorrow we go to war.

And I might die.

Jovan might die.

Sanjay, Olandon, and Blizzard might all be dead.

"Seriously, Sin, it's the stupidest thing I ever saw," Ice snorts.

I glance to the side and burst into laughter. Sin has tried to make up for the fact he only possesses half a head of hair by combing the remainder toward the bald side. I snigger with everyone else.

Dare I say it: Sin looks hurt by our amusement.

Shard approaches, loosening a dagger from his belt. "Now Sin, this is for your own good."

There's a moment—a short one—where Sin is confused. Then he understands what Shard means to do. "You wouldn't," he accuses.

Shard nods to Blizzard, Wrath, Ice, and Avalanche, who close in slowly.

I only see glimpses, mostly a tangle of limbs—and Sin's high-pitched screams. Blizzard is making odd shushing noises as though the sound will soothe the man being forced to have a haircut.

I shake my head and walk in the direction of Jovan's tent. I'm accosted on the way by a red-faced Sanjay. I smooth my features. I've been waiting for this.

"You put me on messages!" he says.

It's not often Sanjay gets angry, but when he does, he really lets loose.

"I did," I say calmly.

"Don't use that Solati shit on me. I'll be going into battle with the others."

Soldiers around us listen with interest. It's okay for Sanjay to speak that way when we're alone, but not with witnesses. I straighten.

"Soldier," I bark. "I am the Tatuma and you will address me with respect."

Sanjay blinks at me.

I continue. "Follow me." It's an order. Even in his indignant rage, Sanjay recognizes my tone. He trots after me into a random, empty tent.

He waits for me to begin speaking once inside, face nearly purple.

"I made Fiona a promise to keep you alive. I mean to keep it." It's as simple as that.

I receive a stupefied look in return. "Do you realize what that does to my balls?"

"Ew!"

"It shrinks them right up," he says. "Olina, don't take away my pride. I want to fight beside my friends and keep my honor."

My tone is cool. "What good is honor if you're dead?"

He flinches.

"A baby, Sanjay. A loving wife. *That* is why you are assigned to messages. It's a task that requires someone Jovan and I trust—"

"Don't give me that," he withers.

I give him a humorless smile. "You're right."

"Do you know how many men here have families back on Glacium?" he asks.

Sorrow fills me. Because, unbeknownst to those on Glacium, many have already lost a family member to fire, or the river, or poison. I meet Sanjay's earnest blue eyes. "I'm in a position where I am able to keep my friends safe. To keep a family whole." My face hardens. "You are assigned to running messages. That is my order, and the order stands."

He stares at me in mutiny. On this I'm unshakeable. And Sanjay sees it on my face. He throws back the tent flap and stalks out without another word.

The exchange hovers in my mind as I resume my walk through camp, and without conscious thought, I wander to where Aquin lays injured. I stare at the medic tent, listening to the flurry of movement inside. Is he dead? Will he be dead by morning?

Minutes must pass as I stand there in indecision.

A loud ringing breaks my trance. I turn away.

I'm not ready.

Instead, I make my way to the edge of the forest.

My mother's palace stands in the distance, tall and dark against the dry landscape. The area between the forest and the palace is desolate. There are no villagers, no housing—no movement.

Inside the walls of the palace, standing in the royal meadow, an entire army waits for us.

They will use arrows.

They will attempt to keep us on this side of the wall as they whittle down our numbers. And then they will sweep through and kill the survivors, cutting off escape. It will take a few months before Mother marches on Glacium, where she will conquer without resistance.

Two hundred Ire folk, eleven hundred Bruma, and three Solati dead. Not to mention the losses on the Tatum's side. All for her greed.

My mother will have other tricks; of this there is no doubt. She's already tricked us once before. I have no idea what her plans might be, and that doesn't sit well with me.

I come to a quick decision. Jogging through the camp, I search left and right for Hamish. I find him up a tree with some other folk. Guess they miss being in the air.

"Want to come and do some recon?" I ask. It's a trick question; Hamish could never turn down an adventure.

Sure enough, he drops from the tree immediately.

We run back to my tent so I can grab my Soar. Jovan is striding through camp, the advisors scuttling in his wake. He turns as we run past and I wave, knowing if I stop this recon mission will be over before it's started.

"What are we looking for?" Hamish pants as we shimmy up a tree.

I balance atop a wobbling branch, strapping myself into the Soar. "I don't want to walk into a trap again. We'll stay high, out of arrow range. I just want to see inside the wall."

He looks down, where a couple of advisors are rushing toward us. "Uh-huh. And everyone is okay with what we're doing?"

I peek sideways at him. "What do you think?"

"That we'd better go now so we can plead ignorance." He drops off the side and I follow him, smiling at the shouts below us.

We pop the wings until we're high above the ground. My eyes stream from the heightened smokiness. It's midday, but smoke pours out of the Fourth, as per usual. Added to the thick layer is the smoke from the fire my mother lit in the Second. We'll have to stay as high as possible despite all the smoke; the alternative is an arrow in the gut.

"Sucks about Aquin," Hamish shouts.

I roll my eyes. "You can say that again."

He opens his mouth and does just that, following it with a quiet, "There's always been something off-kilter with Hayce. I knew he held on to the injustice of Aquin deserting him, but all Ire folk not born in the Ire do. I thought letting him stay with Aquin for a few weeks at a time and allowing him to explore Osolis as a trader would help him heal. None of us suspected he was using his time on Osolis to kill Solati."

I shake my head. "The Ire isn't to blame. Only my mother and Aquin."

I survey the ground below us with blurry eyes. Abandoned. Surely, not all the villagers have moved to the other side of Osolis? There are only half the previous number of villagers there. Had so many died in the civil rebellion?

"What can you see?" I ask Hamish.

"A whole heap of nothin'," he replies.

That matches what I'm getting. The Third is empty. Completely empty. "Okay, let's go to the palace."

"I want indemnity against King Jovan first."

I laugh. "If I could give it, you'd have it."

"It sure seems as though he's wrapped around your undersized hands."

I glance down at my hands. "They're not undersized!" I glare at him, only to see him grinning.

We climb until we begin to cough. A shudder runs through me as I remember my near-death on the ledge in the Oscala.

We should be out of arrow range, but I can't be certain; it is hard to gauge the distance from above.

My childhood memories have prepared me for what I will see when we reach the palace. Inside the high Kaur walls lies a vast meadow, and past the meadow lies a manicured garden. The meadow will be dry now and emptied of hay.

And full of the Tatum's Army.

I hold my breath as we circle over the meadow on silent wings. I open and close my mouth half a dozen times or more before Hamish finally voices what I can't say.

"I thought the army was supposed to be here," he calls.

I wipe my eyes on my shoulder and squint. "Let's drop a little lower."

They have to be here. There's nowhere else to be.

What is my mother up to? We drop ten meters, just below the smoke barrier.

"There's no one here."

I hear his words, but still circle further. Searching for Mother's men. They could be in the palace, I suppose. Strategically, that made little sense. The wall was a better place to make the first stand, leaving the palace as a retreat point when the wall was breached.

Something is going on.

We circle the palace twice. I'm sure we are sighted. In that time, we encounter no one. See *no one*. We return in silence, dropping as we near the tree line.

A deep ripping sound jerks me from my musings. This time I know exactly what it is.

I hurtle toward the ground. This tear is larger, much larger. As the trees draw nearer, I squeeze my eyes firmly shut. This is going to hurt.

"Oof." The air leaves me as my Soar is grabbed from above.

Hamish's Soar isn't designed for two. I raise my hands to protect my face as we sink down into the trees.

"Ow! Veni!" Hamish shouts, as branches scratch us from every direction. At least he has some cover! I wince as a twig whips across my arms. When we make it through the canopy, I grab at the closest branch and latch on, hanging by my armpits.

"Let go!" I shout over my shoulder.

Hamish abandons me to the branch, and I hear his Soar scraping on tree limbs as he continues downward.

I rest for a long moment before swinging my legs over the limb. *Who shot me down? Is Hayce free?*

"That was close."

I look down at Hamish on the forest floor and grin. "Thanks. How many times is that now?"

"I've lost count," he returns drily.

A crashing noise comes from the bush. With a start I recall the fact I've been shot down. "Hamish, *hide.*"

It's lucky the person turns out to be Jovan, because Hamish hadn't begun to move.

Though he might be wishing he had by the look on Jovan's face.

Sheepishly, I slide down the tree and try smiling at Jovan, who has clearly been waiting for me to return from my impromptu scouting trip. He doesn't twitch a muscle in return.

"So… we found out some stuff," I say.

"Indeed."

I shiver at the quiet menace in his tone.

"Before or after you nearly died?"

"Is Hayce free?" I ask.

Jovan's eyes glitter. I can see Hamish sneaking off behind him. Traitor!

"He is not. I am capable of securing one prisoner."

I blink. I wasn't implying that. "Well, I was shot at. That's why I fell. If it wasn't Hayce, who was it?"

This seems to interrupt the king's stalking anger for a moment. His eyes turn to the clearing, the blue orbs piercing into every shadow of every tree.

He grips my elbow, voice lowered. "Come. We will discuss this back at camp."

What is going through Jovan's mind? I crane my head to search behind us. But it's hard to do as I'm being forced out of the clearing.

"Stop it. I can walk myself." I jerk my arm from his grasp.

He rounds on me. "Do you ever stop to think before you put yourself in danger?" He takes a deep breath, closing his eyes briefly before stomping away.

We don't talk as we jog back to camp.

He's angry—and that's fairly normal for him. But this anger seems excessive.

I glance at him. We're going into battle tomorrow; perhaps that set him off? I can imagine he's running through a list of the men he may lose tomorrow.

I realize I haven't been here for him. Absorbed by my own problems, I haven't stopped to consider the fact that this man is carrying the fate of hundreds on his shoulders. I pull him to a stop as the camp comes into sight. He resists my touch at first, but I take a firm hold and pull.

He lets me win in the end. If I were a lesser woman, that might bother me.

"Jovan, I'm sorry."

He arches an eyebrow. "Is this a new way to get back in my good books?"

I don't smile. "You're feeling just as much pressure as I am. I'm sorry I haven't been there for you."

"What are you asking?" he says brusquely.

My brows furrow to think about it. "I'm asking if you're all right."

He turns away, rubbing his stubble. "My brother's killer sits alive in one of my tents. Over thirteen hundred people could die tomorrow if I make the wrong choice. More, if you count the Ire. There is no doubt the Solati are better strategists than us. We're in their territory." He sits heavily against a tree. "Glacium has never won a battle on Osolis."

"Until now," I say.

He looks up, exasperation etched all over his face.

"You have a team of the best helping you to make those decisions.

Your men trust you. I trust you. And not because of *who* you are. Every person camped in front of you trusts you because you've earned it. Because you are strong, smart, and fair. They respect you, and fight for you. Tomorrow, you'll do what you do best, and more, because that is who you are. And that is all you have control over. The choices you make."

"And if I make the wrong one?"

I reach down and try to pull him up. He tugs me down onto his lap. "You won't," I decide, chewing my lip. "But I'll be there to help you. And you'll be there to help me, just in case."

His eyes soften.

I push his light brown hair back from his face. "Plus, you can just be the first Bruma to win on Osolis."

His eyes twinkle. "Simple as that?"

"Don't see why not," I say casually.

I hold my expression firm until he smiles. I punch him, standing. "Come on, king. You must return to do your kingly things."

He rests his head back on the trunk briefly. "You were doing so well before you said that."

I snigger, leading the way.

"And... thanks. I needed that."

"And I needed you to stop being angry at me." I sprint off, laughing, knowing I won't be able to escape Jovan's clutches for long.

CHAPTER TWENTY-NINE

THE LAUGHTER DOESN'T last.

By that night, I'm wondering if it ever happened.

The representatives from Osolis, Glacium, and the Ire talk well into the evening about the absence of the Osolis army at the palace and the subsequent attempt on my life. My gut tells me it must be someone else from the Ire. I'm sure not everyone agrees with what I'm doing. It could be a friend of Hayce's; it could be someone who hates that I've revealed the Ire and involved them in this mess.

I skirt around the issue, seeing Adox is uncomfortable. I don't want the Ire to feel we're singling them out.

Needless to say, we don't get anywhere. It's just as I'm ducking out of the tent around midnight that I spot the senior medic—I can't remember his name—hovering to one side.

Dread pits in my stomach as I guess he's come to tell me Aquin is dead. I approach him with dragging steps. He shuffles nervously, clearly afraid of delivering the bad news.

"Spit it out." My tone is unintentionally harsh.

The medic's eyes widen. "Uh... well... I..."

"He's dead, isn't he." Even I can hear the sorrow in my voice. I should have spoken to him when I had the chance.

"No. No!" The medic rushes to reassure me.

I sag in relief.

"That is to say, Aquin wanted me to give you a message. Uh, but I'm not sure what it means; he's hardly lucid the majority of the time."

I close my eyes. Solis save me from rambling. "The message?" What could Aquin possibly have to say? It better not be an apology, or I might go and scream at him.

"Aquin said to tell you, 'They're behind you.'"

The blood must drain from my face because the medic steps forward. I grab his hand.

"Was there anything else? Did he say anything else?"

He winces at the tight grip I have on his fingers. "That's it, I swear!"

Our exchange attracts attention. Jovan strides toward us, drawn to the stress in my voice from inside his tent. I turn to the medic.

"Take us to him."

The king walks beside me at a fast clip. I jog to keep up with the two men.

Jovan knows better than to ask questions. He knows there are few things that would cause this reaction in me. I'm grateful for the understanding we've forged over many months of shared hardship, because I'm incapable of speech at the moment. If Aquin is saying what I think he's saying, we could all be dead by morning.

It overrides the churning in my stomach at seeing Aquin again. Or maybe it's the excuse I need to give him my forgiveness.

I'm not prepared for what I see. Aquin lay slightly propped up on bundles of dry leaves. It isn't Aquin, though; it's a person half the size of the man I saw mere days ago. How has he become so thin, so quickly? The color in his face is gone. It appears a ghastly white in the low light available and he is utterly still. I could be convinced he's dead already. Aquin is dying. I don't have to see his wound to gather he's fading from this world.

But I'm so angry! Or maybe I just think I should be angry. Is it ridiculous to hold on to the hate when there are only moments left for us to reconcile?

I stride to Aquin's side. His skin is cold. The frail replica of my trainer shivers at my touch and cracks his eyes open.

"Aquin," I say softly.

He licks his lips. I clamp down on a moan at their cracked and bloodied appearance.

The medic drips some water down his throat. Aquin chokes a little at its passage.

"What is his wound?" I ask.

"A dagger too close to his heart."

Hayce is going to die. No matter what good reasons he has to have a vendetta against his father and myself, he is deranged, and a danger to all. He cannot go free.

Jovan crouches by my side and drapes a warm arm across my shoulders.

An iron grip clamps down on my wrist. I look back at Aquin and start when I see the wildness in his eyes. "Lina," he says. "They are behind you."

"Who is, Aquin? How do you know?"

The medic whispers low. "I've been giving him updates in his lucid moments. It seems to calm him."

It sounds like Aquin has been receiving his own report.

Aquin arches off the bed, pulling his face close to mine. His eyes are clear. "They shot at you. The garden is empty. They are behind you."

Jovan has tightened his grip to near-unbearable levels as he absorbs the horrible implication of Aquin's words.

"But why would they try to shoot me down?" I whisper. "It could only reveal their presence."

Aquin slumps back onto the bed, his eyes struggling to focus. It took everything he had to warn me. "A mistake that will save you all."

His eyes droop closed. I turn to Jovan and we stare at each other, not hiding our shock, or the complete indecision we have about our next move. If we ignore this, everyone will die. If we act on this, and Aquin's guess is incorrect… it could mean our deaths as well.

It turns out my trainer isn't unconscious. He says one more word.

A word that tells me what we need to do.

"Run."

Jovan and I move through the camp, waking the council members. We must be subtle.

If Aquin is right, the Solati must have been camped in the Kaur forest since we escaped the trap in the Second Rotation. The army itself cannot be very close as our scouts haven't spotted anything amiss. But the Solati will have eyes on us.

We're gathered in Jovan's tent. I sit, tapping my finger impatiently as the king explains the dire situation. There's immediate uproar. I stand and glare at them until they shut up. That's *just* what we need—loud, outraged noise.

Adox stares at me. He understands the outcome of this just as well as Jovan and I do. "We need to move."

"But to where?" Drummond puts in.

I glance at Jovan. We've only had a few minutes to discuss this and I'm still not sure if it's the right path. "They'll be planning to trap us between the forest and the palace wall. But Mother wouldn't have left the palace unguarded. More likely they've just split the army in half."

I'm overridden by Hamish. "We should send the Ire folk out to scout."

"No," Jovan interrupts. "They'll attack as soon as possible if they think they've revealed themselves. We got lucky after Olina was shot down. They didn't expect Aquin to guess their plans."

"Solati always attack at dawn," Olandon says.

I peek at my brother and see his eyes are dark with worry. He's right. We have a few hours to move. We can be assured Mother's army is on their way.

"We prepare for the worst-case scenario," I say.

"That the Solati are already on their way." Jovan circles the table toward me.

My voice is grim. "Jovan and I have decided to mobilize the army immediately."

Roscoe has remained silent until now. "Where can we possibly retreat? The Fourth and Second either side are uninhabitable at present due to fire. And according to Aquin, there are soldiers behind us. If Olina is right, part of the army is behind, while the remaining portion is within the palace wall."

I avoid his gaze. "My mother won't have left herself defenseless. We take the palace walls before first firelight. Hopefully we can disperse one of the armies before they trap us."

Olandon stands, tense. "If we send Ire folk to take out the palace sentries, I believe we could get close before we're noticed."

It won't be that easy. "Whether we are noticed or not, we must leave now and make for the wall with haste. I hope we will have a few hours to conquer it before the other army arrives to attack."

"There are a lot of 'I hopes' in that," Adox muses gravely.

I don't say anything in reply because he is right.

"We stay, and we could die. If we leave, we will be launching the same attack we were going to—just earlier."

"With a flustered army, in the smoke and the dark."

I narrow my eyes at Drummond. Who woke him? It certainly wasn't me. "It can't be helped. All of us must show confidence. The soldiers will react based on *our* behavior. Be decisive and direct."

Every man in the room is looking at his lap. I myself wonder where I'm going to find this confidence I speak of. A scared army is a dangerous army, indeed.

King Jovan returns to his seat, and all eyes focus on him. He sprawls in the chair, one leg out, one hand laid flat on the table in front of him. "Spread the word. Do it quietly. Anyone causing unnecessary tumult will be punished. We are sneaking up on the Solati. We leave in an hour. Take only what we need to take the palace walls. Leave all else."

My mouth is dry. This is happening. It's actually happening.

"In one hour," Jovan finishes, "we go to war."

CHAPTER THIRTY

I SNEAK THROUGH THE plain between the forest and the palace, my footsteps a whisper on the dry ground. I don't know why I bother masking my footfall with the army at my back. There's no way the palace will miss our approach, especially as the Ire were unable to take out the sentries thanks to the thick smoke.

It took less than an hour for us to leave. If we're lucky, the Solati in the forest have missed our departure.

Speed is our ally; hesitation, our death.

Glacium's army is a sight to behold, the men bare-chested and tight with fury. Most have swords, but there are axes and spears, and some of the Outer Rings men have large hammers. The tall, muscled men stalk toward the palace, each of their faces filled with the savageness they are renowned for.

Jovan gestures to Malir and Rhone. I watch as his order ripples through the men. In the next thirty seconds they are spreading wide across the plain. We'll use our numbers, attacking the wall from many points while we have the advantage.

My breath comes fast as we draw closer.

Olandon is to my right, with Rian on his other side. Shard and the barracks members creep on my left. Sanjay is behind me; my plan to keep him from the battle is now in shambles.

"Shard," I whisper. "I want you to protect Sanjay during battle."

"My orders are to protect you."

"And I'm overriding those orders."

He contemplates it. "My answer is no, but I'll designate Ice and Blizzard to the job."

"Done." I sincerely hope my vow to Fiona is one I can keep.

Another order goes out, and it's as though the entire army shudders. I feel it passing through me, too—a shiver of foreboding.

"Charge!" The scream goes up. I don't know where it comes from, but I'm shouting it, too. Gone is the careful picking through the plain as eleven hundred Bruma, two hundred Ire folk and three Solati erupt into a chaotic sprint in the most primal of all calls: survival. There's no honor in it, whatever our intentions may be. It is what it is. We want to live. And we are willing to kill for it.

With my friends either side of me, I charge, covering the rest of the distance in the next few minutes. The black palace walls loom, and I recall how many times I've walked through without thought. The walls are twice the height of Avalanche. Beyond the wall is a meadow, a sweeping courtyard, and then the dark and elegant palace itself.

One thing is different: A heavy gate has been erected, blocking our way. I'd expect no less of my mother.

The Ire folk will not be able to fly for another hour. The smoke is too thick. It is the single disadvantage we have in attacking overnight. As I reach the wall, I hear the sounds of the army within; the shouts, the screams.

"Cover!" comes a bellowed order.

Shard and Olandon's shields cover me from both sides, and I jerk at the five loud thuds atop it as arrows embed in the wood.

"Loose." I recognize Malir's voice.

Our own arrows are volleyed in return, and a frantic scrambling on the other side can be heard. It is the first time in history Bruma have used archery in battle.

I grin at Jovan like a maniac, high on the thrill of the fight. He grins back, just as unhinged.

Our wooden ladders are pushed against the walls. I watch as the men trying to climb are mowed down like vermin by the archers. I can help with that.

"I need my bow and arrows," I call to Olandon over the clamor.

Rian passes them along.

"Stay here," I call. Our men are being slaughtered trying to get those ladders up. If I can interrupt the precision of the slaughter long enough to get our own archers in place, then we can get the upper hand. "Make sure our archers are ready to climb."

It's worth the risk.

No one expects me to leave the shelter of the shields and make for the wall. Possibly because few others would do what I'm about to do. Surely, my friends should know me better by now.

I sprint for the closest ladder. It sits to the far left of the wall where we are positioned, out of the worst of the onslaught. I leap over the growing piles of Bruma bodies at the base of the ladder. One man clings precariously to the top while four men struggle to hold the ladder in place against the Solati pushing at it from the other side.

The arrows are coming from the palace towers. They'll have their sights trained on the tops of the ladders.

There are shouts behind me—specifically for me, I imagine.

I dance up the ladder, pushing the man at the top off. No need for him to die, too. But I don't climb to the top of the wall there. Instead, I grip onto the Kaur wall with my fingers and swing my way along until I'm halfway between two ladders.

My next move has to be quick. I glance over my shoulder; the quiver is full. How many archers are in the palace towers? If I can get one, or two, it will take a moment for new Solati to take their position.

All we need is ten seconds to press our advantage.

I take a deep breath.

Pulling myself up, I immediately launch to the right, toward the gate. I wish I'd had the foresight to tie my robes up as they swish around my legs. There's no time to stop now.

Still running, I unhook my bow, dodging at random intervals. I drop to the wall as a spear hurtles at my head. In the next second I'm back up, and I've spotted my first archer. Drawing an arrow, I focus on the tower window for a precious moment before loosing.

I have no way to confirm if it flies true. I'm too busy moving. A whir of an arrow sounds to my left, and I jerk my head back just in time.

There! Number two. The openings—windows, as a Bruma would call them—are square holes in the black palace wall, designed to ventilate the rooms and provide light. Every room has one. And now they are used as vantage points to shoot us down.

I select another arrow. A dagger flies past my leg as I shoot. Wide. I select another arrow and loose.

I'm directly over the gate now. I risk a glance back at the second tower. No more arrows are leaving the opening there.

A few of our men have made it onto the wall.

"Send more up," I scream over my shoulder. I doubt anyone hears.

An arrow sinks in the wood just below my foot, and I shoot on instinct. This time, I do see the effect. The Solati tumbles from the tower, falling to his death on the cobblestones thirty meters below. Wincing, I look at my mother's army below for the first time.

Her military is garbed in their fine uniforms; leather straps crisscross over their long-sleeved white tunics. Their loose trousers tuck into knee-high laced boots, and a wide belt encircles their torsos. Leather arm guards protect their forearms. Each soldier possesses two daggers, a sword, and a spear. They look dangerous and well-trained—as I know they are.

Many of them stare at me, and I wonder why for a moment before I put myself in their sandals.

I'm wearing robes. They know who I am. They've guessed I'm the Tatuma. I don't know if they see my eyes, but they see I am not maimed, or grotesque, and they see I can fight.

I don't give a single shit what they see.

I scour the dark towers for more archers. Moving on the wall is harder now. Many of our own archers are up here and have taken care of the other towers. I approach a ladder, intending to make my way back down. But a movement in one window catches my eye. I focus on that opening, and bile rises in my throat.

My mother. I can't see her face from here, but I recognize the color of her hair. And the person standing next to her: Cassius.

That is all it takes for me to lose my focus. I have to get off the wall.

I race to the nearest ladder and slide down the outer edge of it. I've done what I'd intended to do. It's a small victory.

Tossing my bow and arrows to Rian, I dodge my way to Jovan.

I expect anger.

"Good work," he grunts, drawing up his shield to protect me.

I raise an eyebrow. He raises one back.

Malir approaches. "My King, the Ire folk have told me they're ready to fly."

"Do it," Jovan replies curtly. "Tell them to clear the gate. And ready the battering ram."

Malir turns aside and repeats the order to three men before sprinting to the Ire folk at the back. I track his movement to Hamish. Adox waits with the injured to one side, out of arrow range.

I scan the ground; we've lost at least one hundred to arrows already.

"Are you ready to take the wall?"

"The wall?" I ask. "Yes." As for what's on the other side of the wall, not so much. I have no idea how I'll react, or what I'll do when I see my mother and my uncle face-to-face.

Leaving the Kaur forest presented another problem: The Ire had nothing to launch off. The last hour has seen them combining a bunch of ladders into a higher platform. This will allow them to climb high enough to take off. It's the best we could do.

I watch as the first of them launch into the sky. Please don't let them die. All arrows will be trained on them as soon as Mother's army sights them.

There is cheering behind me.

Jovan and I look behind as the battering ram is carried through the middle of our army. I shout with the rest of them, and Jovan lowers his shield, smashing his sword on the side of it.

His men take up the drum with vigor, beating their weapons on their shields. The sound is terrifying. It tells the Solati we are coming for them. I hope my mother and uncle are cowering, unable to hold their cocky expressions in front of the court. I hope they feel the tendrils of twisting fear unfurling to suffocate them.

The first booming blow of the battering ram hitting the Kaur gate echoes across the plain. The king moves to the middle and takes up his position on the ram along with the fifty others already there. Shard and Olandon step up to me, taking Jovan's place.

I watch the Bruma work, and work. It's a battering ram, and there are fifty men. But they're attempting to break a Kaur gate. Arrows whistle overhead. The people of the Ire topple from the smoky air into the clutches of their enemy. If they do not die from their wounds, or the fall, they'll be killed as soon as they land. I wonder if Adox regrets everything in this moment, because my heart is weeping with their screams.

It is all needless. It is all because of *her*.

Crack. The batter of the ram is rhythmic. The men grunt in unison. Soon we will be through. The rest of the army knows it, too. Rhone shouts at the men, positioning them around the battering ram, while Malir directs others to the base of the ladders. We'll use both to overwhelm the army within.

The archers on top of the wall work tirelessly. Some fall, while other pass up a steady stream of arrows.

A shout of victory goes up as the gates crack. I lean forward onto the balls of my feet. *Crack!* Nearly there. But a different sound is making its way through the Bruma. A sound of alarm. Shard is shouting back to Avalanche, and the huge barracks man is pointing back to the trees.

"The rest of the army is here," breathes Shard.

"We don't have long," Olandon says.

I stare at the battle lines exiting the forest. "Ten minutes at most."

Malir and Rhone are already aware of it. The news is passed to Jovan. *Crack.*

Another victorious cheer. We need to get through, *now*.

With a splintering groan, the gate bursts open.

Shields are raised as a flurry of arrows fly through the gap. The men at the front of the battering ram fall dead, bodies turned into pincushions.

I watch the cascade of Solati exiting the tree line behind me. My eyes widen. We've only been fighting a quarter of their force inside the wall! Hundreds of highly trained Solati charge toward us.

Our men climb the ladders in torrents as Jovan leads the push through the gate. The battering ram is thrown to the side, the way open.

The Ire sweep down in waves, focusing their fire on the areas just inside the wall.

The screaming is at fever pitch. Bruma pour into the palace meadow, roaring, enraged with the passion of battle.

I'm scooped into the throes of the crowd pushing inward. But can we possibly get everyone through in less than ten minutes?

Time is running out.

As soon as I'm forced through the shattered gate, I search for Malir. "Malir, we need to have the archers facing outwards to cover the men getting inside."

There's too much to do; we still need to erect a barricade. The battering ram! We can't just leave that for the Solati to use.

"Olandon, we need that battering ram inside."

He nods and uses Ashawn's shoulders to leap for the top of the wall. I expect him to shout down orders. I don't expect him to disappear over the side himself. But he is my brother, I suppose.

Unwillingly, I find my eyes drawn to the palace, to its elegant curves and proud towers. The towers are taller than those of Jovan's castle, but the royal abode is sleek where his is sturdy. Our palace is built for vanity, not war. There are three main floors to the palace, amid the numerous towers. I assume the court must be watching from the second or third level, but they stay out of sight. My gaze falls to where Jovan fights in the middle of his men. Beating his way across the meadow toward the palace. That is where I need to be.

Shard trails after me as I sprint to Jovan's side, drawing my twin swords—a gift from the man I plan to fight beside.

The Tatum's army is trying to stall us. They want to give the rest of their army time to catch up. This is the moment that will tip the balance toward victory. It all depends on whether we can get inside in time. It depends on how quickly we move, and how quickly the Tatum's army crosses the plain.

Jovan's blue eyes flicker, but that is the only acknowledgement I register as I engage in battle with a woman in front of me.

She's one of my people, of course. But I only see an enemy in that moment. The heat of battle is overwhelming. And if I weaken and leave wounded, they might survive only to kill one of my friends. I have no friends amongst the Solati. Only people who wish to kill me. I draw my blade across the woman's throat, blinking through the blood that splatters across my face. With a cry, I leap over her, clashing blades with two men. One of them is inexperienced. Jovan joins me, and I spin behind him as he slashes wide with his sword to give me time to gather myself. I twirl around his other side, bending low to slash through the calf of the young soldier. Jovan stabs him through the chest as I come up and finish the other.

Fighting beside him is easy. Entirely different from when I've fought with Olandon. More spontaneous; dangerous and thrilling.

His watch fight around us. The barracks are also in the mix, minus Blizzard and Ice, who protect Sanjay elsewhere. I have no idea where Olandon is.

The battle becomes a blur. The ground shakes, and I glance back to see the battering ram has been dropped inside the walls.

"Get the barricade up," roars Jovan. "Now!"

The Bruma closest hurry to grab anything that might aid in blocking the gate. Ladders, shields, and broken Kaur wood is propped up, then the battering ram is rolled in front. The Bruma on the walls pull up our ladders from the other side.

As I watch one is flung from the wall, a spear embedded firmly in his chest.

"They're here," I whisper.

Jovan bellows orders, and I wonder how he does it. I can only focus on the next person in front of me. We're about three-quarters of the way across the meadow—not in as bad a position as we could have been, in that we are not trapped outside, but we are still between two armies.

Minutes go by and there are no attempts to scale the palace walls.

The Solati were too cocky in their assumption that nobody would guess their move. They have no equipment to break through. Their arrogance is a strike in our favor!

I wipe at the sweat and blood on my forehead. A hand pulls me back. I follow Jovan into the middle of the battle. Hands on my knees,

I take stock. The beautiful meadow from my memories is awash with blood. Weariness blurs my vision. I haven't slept in a long time.

Jovan is also panting. "How many inside?"

One hundred Solati sit between us and the palace, still protecting their Tatum. "Not many," I gasp. "They've thrown everything into this plan. They must have been caught off-guard when we didn't perish in the fire. She'll have the Elite, I assume. A handful of guards, as well as the court."

Jovan signals Rhone. I have no idea where Malir has gone. "We'll storm the castle with four hundred men and leave you the rest. I want you and Malir to remain out here and direct battle."

Rhone's eyes darken. "Yes, my King."

"We will send out the troops we don't need as soon as the palace is conquered," I add. Four hundred is a lot. But I can see Jovan's reasoning. A show of force could cause the court to submit and prevent a third battle within the palace itself.

Nerves roil my stomach. This is it.

"Give out the order," Jovan commands. "And good luck."

Rhone looks down at me and I try to decipher the intensity of his expression. "Good luck, Tatum." He bows slightly. "My King."

Jovan's army slowly divides as the order is taken up. Shard works to separate the force into the correct numbers.

The majority turns outward, toward the bulk of the Tatum's army. The Ire have landed inside the gate for the moment, their job done.

I, along with the king of Glacium, turn inward—to the palace and uncertainty.

CHAPTER THIRTY-ONE

*W*E SPREAD WIDE, and close in on what's left of the Solati force between us and the palace. The numbers are in our favor.

I can see some of Mother's force breaking off and dashing for the castle.

They will barricade the palace entryway. However, there is a crucial difference between the castles of Glacium and the palaces of Osolis. Glacium's are built for war, and Osolis's are built to be pretty. Without archers, the Bruma were never a real threat on our home ground. Therefore, the palaces did not need to be battle-ready.

I enjoy that the arrogance of my forebears will be the means of my mother's destruction.

Arrows rain down on us intermittently. There's a to-and-fro as Solati archers take posts above us, and our archers take them down. Slowly, agonizingly slowly, we pull tight the noose, creeping forward one foot at a time. We no longer fight on the dry ground of the meadow; now, we fight on cobbled paving. Close. So gratingly close. No history book will tell you how battle plays with time. This battle could have taken a matter of minutes. But it feels like hours as my arms burn and my chest aches. As soldiers on both sides push past their endurance.

Another battle to get inside the palace still awaits once we get to the door itself. Ducking to the back for a rest, I take a moment to gaze upward. The window openings are now empty; likely Mother's men are racing to hold the door against us.

The upper levels will be bare...

I pull a few men back. "We need four ladders. Take men to get them."

I dodge around others until I find Jovan. "I suspect the upper floors will be empty. I have an idea."

"Does this idea put you in danger?" he asks.

I shrug. "No more than usual."

"Then, no."

I roll my eyes. "Listen. I can climb up to my tower. Get in through the opening. I've done it thousands of times. I can do it with my eyes closed. The archers will protect me. There's no one up there to shoot me down, anyway. I can make sure the second level is clear."

He's listening now.

"I've sent men back to get ladders."

His eyes hold my own before scanning the upper levels himself.

"We distract them at the door while we attack from above. We can catch the remaining soldiers unaware in the entry. They won't present much of a problem in that narrow space, believe me."

Jovan pushes me back and deals with a Solati who has made it through four rows of Bruma.

I grip his wrist afterward. "This is a good idea."

He grunts. "It is, Lina. Except for the part where you get shot by an arrow and topple to your death."

I open my mouth to tell him he hasn't got a choice when he swings the massive shield from his own back and slings it over mine. My legs sag with the weight and I glare at him.

"You expect me to climb with this?" *Is he serious?*

His returning look tells me he's perfectly serious. He brushes my forearm with his thumb and swallows hard before pushing me forward.

The room where I spent my teens is on the third level of the palace. Only twenty hand-holds from bottom to top—with a bloody heavy shield on my back. I think Jovan's forgotten he's stronger than I am. But he'll never forgive me if I take it off.

I reach high to my left. There's a groove there.... I feel for the right spot. Perhaps I'm a little rusty. My eyebrows furrow. Where is it? I lower my hand a few centimeters and find it. I've grown taller? Must be all that meat I've eaten. I'll have to remember that on the way up.

I climb.

Six holds, eleven holds. *Thunk.* An arrow embeds in the shield at my back. I wince; Jovan will be losing it down there. Fourteen, nineteen, *thunk, thunk,* twenty!

I grip the edge of the opening and swing myself up. Not gracefully— I can thank the shield for that. The coast is clear, but someone obviously shot that arrow. I can't rule out an ambush.

The ladders will only reach to the floor below me. That is where I need to check.

Despite the urgency of the situation, I can't help pausing to gaze around my room. I *lived* here? The plainness of the room disturbs me. It's empty. A bed, a trunk, two fans, and a basin. It is devoid of warmth; I can see why Olandon was always on me to decorate it. It feels brittle.

I shake it off and approach the door, swinging the shield in front of me. My arms tremble from holding it. As soon as I'm out this door, the shield is getting ditched. I grasp the lever and take a breath. Let's hope there isn't a legion of soldiers on the other side.

Nothing for it. I jerk the door wide open and charge out.

…Into an empty hall.

"Huh," I say, bemused.

I lean the shield against the wall. I'll start with the tower farthest from the entrance hall. Then I'll have backup to take the others by force if necessary.

As I navigate the black halls, it's like I never left, but at the same time it is utterly foreign. The dark passages are haunting and full of screaming memories. It's like a close friend is telling me the details of their nightmare and I can picture what they saw, but cannot feel the same terror.

The sight no longer holds horror for me, just the heaviness of regret.

Skimming on light feet, I make my way to the servant stairs. The upper levels are empty. I was right; everyone is probably downstairs. Though I expect to encounter *some* of my mother's soldiers on the floor below. I wrench open the way to the stairs and take them two at a time.

The door to the first tower is up ahead on the right. My pace slows, and I creep forward on the balls of my feet.

A clanging noise rings out from the room, heard clearly over the thrum of battle outside.

I jerk back. What on Solis? It's followed by a heavy thud. Gripping my short dagger, I creak open the door.

…And blink at the sight before me. The palace cook stands over an unconscious guard, pan raised high. The haggard woman freezes in this position, just as I freeze. For a moment neither of us speaks.

She knocked out the archer with a pot? I lift my eyebrows and grin. "Thanks," I say.

The cook lowers the pan slowly. "You are welcome, Tatum Olina. They killed my sister; they deserve no less."

Remorse floods through me. The matron of the orphanage was the cook's sister, strung up on the Oscala like a common criminal. "She was one of the kindest souls I ever knew… and I'm sorry. If she hadn't helped me with the apples, she might never have died."

The cook's face turns fierce. "And if I'd never given you the apples, she wouldn't have died either. My sister died doing what she believed was right, Tatum. Don't be a fool, regretting the past."

Not many people would talk so bluntly to royalty. In fact, I can't think of anyone—not even my brother, really. The soldier stirs. Before I can take a single step, the pan is thrashed across his head once more. He lies still.

I race past both of them to the window opening. I spot Jovan and wave my arms. It takes him a while to see me; possibly he is distracted by the two men taking him on.

The ladder is put in place, and the first of the Ire and Bruma soldiers begin to climb. I wait until twenty or so are in the room. I gather five who seem to hold their weapons like they know how to use them. "Follow me."

In the second tower is a dead archer. Someone shot him in the eye, and he hasn't been replaced.

The ladder is propped and my chest tightens as we draw closer to my mother. What will she say? What will *I* say?

This time I take ten men. And a lucky thing, too: There are three in tower number three, and they're expecting us. They probably figure they can die here, or die down in the entranceway.

"Wait!" I command as a watchman to my left draws his sword. I face the three Solati. "I have no desire to kill you needlessly. Soon I will be Tatum. Surrender, and I will let you live."

Without a word, the two men and woman fall to their knees, weapons thrown in front of them.

"There are more of us in the next room, Tatum Olina," one of the men says.

I nod. "Restrain them for now," I tell the Bruma soldiers. "Do not harm them, or I'll put Avalanche on you."

Someone gulps.

As more Bruma climb into the second level of the palace, I drag a few to the side. Olandon enters with this group. I pull him in for a quick hug. The three restrained Solati watch us with curiosity. "Brother, you will come to secure the final tower."

"Count me in, Tatum Olina."

I'm tempted to roll my eyes at his formality, though I'm aware he must show respect in front of the other Solati.

"Where is King Jovan?" I ask.

Olandon grimaces. "He said to inform you he'll be up last."

I dash to the window. Only half of the men remain down there. Sure enough, Jovan still swings his goliath sword through the air. "That's really what he said?" I ask.

"Take out the words over one syllable and insert a few swear words."

I snort. "Don't let him hear you say that."

He grins, face streaked with dirt and blood.

The fourth and final towers are nearly full of Solati.

"They've been sent up to kill you," Olandon whispers.

I have such a lovely mother. I repeat my proposition to the group of fifteen. One decides he doesn't like it.

A minute later, I repeat the offer as I wipe the man's blood from my sword.

Everyone accepts.

I stand outside in the hall as the Solati are trussed up for safekeeping. The halls are jam-packed with Bruma and Ire folk. I squeeze between the battle-streaked bodies and wait. He doesn't take long.

There is a booming command. "Move." And then *somehow* the crammed masses make way for the huge frame of their king.

His face is tense.

"What happened down there?" I ask.

"We captured the last of them. The other armies are at a standstill. The Solati have drawn off, unable to scale the wall. I left one hundred down there to stop the Solati from exiting the palace," he pants. "What can we expect downstairs?"

I turn and spot Avalanche. "Avalanche. Can you grab me one of the Solati prisoners?" I call out.

He lumbers to do as I've asked, squashing a small man from the Ire against the wall. All levity is gone a few minutes later when he drops a weedy-looking man at my feet—good pick. Avalanche looms over him. I truly don't think he means to; he kind of can't help it with so many people around.

"I need to know what is downstairs. You can help me." I stare the weedy man straight in the eyes. It's easy to see what's going through his head. Solati are raised to mistrust blue eyes. This man is trying to override his natural response to my face, and reconcile who I am with my appearance, in order to live.

He makes the correct choice.

"Archers wait at the base of the stairs, court is in the dining ring, and the rest of the guard are probably split between holding the entrance and protecting the court."

"How many?" Jovan growls.

The Solati's face remains smooth, though he does gulp under Jovan's gaze. "I... I think around fifty."

Jovan and I exchange a look. That's good for us, *if* the man is telling the truth. I nod at Avalanche, who hauls the man away. "We should target our forces at the entrance and let the rest of your men inside."

Jovan wipes his brow, surveying me. "Agreed. And then take the court."

I glance away.

"Are you ready to do this?" he asks.

"To kill my mother?" I raise my brows. Can anyone ever be ready for that? "Yes. Maybe."

He shakes his head. "You better decide quick. And I want you to stick close to me. Got it?"

I narrow my eyes. "How about you stick close to me?"

He catches my mouth in a kiss. It's over before it's begun and I almost pout before remembering where we are. "I can settle for that."

I huff, glad my red cheeks are covered in grime. "Well, let's not just stand around all day."

There are a few chuckles as I squeeze my way to the front.

"Shields up," I call.

The staccato thud of twenty shields hitting the ground echoes through the hall.

"Open the doors," I call.

As soon as the door opens there is a tightening of bowstrings from the bottom of the stairs. The Solati are ready for us.

Jovan studies the size of the stairwell. It is wide enough for four men standing shoulder-to-shoulder, and three heads higher than Jovan's frame. I know that it gently curves down to the ground floor of the palace, and the steps are narrow, but not steep. At the bottom is the main thoroughfare of the palace. The dining way sits fifty meters to our right, once we reach the ground floor. And the entranceway sits another fifty meters past this.

If I were short on numbers, this is where I would funnel the enemy through, to render their extra men useless.

Jovan's voice rings out over the thudding. "This needs to be quick. You go down in fours, two shields high, and two shields low. That should prevent any of their arrows slipping through. Once you reach the bottom, spread out into barrier formation."

Jovan talks aside to Shard, Avalanche, and Sin. They disappear through the ranks with his message.

The men nod, focused on the task.

"For Glacium!" Jovan roars

"For Glacium!" they chorus back.

I wince as the second floor fills with roaring and shouting. The twenty shields and their fighters move in front of us, pushing down the stairs in rows of four—two holding their shields high enough to scrape the ceiling, and the other two holding their shields low enough to touch the floor. Jovan slides in front of me, and then I too am caught up in the steady push down the wide stairwell.

The sound of arrows striking shield starts right away. Solati sit at the bottom, likely wondering what on Solis we are doing.

The Bruma soldiers ahead of us reach the ground floor, and I hear the sound of shields being stacked on top of one another, but cannot see what they're doing.

Finally, I crouch at the base of the steps and see what is making the clanging noise.

Jovan's soldiers have formed an arc of shields—an impenetrable semi-circle. As more men reach the bottom of the stairway, the circle widens, each new Bruma adding his shield to the tight formation.

The arrow fire has stopped and footsteps on the other side are running away to each side. One Bruma checks if the coast is clear. Jovan whispers an oath as the watchman falls dead, arrow straight between his eyes. Another Bruma takes his place.

I watch Jovan as he directs more men into this "barrier formation."

As they're added, our shielded mass swells into the thoroughfare, spreading, until the apex of our circle reaches the far wall.

"Split," the king booms.

In total synchronization the semicircle of Glacium shields splits at the peak to create two curved lines of soldiers, twenty men on each side. A clear space now extends from the stairs to the opposite wall.

"Push!" comes the next shouted command from beside me.

The two rows of men begin to push in opposite directions down the hallway, making the available space at the bottom of the stairs larger.

I watch the whole display with wide eyes. This is incredible. Jovan smirks at the awe on my face, drawing himself up to full height.

Men.

Our army files into the space from the second floor at a faster rate.

"Which way to the entrance?" Jovan calls out.

I point to the right.

"Right march!"

It's awkward. We move at a tediously slow pace and frustration has me itching to break out of the shield's protection.

"The dining ring is coming up on the left," I say.

Jovan nods. It takes ten minutes to push the shields up against the entrance to the dining ring, effectively blocking anyone inside. And that's when, finally, Jovan lifts the shields.

"Charge!" The cry goes up as we race down the hall to the entry. Shard jerks me so I'm several rows back.

A few Solati fall victim to hurled spears. They scramble to open the entranceway. Some fall to their knees in surrender immediately.

For others, it takes opening the heavy doors and seeing they are surrounded by a horde of Bruma on both sides before they acknowledge defeat.

I suppose I should be happy, but I'm coiled so tightly at what is to come, I cannot celebrate. Fifty men, the Solati said. There are thirty here. How many were at the base of the stairs? I guess they made for the dining ring.

We secure the prisoners in a side room with ample guards.

The first floor is clear, but my breath comes faster now that the action has paused.

I approach the men breaking down the doors to the dining ring, trying to keep my stomach down. My thoughts are stupid but I can't help them. I glance down at my robes and see they are torn, bloodied, and bits of my thighs are showing. My hair is up, but I have no doubt it looks appalling. And my mother will be perfect, probably wearing canary-fucking-yellow. What if she makes me look like an idiot in front of everyone? In front of *three* worlds. In front of Jovan.

A water flask is waved under my nose. I stare up at a bald Sin and choke back a laugh.

"Here," he says gruffly. "Wash your face."

I dart a quick look around and then do as he says. He studies me critically, and splashes some water onto his hand before smoothing my hair back. I hope no one is watching this.

He stands back with a nod and then looks down at my robes. "Tie it up to the side," he says.

Is he daft?

He runs a hand over his head. "You've been in battle. All day."

I wince.

"Exactly. You can pull off the warrior look right now, just not a half-warrior, half-Tatum look. You've got to commit."

I sigh heavily. "Do it."

He ties the robe up.

"Not that high," I snap.

He strokes a finger down my leg. "We still have time, you and I."

"No," I say. "We don't. But if you like, you can be my valet when I'm Tatum."

His eyes light up on cue. "Really?"

"Really." I regret the words as soon as they're out. Sin loves to extract promises right before battle. Still, I can't see him following up on this one.

The watchmen shift ahead, moving into the room in the same way Jovan directed them down the stairs. I feel better now. As good as I'm going to, anyway.

Cassius is dead meat.

There are screams in the dining ring, crying, and the scrape of wood on the floor. But no arrows are loosed. I hear no metal ringing.

Olandon peers at me, and I see the same thought process running through his head. "She left the court to die."

I shrug in response. Wouldn't put it past her.

Jovan is next to me and hears. "Are there any guards?"

"Doesn't sound like it. Let me look."

He clamps a hand around my waist and draws me back into the midst of the men. "Lower shields!"

CHAPTER THIRTY-TWO

*N*OTHING HAPPENS.
No one falls down dead.
No one moves.

Finally, after a shared look with Jovan, I push to the front. That's when the sound starts.

I don't worry about what they see, or the connection they make as they stare between me, Olandon on my right, and the king on my left. I stare back at them in bafflement. Really? The court is still dressed up. There's a war on! I glance sideways at Olandon, whose cheeks turn red. Does he see how ridiculous these people look? Their bright colors, their elaborate hairdos. They look like they're going to a feast, not battle.

"…Quaint," Shard whispers behind me.

Only the court members sitting in front of me stop the laughter from bursting from my lips.

I care for them about as much as I always did. That is to say, I don't.

I stride up to them, looking at their faces, veil-free for the first time. I give them a damn good chance to see my own. I'm not surprised to find I feel the same way about them as I always have. I feel nothing but contempt.

They gaze at the child they ridiculed from birth. And I glare them into shame. I don't greet them; I don't smile; I just let them see the condemnation on my face.

And then, in a pleasant voice, I ask my question.

"Where is my mother?"

The torture room.

How fitting. And how typical of my mother to leave her "dear" court behind while she locks herself and Cassius away with protection.

My stomach drops at the thought of my uncle. I glimpse at Olandon's grim expression as we race through the halls with a small contingent at our backs. He will also be fretting about what comes next.

I wish all of my friends were with me. Half of them still fight outside and I have no idea what has become of them. Is it possible that we'll all make it? I renew the energy of my pace, finding some deep reservoir that somehow is not yet depleted.

The torture room. The scene of some of my most horrific memories. The wood is drenched in my blood, literally. The stained carpets there have been changed so many times they could cover the floor of Jovan's massive food hall.

The torture room sits at the opposite end of the palace, on the ground floor, at the base of my childhood tower.

We get to the far end of the first level, passing the entertainment areas, the fountains, the artwork. It disgusts me—I want to get to what awaits at the end. The faster I get there, the sooner this war will end—and the more likely my friends outside will survive.

But my throat is tightening, making my breath wheeze. It's funny—no matter how much you change, your body sticks to old habits. My habit, in this part of the palace, has always been to panic.

And so I do. I tell myself I'm not a little girl anymore, but the Olina deep in the recesses of my mind still expects to get beaten and humiliated.

I stride beside the king.

He looks down at me. "What's the outlay?"

"Circular room," I gasp. "Raised platform up to the right. Soldiers are usually spread around the outer wall while Mother and Uncle Cassius watch from above."

He stares ahead and doesn't respond. It takes me a moment to realize I've let the wrong words slip out.

This time it's Jovan who speeds up. Even my legs can't keep up. He disappears around a corner, and I know we've left the rest of our force far behind. It's normal for emotion to get the better of *me* during battle.

But how long has Jovan been waiting for this moment? His stride ahead of me is predatory and more powerful than I can match. I doubt he even realizes he's sprinted ahead. It is battle rage, bloodlust, and it has taken over his actions. I know the feeling well.

And then it strikes me. *That's* why Jovan has been so calm over Hayce's capture and Aquin's confession. He isn't after the person who killed Kedrick—he's after the person who ordered it. He's going for the source. Is he unleashing the suppressed emotion over his brother's death that he has controlled since hearing the news?

My feet stumble slightly as I reach the segregated hall and see the torture room doors are flung wide open. Jovan is nowhere in sight. I didn't think he would *enter* alone!

Real panic chokes me. "Jovan!" I cry. All reason gone from my head, I fling myself into the room, eyes wide as I search for him.

And when I find him, standing in the middle of the round space, I can only drink in the reassuring sight, completely unaware of my surroundings.

For a second, I thought…

Then the smell hits me: rotten blood. A lot of it. And I see that Jovan is staring at the floor. Or more specifically, staring at what he stands on.

Bloodied, reeking carpets cover the room. They're overlapped on the ground, hung from the walls, strewn over the balcony. Every inch. Every space.

And all of it is mine. What's more, Jovan has guessed it. He is completely still. In the state of mind that draws in the air around him and chills it to menace. I can sense his rage accumulating, but all I'm worried about is keeping him safe.

Footsteps pound behind me as I scan the room for life.

The guards stand in a single row, circling the edges of the room, as I described to Jovan. The circle is only broken at the entry. Each soldier has an arrow, nocked, at the ready. Their sights are trained on Jovan. *No.* I blink back a fresh surge of panic.

And there, up on the inward-facing balcony, the same eerie expression covering his cruel face, is Uncle Cassius.

Our men are close; I hear their shouts. Cassius knows it, too. He wastes no time. It's the first time I've heard him speak in half a revolution, but his nasally, thin voice hasn't changed in the slightest.

"You have a choice to make."

I'm so glad not to be frozen in fright I don't immediately heed the words. Even months ago, on the Oscala, the sight of my uncle gripped me with fear. It's not even that I feel stronger within, but that Jovan is here. He's the only difference. And I realize I'm so worried for *him*, I can't be afraid.

I casually stroll in front of the shaking Jovan, who still stares at the stains under his feet. "I'm listening," I say.

"Your... *soldiers* are willing to listen," he asks.

"The soldiers who broke down the palace defenses and obliterated the Tatum's army?" I ask with a tight smile. "Yes, Uncle. They are." I relish in the way he jerks before turning to stride to the door.

Olandon nearly bowls me over, rounding the corner as I step back to the room's entrance.

"Brother." I steady him with a sharp look. "Our dear uncle would like to speak to us."

Olandon's eyes dart behind me, to Cassius, and back. I shift my eyes to the middle of the room, and though he does not move his gaze, Olandon is seeing where Jovan stands—in danger.

I address the others, subtly squeezing Olandon's arm. "Wait here."

I return to Jovan's side. "Get on with it, Cassius."

"You have returned from Glacium well-mannered, I see."

"You seem content to insult me from that high platform. Could it be you still feel the pain of our last exchange?"

His anger flashes across his face. No doubt he is remembering the day I finally lost my temper, just before Kedrick's death, and beat him to a pulp. If his expression is anything to go by, he hates that memory almost as much as I enjoy it.

"You are brave to remind me of that while I hold you and what I assume is the king of Glacium within my circle of archers."

I shrug, but sweat breaks out on my forehead. I've never had to try so hard to remain emotionless in my life. "We've won. Whether Jovan and I live is immaterial. If you shoot us, Tatuma Olandon and Prince

Ashawn take our place. And if they die, two more take their place. No matter who you kill today, you have lost."

I meet his gaze with arched brows, letting false amusement shine through my eyes. And he seethes when he spots it. Without realizing, he has stepped forward to grasp the balcony's balustrade.

He shifts his gaze to Jovan. "Is he mute? Or simple?"

What *he* is, is very close to tearing Cassius limb from limb—but I don't think I'll warn my uncle. "You're stalling. What is this 'choice' you give me. I'll entertain you, for now."

I wonder which side the guards are on. All of them are fresh Elite, which might mean they don't hold the same blind loyalty as the men before them. Are they like Rian? Or like Cassius and Hare?

"I give you this choice, Tatuma. You can continue up to your old tower. By yourself. And speak to your mother."

Jovan's head snaps up. He fixes Cassius with both eyes. My uncle starts before he composes himself. I snigger loudly. In Solati culture, he just shat himself.

"A choice usually implies two or more options." Jovan's voice is unrecognizable. He moves behind me. So close he could cover me completely if he chose.

"Ah, you *do* speak." Cassius claps slowly. The corners of his mouth tug up like a marionette's.

Jovan waits.

Cassius smirks. "The other is that this room turns into a bloodbath."

I gesture around. "I don't see why that would be a problem. You've put down carpets to make the cleanup a little easier. I'd hate for your bowels to spill all over the polished Kaur wood."

His nose wrinkles in distaste. "You always were unrefined. Unfit to wear the mantle of heir. A disgusting, ugly—"

"Aunty Jain says hello."

He blanches noticeably.

"Your wife, Cassius. Tortured and exiled to the Fifth... Have you forgotten her screams? I assume you did it yourself. Tell me, did you lose your mind as Jain lost hers? Could it be that your wife had the last laugh?"

His chest rises and falls quickly. "I have no wife."

I open my mouth to press on the crack appearing in his façade, but Cassius rushes on.

"You'll notice the rugs, niece. I'm sure you like them. You might even remember some of them. I've kept every one you've bled onto since you were two."

Jovan has been vibrating for the last five minutes. But with those words he becomes predator-still. My uncle has sealed his fate and doesn't even know it.

However, Cassius's two options have given me pause. There are nearly one hundred men here, many of whom will die if this erupts into a skirmish. Jovan and I are placed in a prime position to be slaughtered, and no matter what I say, I know in my heart we are the best people to rule in the wake of this war. If I go up and talk to my mother, it could avert more death. Though I highly doubt my mother is alone up there…

I lift my left hand calmly and stroke Jovan's forearm. When the battle is done, and the war is over, all I really want is for him to be safe.

"There has been enough bloodshed for one day. Hear me, Cassius. If it's a trap I walk into, you'll die very slowly." He's going to die slowly anyway, but I watch his reaction for any flicker of a lie.

"Niece," he simpers. "Your mother merely wishes to talk."

If he does lie, it's good enough that I cannot detect it. I cross to the door. Every fiber in my being tells me to throw myself in front of Jovan. "Very well. Your men will drop their weapons as soon as I enter this door."

Cassius grins. "Of course."

I grin back and turn to address the Solati soldiers in the room.

"The palace is overrun by King Jovan's army and the forces of the Ire. We have offered amnesty to all captured Solati soldiers. You will be given the same option for safety and life should you behave with honor in the next moments. If you are stupid enough to choose the losing side, then you deserve death."

I walk through the door and start up the twisting staircase leading to my mother.

Chapter Thirty-Three

S HE SITS IN what used to be my favorite perch; in the single opening.

I'm in the highest tower of the palace—my childhood prison. The room where I cried, screamed, and was alone for the first ten years of my life.

To my surprise, there's no one else here. My mother isn't stupid. She must have a trick up her sleeve.

I circle toward her, waiting for her to honor me with her attention. I don't bother with a greeting, and I'm glad she doesn't acknowledge me immediately. It gives me a chance to absorb that I'm standing in front of my mother after all this time.

Her chestnut hair is coiled at the nape. She's slender and tall. Poised and evil to the core. Responsible for the death of hundreds. A murderer in the most depraved sense of the word. Then she turns to face me with an ethereal movement of her head. And for the second time in my short life, I see my mother speechless.

The first time was when I gave my ultimatum and stood up for myself. I'd told her if she laid another finger on me, I would show everyone my face. I hadn't known I had blue eyes back then, but Kedrick had shown me Mother's terror of the veil coming off. If only I'd realized it years before.

Today she is speechless because she is seeing my face. I let her stare, wondering why she is so fascinated.

"All I ever wanted was your love."

"And it was too much for me to give," she says softly, making me realize I've said the words aloud.

I choke on a laugh. "I would have settled for neutrality, then." I understand what I need to ask her. What I need for closure. "Why did you have to hurt me when you could have ignored my existence?"

She stands. "How your eyes reminded me of him. The instant I saw them, I felt my prior self slide away like wisps of smoke. He was the first to ruin my life, and you continued his work. I hated everything you reminded me of. I was terrified of what I could lose. I detested the way your cry made me feel."

"And yet you went out of your way to make me cry," I say dully. This is the most candid discussion I have ever had with my mother. Perhaps we both realize we will never speak again. "How can you blame others for your own actions?" I shout. "You made my life hell because you slept with Roscoe! You did that! Just as much as he."

It's like I've slapped her. Her lips curl back. "Do not speak his name," she hisses.

I fold my arms as her face twists. "I wondered where the real you was. Aunty Jain and Aquin were right: Roscoe broke you."

She gasps and clutches at her chest. *Really? It's been twenty years.*

My mother cries. "I loved him with every piece of me. And he left me, like some common villager."

I sigh. "You may not look like trash, Mother, but you are on the inside. I imagine that's why he left."

She gapes at me, her tears drying immediately.

Yet, I'm not sure that performance was entirely false. "I won't fall for that bullshit. But it might interest you to know that Roscoe has a family on Glacium. I have a half-brother called Adnan. Actually, you met him during the peace delegation. He sat with us for a couple of dinners. Both of them are outside."

This time the blanching of her face is real.

I feel no remorse whatsoever. "You made every second of my childhood horrific. You filled it with fear, with loathing, with self-doubt and hurt. I yearned for you to love me, confused when you sought to hurt me and not my brothers. You made me feel something was horrifically wrong with me and I have hated you for it every second of every day. And yet, at any point in my life, if you had admitted your mistakes and made pains to earn my forgiveness, I believe we eventually could have loved one another. We could have been a mother and daughter."

Her eyes flicker.

My voice becomes hollow. "Even now there is a part of me hoping it was all an act, that you were forced somehow. But that part of me is small, as is the sane part of you. If there is a mother inside you at all, I want to tell her not to worry; despite your best efforts to break me, I overcame the fear, the loathing, the hurt and the self-doubt you instilled. I want to assure the remaining sliver of the person you were, that I will go on, and your evilness will become nothing in time."

Even if I could forget the needle marks on Oberon's lips, or the multitudes of starved villagers. Even if I could forget watching Kedrick die, and the bones Cassius broke on her orders, or the torture. Even if I could forget all of that, I could never forget I was veiled for the first eighteen years of my life.

I could never forget the girl with the slit throat.

I could never forget the agony of the guilt that comes with abuse.

She stares at me. "I knew you would be beautiful." Her breath catches. "That was my torture; if you had to wear the veil, then I was not allowed to peek."

Rage unfurls deep in my stomach. "How difficult that must have been," I wither.

Her eyes sadden. "It was."

I move closer to her. I'm still not sure how I will kill her. Nothing seems enough, and I hate that a piece of me doesn't want to do it. What's wrong with me?

"Nothing is wrong with you," she whispers.

For a moment I get angry, thinking I've spoken aloud again. But her eyes are distant, focused on memories.

"You were perfect from the moment I first held you. And you are now, even though you are half his. Strong, and capable. A leader that the people will respect and die to protect."

A lump rises in my throat. How I've longed to hear these words.

Every second of every day of my childhood. "You try to trick me." My voice cracks.

"My words are no trick," she says, getting to her feet. "But it did not matter that you were perfect. A perfect baby was not enough. Not one with blue eyes."

"And your ambition, vanity, and greed was enough?"

She looks over my features once more and smiles sadly. "They were all I had left. All I could trust in."

I find it curious she does not include Cassius in that list. "And your brother?"

"No one hates him more than I," she whispers, tears shining in her chestnut eyes. "He knew the truth. Keep your friends close…"

"…And your enemies closer," I finish.

"Are your brothers safe?"

"If you deserved to know, I'd tell you."

She smiles that same ghostly smile again. "They will be well under your care. You were more of a mother than I could ever be."

"And yet you kept having children." I take another step forward. Only a few paces separate us.

"It was good for my image."

Loathing fills me. "You are empty inside."

She stares at me, and I cannot help shivering at the endless pit I see in her eyes. My mother leans out of the opening. She looks back at me over her shoulder. Her tears are real.

"My daughter, you should know by now; some people break under pressure while others merely bend and bounce back."

In the quickest movement I've seen her make, she places one foot up onto the mantel of the opening.

I rush forward, a scream stuck in my throat as my mother throws herself from the tower.

I stand by the opening, my head buzzing.

…She threw herself to her death. *She threw herself to her death.*

A muted thud reaches my ears from far below and I flinch.

I approach the opening with dragging steps, not believing what Avanna has done. *Or was she Ovanna in the end?*

I lean forward on both arms.

And with a deep breath, I peer down.

My mother landed head-first.

There's nothing recognizable left of her face. She is not beautiful in death. I doubt anyone would be after falling from such a height.

...*She didn't scream.*

It is not my favorite memory, but it is one I will always have.

The door slams against the wall.

Weariness piles atop me. I feel every bruise and sore muscle. I have no energy to turn, and I know who it is.

"Where is she?" he asks. I point down, out the opening.

He crosses the tower room in four strides and peers down. Jovan whistles low. "She's dead?"

"Pretty certain, yes."

I'm glad he doesn't touch me. I don't want to be touched.

"What happened?" he asks, moving to sit on the small child's bed in the corner. My old bed.

"She talked. Then she jumped," I say hollowly.

"And somehow, after everything she did to you, you feel bad."

It doesn't make sense.

Jovan looks around. "This is where she locked you?"

I nod, crossing the room. I won't sit on the bed. I spent too much time lying there, crying. Instead, I stand close to the door.

"I wish I could have thrown her from the window myself."

Tears pool in my eyes as I stare at the floor. Her words before she jumped are battling in my mind. I think it's worse that she showed humanity at the end. It makes it harder to see her as the monster I knew, and draws instead an image of a young woman who was forced to do horrible things to survive, things that twisted her beyond recognition over time. "What happened downstairs?"

Jovan stands, wincing. He looks about as sore as I feel. "Your speech proved rather effective. Most laid down their weapons. Then I broke most of the bones in Cassius's body. Slowly. Then gave him to your brother for a turn." He pretends to think. "I heard the word 'peeling' as I left."

"My mother hated him," I say in bemused wonder.

He stops at that information. "Really? And no one ever guessed?"

I glance past him to the opening, reliving the moment she jumped. "One mistake, and she was torn from her child, forced to marry, impregnated, and lived in constant fear of discovery until it consumed her and spat back out a bitter, evil replica of who she once was."

I turn and we make for the doorway in silence. I face him as we reach the doorway and move into his arms. We're both filthy and weary. There are urgent issues to attend. A world and its people to secure. Yet we stand like this for an age.

I could almost sleep if Uncle's screams weren't so loud. They're quite enjoyable to listen to. Olandon has waited a long time for this. I just hope he doesn't finish him too quickly—not after what he did to my boys.

"Lina."

I peek up through wet lashes. My heart breaks at how handsome he is. He still takes all thought from me.

"You did it."

My mother lies broken outside; my uncle is screaming and will soon die. The villagers are safe. Osolis is mine.

Everything I've set out to do has been done.

And yet more tears fall.

A particular tortured scream reverberates through the tower and I begin the trek back the way I came. I pause and harden my expression before swinging the door open.

...It's lucky the carpets were down.

Cassius is a mess. I swallow back bile. This is one side of fighting I'm not accustomed to. Nor do I wish to be. In Cassius's case, I'll make an exception.

"You've done a good job of him," Jovan says, eyeing my brother's work.

Olandon nods, breathing hard.

I approach Cassius and—I've got to admit—I also like what I see. Not the shredded skin. I like what I see in his eyes.

Defeat.

Gone is his smile. Gone is any semblance of hope. Gone is the want to carry on.

Cassius took two of these things from me. But he never could take the third away. Not with twenty years of torture. And I have crushed him in less than two.

"You made my childhood rather unpleasant, Uncle," I whisper to him. It is hard to tell if he hears me. "Do you know my first memory is of your face, and the hate I feel for it? I've feared you most of my life, yet looking at you here, I wonder how I was fooled by the fragile cover you placed over your coward's heart, and your coward's mind."

Cassius's eyes flicker to mine. "Kill me," he pleads. His tears create tracks through the blood on his face. He cries.

And I revel in it.

"It was your mother," he gasps. "I m-merely did what I was bid."

"Your sister is dead," I say simply. "A quick death, from the tower opening."

"Yet you torture me, niece. That is not justice."

I bring my face inches from his, and my uncle avoids my intent gaze. His eyes flicker side-to-side.

"My mother is responsible for many heinous crimes, none of which have escaped my attention. And yet, it is possible she was a product of how she was treated. *You* chose to follow her down that path. Having knowledge of her secret gave you power, and you enjoyed every moment of it, wielding that power against the defenseless. You are dirt. You are poison. You are no worse than her, nor any better. So why are you here, balancing on the edge of death?"

I lean back and bare my teeth. "Because you fucked with my boys."

I turn on my heel and stride to the door, calling, "Beron and Chave send their regards, Uncle." I look back at my brother. "Draw it out as long as you can. Then chuck him in the Fourth fires alongside Avanna."

CHAPTER THIRTY-FOUR

I STAND BEFORE THOUSANDS, staring out to where the river flows behind them.

The last few days have been chaotic. I've barely registered anything. Yet here I stand, about to say goodbye to those we lost.

A message was sent to the Solati army outside the palace walls. The remainder of mother's army surrendered to their new Tatum.

I am now Tatum Olina.

My mother and uncle were thrown into the fires of the Fourth without ceremony. Olandon chose to interpret my order his own way, and threw Cassius into the fire while he was still very much alive, though he hadn't wished to be for many hours prior.

"Today," I say strongly, "we stand beside a people who we've been told to hate. We were taught to hate them by those who valued greed and hate more than the lives of their own people." I turn and dip my head to Adox, who sits to my right. "You also stand beside a people previously unknown. A race of people forced out of our worlds, not because of who they were, but what they represented. But we were wrong!" I sweep my hands upward and my black robes slither down my arms. "They represent *strength*! We are stronger *together*. This day marks a new beginning for all three peoples."

I smile as Jovan and Adox stand either side of me.

"No more war!" I shout. "Peace has been hard-won, costing many lives. And we will respect the blood and the sacrifice of those who died to achieve it by holding fast to this peace. This is our future. Three races, unified."

I take Jovan and Adox's hands and grip them tight. Emotion is tight in my chest as I look out over our people. The three races look at each other, some smiling, some uncertain, some wary. But what matters is they are looking at the people around them *like* they're people. It is more than I had hoped.

Jovan and Adox return to their seats.

I hold my hand high for silence. "I would like to take this time to pay tribute to Prince Kedrick. His ideals of peace were laughed at by Avanna. And yet see where we now stand." I scan the somber crowd. Mostly somber. Several court members are blatant in showing their disdain. "I honor Kedrick for his actions that day. He will be in my heart and mind forever as the man who sparked peace. We will remember him."

A lump rises in my throat at the thought of what I must next do. It takes me several moments to battle it, and I know the members of court judge me.

"We will also remember our dead: Bruma, Ire, and Solati alike. To those of you unfamiliar with Osolis, it is our custom to honor our soldiers in a certain manner. King Jovan and Adox of the Ire folk have agreed to send off their fallen fighters in the same way. Please follow our procession."

I take a shaking breath as I step down from the podium. Jovan falls in beside me. Adox is helped onto a dromeda and takes my other side.

Olandon and Ashawn walk behind us, followed by those in descending rank. Thousands of us walk beside the river as the rafts transporting our loved ones pass by.

Malir's body is on the first raft. Hundreds will follow him, but he is at the front, in the position he held in our hearts, and in the hearts of the army he commanded. Eight hundred of them still live.

The survivors stand in silence on the shore of Lake Aveni, watching as my brother fires the first flaming arrow.

A moan is drawn from my lips as Malir's raft flares with flame.

He was a man who commanded respect. And I cannot believe he will never speak again. Or see his Sadra.

I weep against Jovan's shoulder unashamedly and mourn the loss of a dear friend who is so alive in my memories, he cannot possibly be dead.

There is one thing I have left to do. I should have done it a week ago.

I stand outside Aquin's door.

He was moved to more comfortable quarters after the battle. There were chances to visit him before now. But I was not ready. Forgiving him was the easy part. That was done when I saw him delirious back in camp before the war.

But saying goodbye to my father... It took time to understand this was a moment I couldn't prepare for.

He is lifeless aside from the occasional groan of pain, or mumble of hallucination. The same medic sits in the corner. He stands as I approach the bed.

"Leave us."

He bows. "Yes, Tatum Olina." The medic pauses in the doorway. "He hasn't got long."

I nod curtly, unable to speak. The door bumps gently shut behind me and I approach the side of the bed where my trainer lies. He's dying. I'd been told before now, but I finally allow myself to believe it. Sobs wrack my body in unrelenting waves.

Blindly, I reach out for my father, grasping his chilled and frail hand. "Aquin, please don't leave me."

He twitches, a large frown riveting his brow. I rest my head on the bed beside his hand.

And I tell him what he is waiting to hear. The reason he has not died yet.

"I forgive you, father."

I close my eyes, still clinging to his hand, kneeling on the floor beside his prone form. And I talk. I tell him everything I can remember of him: of the first time he taught me to punch; of the secret smiles he would give me after telling Olandon off; when I didn't mind scraping my knees in training because afterward he would fuss while pretending not to care.

"I love you," I tell him. "No matter what you did. I know it was all for me."

He has been the steadiest, most stable presence in my life. I owe him for that, no matter what mistakes he made. I am who I am because he cared.

Even when I'm empty of tears, I stay, tricking myself into believing the twitching of his fingers means he will wake soon.

"Lina." A whispered voice comes from above my head.

My eyes don't want to open; they're swollen closed. Wincing, I grip my neck. Where am I?

"Lina." The voice comes again. A hand squeezes my shoulder. "He's gone."

I lift my head. And as I do, a hand slides from the top of it, onto the bed beside where I slept. Aquin's hand had been on top of my head.

My trainer looks more peaceful in death than I've ever seen him. It strikes me his life was not easy. But he will be with his loved ones now. And Malir. With Flurry, and Kedrick. All the people we've lost will take care of each other.

Jovan picks me up and takes me to the chair. "He shifted his hand during the night. The medic said he died shortly after."

I think he expects me to cry, but I have nothing left. And strangely, though it seems odd when I have lost so much…

I am at peace.

CHAPTER THIRTY-FIVE

I SIT IN THE dining ring.

At the same middle table where I used to sit beside Avanna. The members of the court watch me on tenterhooks, slowly nibbling away at their food. Jovan isn't impressed with the diet here. He mainly eats apples, though I'm not sure if this is to mess with me or not. I've lost my appetite for them.

I placed Shard and Satum Jerin—the only Satum I ever liked—in charge of dispersing food to the villagers and redistributing my people to their homes. We'll have to take care during the next rotation until we get more harvest, even with the extra food that Jovan and the Ire collaborated to fly in.

Needless to say, I made sure none of these extra rations went to the court.

The king and I are unbending in the respect we show to the other races. Our people know what is expected, and any who step out of line are dealt with. It is more than I'd hoped for, but I wonder if it will hold.

Yesterday, the Glacium forces began to withdraw through the Oscala.

Jovan has said he'll leave two hundred men here for as long as I need them. I'm grateful for the numbers as I watch the court conspire. Fear of change drives them to consider drastic action. Considering their precarious positions in the palace, they're smart to feel this way.

It is nothing I didn't expect, and I take it in my stride—all my food is tested for poison by random members of the court.

"Tatum Olina?" a voice prompts uncertainly.

Roscoe addresses me from across the table, his blue eyes twinkling. The kindness there is hard to reconcile with his past. For now, Adnan's father is no one to me. As far as I'm concerned, my real father is now dead. The only parental figure I wish to know further is Aunty Jain.

"Roscoe," I answer.

"I... I just wanted to say that I'm sorry about Aquin. He was dear to you."

I inhale sharply. Dear to me? Aquin was my *everything*—friend, father, trainer, and advisor. Bitterness churns within me and it has nothing to do with Roscoe's words. I need him to know what his actions did to Avanna. "Do you know what my mother said to me before she jumped to her death?" I haven't told this to anyone. The table falls silent.

I speak quietly enough that no one else will hear. "She said, 'Some people break under pressure while others bend and bounce back.'" I stand from the table. "I wonder what life could have been if Avanna wasn't broken."

Realizing I'm about to lose control, I sweep from the dining ring.

I'm furious at Roscoe. I'm furious at Avanna because somehow she's earned a smidgeon of pity from me, and I'm furious at myself for reacting so childishly. It isn't fair to blame Roscoe; I know that. How could he have known that a single moment would lead to this chaos?

My mother made her choices. Aquin and Hayce made theirs also. Yet hurt and anger thrash inside of me, compounded by my grief over losing Aquin and Malir, and it targets my only living parent.

I take a dromeda out, and gallop to Lake Aveni.

When I return, the smoke is pouring into the sky. Jovan waits for me in the stables.

He eyes the heaving dromeda with mistrust. I dismount and begin to brush the steed down. I worked her a little hard.

Jovan leans against the wall of the box stall. "We need to talk."

The hand brushing stills for a moment before I resume the steady downstrokes. "What about?"

He snorts. "You know what about. Us."

Dread fills every part of me. I knew it was coming. We are meant to be together. I feel the truth of it right to my very soul, but...

"Jovan, I love you…"

"But it's not enough," he says bitterly.

I jolt at the words and stare at him, wondering if he's chosen those words on purpose. He wasn't there when my mother uttered them. The coincidence shocks me to the core.

I'm not like my mother. "It is enough for me," I say. "It will always be enough."

He knows there's a "but."

I put the brush down. "I—"

He holds up both hands, and I clamp my mouth shut at the panicked edge in his eyes. "Hear me out. I'm not sure if you've considered we can rule both worlds."

My heart sinks. I've thought through our options. There's only one path we can take. "And where would we live?"

"Half the time in Glacium, half here. It hasn't been done before, but we could make it work."

Doesn't he see how much I need him? "It is too unsettled. It would allow our conspirators to gain too much traction in our absence. And, I believe, would create discontentment in the people."

His face smooths, and I hate that he's done that to me. "And I'm just supposed to wait, how long? Until you decide you want me?"

I take a step forward, and he takes one back. "It's not like that." I place my fist over the middle of my chest. "You have no idea how much I want you. How much I need you."

"How much you needed me to claim Osolis?"

It's like he's slapped me. I know he's hurt, but does he think I'm just going to kill the previous Tatum and then leave my people to flounder? I blank my own expression, and see his eyes glint as I do so. "It was you who lectured me on responsibility so long ago. This is me doing it! I can't leave them now."

He needs to hear me out! The stabled dromeda stamp in agitation at our raised voices.

Jovan's words churn in my mind. Does he honestly think I've used him to get here? I wait for him to apologize. After a few seconds, I realize he's not going to. And I refuse to speak until he does.

We exchange our neutral expressions for another long moment. Is it over? Just like that?

"And I'm just supposed to wait, how long? Until you decide you want me?"

He won't wait for me. So there's no point in talking. I study his carved features. His beautiful, all-knowing eyes that once scared me. The curves of his chest where I have rested my head more times than I can count.

And I wonder when we stopped talking, or whether, at some level, we understood talking could not change the future.

He's gone by breakfast the next day.

Everything else I can survive, but without Jovan, what is the point? I never deserved him, and he has realized it. It's too late. I cry myself to sleep at night, and dry my tears during the day.

"I can't believe you're watching this," Olandon whispers in my ear.

We sit on the raised platform overlooking the back courtyard, where a tragic play is currently in its millionth scene. I can't believe it either. "Satum Jerin advised we continue as normal a routine as possible."

He sniggers, and I ignore him, looking at the stupid court.

I breathe a sigh of relief at the announcement of the halfway interval. But a disturbance soon interrupts the low murmur of talk.

For a moment, I'm exceedingly grateful for some excitement. Then I see who it is. Ogeorg, the fat Satum of treasury—my least-liked Satum—walks up to the front of the stage. I fix my eyes on the fat Solati. The food shortage on Osolis doesn't seem to have affected him in the slightest. In fact, he profited rather nicely from the starvation of my people.

"You have something to say, Ogeorg," I call down.

"Tatum Olina, I do. I wish to draw your attention to a prisoner being starved in the dungeons."

Hayce was still there. I'd left him there to rot for a while. I don't break from Ogeorg's gaze. "I find it interesting you were in the dungeons at all, Ogeorg."

The man throws a look at the court audience. I've been waiting for this moment. "Landon, watch who he's communicating with."

"Merely passing through." The Satum smirks.

Is that the best he's got? That Hayce is starving in the dungeon?

I smile at Ogeorg and stand, making my way slowly down the curved stairs from the royal balcony. My blue robes, chosen by Sin—who demanded I hold true to my valet promise—kick out in front of me.

"How remiss of me," I say as I near Ogeorg. "And how kind of you to point it out."

"That is not why I've come, Tatum Olina. I could not stay silent. The prisoner has told me you killed Aquin. I'm sure this cannot be true," he simpers.

I see the triumph in Ogeorg's eyes and realize this is his true plan. He's wheedled the story of Aquin's death from Hayce's lips. A complete lie, though the Satum has taken it for truth.

"You surely did not kill Osolis's beloved Aquin." Ogeorg feigns shock well. There are gasps from the court, and sounds of outrage—from his supporters, no doubt.

I find it boring. "Brother," I call out. "I forget, can you recall who stabbed Aquin in the back," I ask.

"The prisoner in the dungeons," he replies. "The man you're starving."

I gaze at Ogeorg with a small smile. "Ah, yes. I remember now. Guards!"

Two soldiers hurry forward. Ogeorg tenses.

"Please bring the prisoner, Hayce, to me," I say. I hum to myself, slowly pacing the stage as I wait. The court is silent. I hope Olandon pays close attention. It'd be great to get all the conspirators at once.

The two guards reappear, dragging a sagging Hayce between them. Kedrick's killer begins to resist when he sees me, and the guards force him to his knees.

Kedrick's killer. Aquin's son. A man who was let down by his father, just like me. And yet I chose to do good. And Hayce did not. I've debated what to do with him. Should I organize a public execution and use it to strengthen my rule? Should I gift him to King Jovan and let him chuck the man in the Dome? But when I threw Hayce in the dungeon, Jovan made it clear he didn't care about the fate of Aquin's son. Only that the assassin died.

The problem is, I respect Aquin's memory too much to torture his son.

In a ringing blur, I've unsheathed the two short swords buckled to my hips and drawn them across his throat. They are sharp.

The assassin's death will help me weed out future assassins.

Hayce's eyes are forever frozen in shock as his head slides off his body. Dispassionately, I kick the body to the ground. Kedrick's killer is dead. Aquin's killer is dead. A man who was broken by his father is dead. Everyone is dead and gone.

I grab a fist of my robes and wipe my sword, gazing at Satum Ogeorg, who does his best not to vomit. The way of the Solati court has always been deception and hidden truths.

Not anymore.

"Satum Ogeorg, you sought to use this man to undermine me," I start.

This drags more gasps from the audience than the announcement of Aquin's death.

"And you have shown me what I needed to see." I reach forward and grasp his wrist. With a quick jerk, I remove the Kaur wood bracelet showing his rank.

I stare into his beady eyes. "You no longer hold the title of Satum of Treasury. You no longer occupy the house of a Satum. You may keep your possessions and no more. How you survive in this world is entirely up to you."

"You mean me to live as a villager," he asks in confusion.

I sheath my swords. "While the villagers starved, what were you doing?"

He scowls at the question.

I turn to the court, still facing the ex-Satum. "No need to answer. I have spent the last few weeks assessing the royal ledgers."

Ogeorg blanches, eyes flickering to someone in the audience.

A kind smile curves my lips. "The penalty for crown theft is execution," I say softly. "I wonder if you prefer this."

Ogeorg falls to his knees. "No, Tatum. I will take poverty."

He'll regret his choice once the villagers get ahold of him. "Of course you will. I have decreed it so. Get out of here. You return under pain of death."

Ogeorg scrambles to his feet. I lift my chin to Rian, the head of the Elite, who stands to one side of the stage close by. "Rian, please escort Ogeorg to the closest village. He is not to take anything which does not belong to him."

Rian bows low, eyes gleaming with promise. "Understood, Tatum Olina."

I watch them go before turning to my brother. "Tatuma Olandon, your findings."

Olandon stands. "Yes, Tatum." He points down to ten court members in the two rows closest to the stage I stand upon. It is where the court of highest position and wealth sit.

Not as many as I'd thought. None of the ten faces come as a surprise.

"Guards, please show these men and women out. They may collect their belongings. Nothing more."

The remaining court stare at each other in shock. They don't think I'm serious. I've wanted to do this for a long, long time. I savor the looks of bewilderment on their faces. Did they think I'd allow them to conspire beneath my very nose? I ignore faint sounds of protest. No one is too loud after the ultimatum I gave Ogeorg. Each of them is wondering how they will possibly survive in the village. They have no skills; none of them have ever worked a day in their lives. They will be forevermore surrounded by the people they've detested and looked down upon. I enjoy every moment of their demise.

"There is a new Satum position to be filled," I announce. "You." I point to a random court member. "Go and get Cook Afranca."

I hum to myself as I wait for them to return.

Cook Afranca approaches me with timid steps. She is not beating a soldier with a cooking pan this time. The material of her tattered and flour-streaked apron sticks out like a forest fire on Glacium amongst the bright, flamboyant audience. It only endears her to me.

"Afranca helped defy my mother for years," I call out. "And though she lost a person very dear to her, she did not give up hope for a better Osolis. She bounced back when she could have broken. And as of this moment, I decree that Afranca, cook of the palace, shall henceforth be the Satum of Treasury."

The cook loosens the tight grip she holds on her apron, a boggled expression on her face. I wink at her and pull her into my arms, whispering, "Look what we started with a single apple."

CHAPTER THIRTY-SIX

Two months later...

I WATCH THE TWINS play in the First Rotation. They remind me of little Cameron, and the troublesome Jimmy of the Ire. Thinking of the Oscala and Glacium immediately leads me to thoughts of *him.*

The twins play upon the Old Lake—the lake my mother filled in at my birth. The grass here is beginning to yellow; it's much shorter than it should be, and the wildflowers are in full bloom. My world is beautiful, and most importantly, it is healing.

I call to the boys, who launch themselves into my arms without hesitation.

"Chave, you're getting too big for this." He's taken off like a weed, and I've never been happier to see it.

"Lina," Oberon asks.

I grin. "Yes, Beron."

"You were vomiting behind the tree."

Of course he saw that. My smartest brother doesn't miss anything. How do I tell him the stress of running a world gets to be too much sometimes? Or that I miss the king of Glacium so much I can barely function? "I was."

He's old enough to gather I don't wish to speak of it.

They run ahead of me as we stroll back through the village. Children run up to me, and I accept their gifts until I can hold no more. A girl giggles as I open my mouth for her to place a baked sweet inside.

Gone is their fear. Gone is their hesitation. My people are still too thin, but they have life in their eyes. Especially the children, who are best at forgetting.

I wave to those I know, glimpsing Olandon coming out of the forest. He'll be returning from Aquin's training sheds. My brother has spent a lot of time there as he mourns the loss of our trainer—though he will not admit that is what he's doing. The old man never did tell me how to work the levers and buttons in his shed, but he imparted the secrets to Olandon for reasons I'm only just understanding. Aquin knew how things would work out.

I enter the palace walls, eyeing the Kaur statue of Aguan in the middle of the meadow. I declared the villager a hero of Osolis after he saved the Glacium army from fire. He'll be remembered forever. The wood from his statue came from the deconstruction of my childhood tower. Both of the palaces are now minus the monstrosity of my childhood and the Kaur has been put to better use. The village orphanages will never need to be rebuilt again. Parentless children will always have a home.

In honor of my rule, I declared an annual day off work. Once a revolution, all in Osolis will gather in the palace meadow for a feast. I have called the gathering a fair, the name for the benefit of the court, so they will remember all Solati eat from the same table. That, in the Tatum's eyes, none is better than another, and none shall be treated any differently from the next.

The twins disappear to the training yard where they go to annoy Rian. My trust in him has been well placed, and I depend on him more and more every day as Olandon is occupied with his role of Tatuma. I believe Rian will make a good regent for head of the guard until Ochave can take over the role.

Olandon catches up to me just before the dining ring. "Sister," he pants. "Veni, you walk fast."

"Maybe you're just unfit?"

He snorts and his eyes widen in horror at the sound.

I burst into laughter as two guards open the doors before us. Those in the dining ring turn to look. Some eyes are friendly—belonging to the new additions to the court. But most eyes are unfriendly—while they're trained on me, anyway. My brother, they like. As they always have.

The three Satums join us for the meal tonight. It's an empty meal, like all others. I'm merely filling my days so I cannot feel. I yearn for Jovan. I haven't heard from him at all, only communicating with Shard, Drummond, or Ashawn. Ash and Shard have visited *twice*.

Satum Jerin pulls out my chair for me. "Well met, Tatum Olina."

I smile fondly. "Well met, Satum Jerin."

I nod at Afranca and Namas, who bow before taking their seats. Namas doesn't like me, but he's smart enough to see his position here is tenuous—and he kisses my butt so I don't get rid of him.

The doors to the dining hall crash open with a boom so loud, everyone in the hall jumps.

I'm standing before I realize it. Only one person opens doors that way.

He's here. My breath thunders in my ears as I look to where the king of Glacium stands in the entrance.

Something stirs deep within me as my eyes run over his frame. He's minus a tunic, but wears his Bruma pants and boots. I don't think Jovan would be caught dead in our robes. My whole body clenches with the want to go to him and kiss him until I combust.

My brother saves us both. "K-king Jovan. What a pleasant surprise."

I would've used the phrase "fucking massive surprise," myself. A note would have been fine. Something in the last two months. I narrow my eyes at Jovan, whose eyes glimmer with amusement.

Olandon orders another seat brought to the table. I slowly sink back into my chair as Jovan strides forward, ignoring the brazen looks he receives. The court wouldn't spare him a glance if he wasn't half-naked, I tell myself. I grip my fork, wondering which woman I should prong in the eyes first.

Jovan doesn't take his seat. Instead, he circles the table to my side and bows low, bringing my hand to his lips. I hear my breath hitch in my throat. Damn him.

He turns to Olandon. "Move."

I hold my breath at the sound of his voice. Desire unlike any I've ever felt sweeps through my body. What's wrong with me? Is it the time we've spent apart, or the fact he's no longer mine?

Olandon eyes the king. "You'll meet me in the training area tomorrow morning."

Jovan chuckles. "You've got it, boy."

Olandon raises his brows. "Technically I'm doing you a favor. And my name is Tatuma Olandon."

"Sounds like a girl's title."

My brother scowls and I try to hide my smile as he vacates his seat. Then I realize he's vacating his seat so Jovan can fill it.

I munch on a crisp lettuce leaf. "What brings you to Osolis, King Jovan?" My voice shakes.

"You," he replies, calmly.

A large hand rests on my thigh.

I brush the hand off. "What do you require?"

"You."

Namas gasps, and Satum Jerin coughs over what very much sounds like a chuckle.

"Does the king of Glacium say any other word, I wonder."

He drapes the offending hand over the back of my seat. Months of work, undone in an instant. Now I'll be the Tatum whore. Great. For some reason I can't bring myself to care too much.

"I stopped at the Ire on the way," he says.

I swallow my mouthful. "You came in a Soar? You hate those things."

His face twists. "Quickest way."

My lips purse to hold in my laughter, and his eyes narrow. "Adox fares well," I ask.

"Is that a question?" he asks.

It's my turn to glare.

He grins, picking a tomato off my plate. My mouth drops open at his rudeness. How dare he?

"Adox is fine, Lina."

I groan aloud as a shocked murmur ripples through the court. Olandon is laughing!

"Brother," I say sweetly. "The king must be tired from his travels. Would you kindly show him to a room?"

"The stables, or guest chambers," Olandon asks.

I tilt my head to contemplate Jovan, replying to my brother, "I'll leave you to decide."

The king winks at me, infuriatingly, taking another two tomatoes before following my brother out of the hall.

"Something funny, Afranca," I snap.

I shouldn't have asked. The newest Satum doesn't mince her words.

She says, "For a moment, I could have sworn your face and the tomato were the same color."

Jerin and Namas gape in horror, but I snigger.

"You're lucky you make me laugh, Satum Afranca."

She chuckles back. "You're lucky you got the best Satum of Treasury on Osolis." She rolls her "r's," the only sign she is village-born.

I stay at the meal for another hour. Partly because if I leave too soon, rumors will run amok. *More* rumors. But mostly because I'm reeling. A chant repeats over and over in my mind. *Jovan is here. Jovan is here. Jovan is here.*

Did he mean it? Did he come for me? Does he still want me? My previous plan stirs deep within me, where I buried it after our last conversation. I have not dared to give it traction, aware that doing so has the potential to ruin me. In the last two months all I've done is hold on. The slightest thing could have tipped me over the edge. I've never been brave when it comes to Jovan.

At the end of an hour, I haven't answered any of the questions. I rise, dabbing at my mouth. My stomach roils as I stand too quickly. Why does he make me so nervous? I twist through the black halls of the palace to my old room. I refused to take my mother's room, instead giving it to Olandon. It seemed a natural solution.

When I throw open the door to my room, the king is there, sprawled out over my bed.

"Comfortable?" I say in an icy voice. It doesn't make sense to be mean to him while I secretly want to throw myself into his arms.

However, I'm unsure of his intentions, and I remember what he last said to me in the stables.

"I could be more comfortable," he growls, running his eyes over me.

"Why are you here?" I ask, moving to perch in the opening.

As soon as I gained control, I decorated this room. Color bounces off every wall. The room is a happy space, and one I spend much time in. Now there is a larger bed, and a more ornate trunk and sink. There is also an obnoxiously sized wardrobe—courtesy of Sin, who will not leave, no matter how many times I suggest it. I assume he's going to stay until he makes his way through the court females, but his behavior of late has been… unusual. I've begun to wonder if something else is going on.

Jovan rolls into sitting position. "I told you."

I look out of the opening, gazing at the quiet village in the distance. "You told me you came for me. But I do not know what you mean."

I hear a quiet noise behind me and start when I see how near to me he's drawn.

He glares. "Can you get out of that damn window before you fall?"

"No."

I find myself thrown onto the bed three seconds later. "I've had time to forget how pushy you can be."

He lies next to me and grabs my chin. "Do I need to remind you?"

I moan even before his mouth meets mine. Talk is over as I press myself to him, desperate to feel every inch of him.

He growls low in his throat. "Lina."

"Shh, kiss me." I bite his bottom lip and drag his head down for another breathless minute.

"Lina."

I don't stop what I'm doing. He's shirtless, but wearing far too much clothing.

"Damn it, I'm not a piece of meat," he says, laughing.

I giggle and pull back, about to dispel *that* illusion when he shocks me.

Jovan pushes up onto his knees and pulls me up till I'm seated. I blink up at him as his face turns grave, and… anxious?

He licks his lips. "I cannot live without you, Lina. I cannot rule without you by my side. I have arranged it all. Ashawn will take my position as soon as you agree to let me stay here."

"What!" I screech.

The king falls backwards. A knock comes at the door.

I gather my thoughts. "I'm okay, Rian," I call to the door.

Then I turn on Jovan. "Are you mad? You can't give up your kingdom. They need you, and Ashawn isn't ready."

"What happened to us, Lina? As soon as we set foot on Osolis, it was like everything we had got locked in a cage. By both of us. I was worried about my men, about winning, so you could take your rightful place on the throne. And after the attempt on your life on the Oscala, I could barely sleep for fear you would be here one moment and gone the next. You were so close to me, just across the tent most of the time, yet I couldn't close the gap between us. Part of me knew this was your journey, and so I stepped to the side, and in doing so made the biggest mistake of my life. I waited too long and didn't see it until it was too late."

"Oh, Jovan, I—"

"After all my careful plans and earning your love, I nearly lost the person I cherish most. It was stupidity, from both of us. We lost sight of what is important. And so, with a message from me, everything will be rectified." His gaze sets on mine. "In short order, I want to be your Tatum-man."

Laughter bursts from my shocked lips before I whisper, "That's not what you'd be."

I can't... Does he mean it? Everything he just said?

He continues. "Anyway, it's possible I'm wearing out my welcome in the castle. I've been a bit out of sorts."

I fold my arms across my chest. "You mean moody? Why would I want a moody male?"

He tackles me to the bed. "Because you cannot be without me, and cannot live without me by your side. Because you are no good without me, as I am no good without you."

My mouth dries, but to disagree would be to lie. I raise a brow at his self-satisfaction. Jovan has always had confidence to spare. I push him away and clamber off the bed. "You will not give up your world, King Jovan. You will return there tomorrow."

Disbelief sets on his features.

Smiling a little, I finish. "I will join you there as soon as I can. My world is more stable, and…" My smile fades. "Jovan, I don't belong here. Maybe I never did. I've known for some time. If you'd stuck around after our fight, I would have told you I'd already decided to abdicate! But you made me angry and then left." I scowl at him.

"You said you wouldn't come back with me." He scowls right back.

"You pig-headed Bruma. I couldn't come right *then*. If you'd given me a chance to explain before you upset me I would've told you!" A tear drips down my cheek. "But after we spoke… you made it sound like you didn't want to wait for me."

Jovan has me cradled on his lap in a flash. "Lina, I'm sorry. I didn't mean anything I said."

I sniff loudly. "You don't actually believe I used you to kill my mother?"

"No." He kisses my temple.

"And you don't actually think I wasn't in love with you?"

"No." He kisses my eyelids.

"And you've waited for me?"

"Always."

"And you don't think you're a better fighter than me?" I snuffle.

I crack open an eye when he doesn't respond. I grin saucily, and he tosses me back onto the bed.

"Robes. Off," he orders.

CHAPTER THIRTY-SEVEN

O LANDON GAPES AT me. He's held the expression for at least two minutes. I'm beginning to worry.

He croaks, and I wait as another minute goes by.

And another.

Finally, his mind begins to work once more. "You… you want *me* to become Tatum." He's nineteen, but you wouldn't guess it from the high voice he uses.

"I do."

"But—"

I shake my head. "But nothing. You're perfect for the role. The villagers like you, the soldiers have the utmost respect for you, and, what's more, the court likes you, too."

"They like you as well," he says weakly.

I raise my eyebrows. That's a goliath stretch of the truth.

"Osolis is unstable."

"That isn't true, brother. The tri-world accords are signed, and strong. The plans for peace have gone along without a hitch. This is the most stable and safe our world has ever been."

Olandon's face turns red. "And it's because of *you*! The people don't want me. They want their savior. They want the person who rid them of evil and hunger."

"Are you saying you had no part in that?" I counter. "You were by my side through it all, helping those who needed it, trekking through the Oscala to save me and nearly dying. You threw yourself over the wall to make sure Mother's forces did not get their hands on the battering ram, which could have ensured our demise." I continue, talking over his attempts to interrupt. "You have overcome your prejudice. You have *always* stuck by my side and put Osolis first, more than I ever will. You are a Solati, and that is something I will never be."

Tears flow down his cheeks.

"Landon." My voice breaks. "In the last year I have seen my brother change from a boy into a man. I have seen you begin to care for those outside your circle. I've seen you become the person I always knew you would become. Aquin saw it, too."

I step closer and take him into my arms. He towers over me now, but he welcomes the embrace. "I've achieved what I wanted to achieve. I have given my people peace."

"That's not enough," he says sadly.

I shake my head and step back, drying my own face. "I'm not meant to be here. The court can sense it; they always have. In time, the villagers will sense it too. And then the fact I'm half Bruma will begin to matter. I know how hard it is for our people to accept all the changes I've asked of them, let alone accept who I am."

He's seen the signs. He stays silent, unable to disagree.

"I do not belong here," I say. "I deserve to find my own peace, too. My own freedom."

Fresh tears pour down his face. "And Glacium is your freedom?"

I shake my head again, staring out of the opening with a smile. Jovan had left that morning, eager to make some kind of preparations for my arrival. "No, brother. Not Glacium."

I strap into my Soar two weeks later. It took far too long to hand over the reins of Osolis to Olandon. I think he dragged it out on purpose.

"You are sure you don't want to take Sin," Olandon asks.

I snort. "Yes. I think Sin has a few things to sort out here. Good luck with that."

"Thanks."

I grin at him.

"Chave," I call.

Chave moves in front of me and I strap him to my stomach—he was grounded from using his Soar after stealing food from the kitchens and storing it on the palace roofs.

Oberon sniggers from his Soar. The twins will join me on Glacium. They no longer trust Osolis without my presence here.

"Give my regards to Adox," Olandon says shortly.

My heart twists at leaving my brother because I would hate to be left on this world. I keep reminding myself he is a different person and wants different things than I do. I see him laughing with the court, joining in on their games, and joking with the soldiers.

This is his world. Under his Tatumship, Osolis will thrive.

"I will," I reply, kissing his cheek.

"Yuck!" yells Ochave between us.

Olandon doesn't pull away. His sad brown eyes shift to my blue ones. "Promise me you'll visit."

"Often, brother. You and Aunty Jain will get sick of me."

"It could never happen," he says vehemently.

I look forward to proving him wrong. With a final glance at the palace behind me, I move to the opening's edge. "Ready, Oberon?"

"Yes," he complains.

I grin and shift to drop from the third floor of the palace.

Olandon coughs loudly.

I turn to him, noting his red ears.

"Do you think you could, uh, say hello to someone for me," he asks.

I dip my head and Olandon leans forward to whisper the name in my ear.

I grin at him as he steps away, face beet red. "I see. Anything in particular you want me to say?"

He scowls. "Hello will suffice."

I laugh and drop downward, the black walls of the palace blurring past me until I level off and begin to climb. Ochave squeals in excitement below me. We swoop low over the First Rotation village, and the children there scream and wave.

The twins boom their hellos back.

I let a few tears fall from my eyes, and smile happily. Because after everything I went through, all the agony, the heartbreak, the broken bones, and the fear—after all of that—I'd do it all again to see Osolis flourishing.

I peer ahead at the Oscala, and the hot air dries my face. "Are you two ready to see some snow!" I shout.

"What's snow?" they chorus.

I grin evilly, and open my mouth to lie. Sanjay will be so proud.

We stop in a cave above the smoke layer the first night, and then at the Ire for two days. I don't want to visit long. Just enough to refresh the alliance with Adox, who's in the process of handing over his rule to the Ire's next leader.

The Ire took a sore hit in the war, just as Osolis and Glacium did. There are many women and children here who are now without a husband or a father. Yet there is a hope and lightness about the Ire that was never here before.

"Will you stay another night, Tatum?" Nancy asks. Jimmy's mother is the most relaxed I've ever seen her. Perhaps it is because Jimmy is behaving, for once.

"Yes. I think I will press on tomorrow morning, however. I am eager to see... Glacium." I clear my throat.

Adox chuckles. "I'm sure you are."

"When will you be back?" Hamish calls his question across the fire.

"Soon, I hope." It is awkward to answer him while he has his arms and lips on another. He's being very obvious about his relationship with one of the nursery supervisors. I cannot remember her name, but she looks at him so adoringly, while he is split between looking at me and the woman in his arms. I hope he is able to return her adoration in time.

I see everyone I care about on the Ire, but though I search for them, I do not see Hayce's family—his wife, or little Cara. I guess they've been asked to stay away, and I wish it were otherwise. Cara is Aquin's granddaughter, after all.

We leave the Ire and my stomach lurches in anticipation of seeing Jovan. I almost lose my breakfast on Ochave's head.

The twins cannot believe their eyes as our Soars fly over Glacium.

I point out all I can, just as excited to be back.

"It's so white!" Beron shouts, swooping down to get a closer look.

"Their trees are the wrong color."

I smile at Ochave's adamant voice and tilt my head. "There are the Outer Rings."

"Is that where you met the whore?"

I gasp. "Who told you that?" *Sin.*

The twins giggle. I sincerely hope they don't understand what a whore is. I swear that as soon as they show any interest in girls, I'm sending them back to Olandon.

"And then we have the Middle Ring."

The twins wave at the staring people, hollering down to them. I'm not sure Glacium is ready for my boys. Though, I'm not sure the Bruma are ready for my permanent arrival either. I wonder what Jovan has been doing to prepare since I last saw him. I've exchanged a few messages with him, but it hasn't been enough to satiate either of us. I long to see him. I just wish I knew what his assembly expects of me. It has been the better part of six months since I was last there.

I point out the Inner Ring as we begin to drop.

Finally, we land on shaking legs in front of the castle's portcullis.

"Tatum Olina," a watchman calls. "The king awaits you in the food hall."

"Thank you. And, just Olina now."

The watchman bows low.

I tuck the two Soars under my arm after extracting us all and shoo the twins ahead of me. They stare at their surroundings with awe. Blazing torches illuminate the courtyard, and the two boys skirt back.

I bite my cheek, remembering when I did the same. "They do not fear fire here."

We all push against the entranceway to open it.

"Solis, this thing is heavy," grunts Ochave.

"It's to keep the cold out," I reply. "And don't curse," I add, hypocritically.

Our footsteps echo down the hall. I prop our Soars to one side of the archway and grab the twins' hands. They cling close to me at the uproarious sounds emanating from the food hall. I soak it up—the yelling, the laughter, the clanging, and the smashing. The Osolis court had been entirely too quiet.

"Come on," I say. "There's nothing to be afraid of. Bruma just like to laugh a lot."

Oberon prods Ochave. "You like to laugh, Chave."

The taller twin thinks about it, then beams. "I do!"

I hardly register the archway as we pass under, carefully watching the faces of my brothers. But, of course, the noise stills as the assembly sights us. I smile around me, wrapping an arm around each of the twins.

Fiona runs to me, and I let go of them to return her embrace. Sanjay isn't far behind her, and I cover my mouth with both hands as I see what he holds.

I burst into tears. "Your baby, Fiona. Let me see him."

Sanjay thrusts his young boy out—Kedir, named after both Kedrick and Malir. He's only weeks old. I wave back the sudden tears that have sprung to my eyes while the happy couple stares lovingly at each other.

Fiona bends down to meet the twins and I turn to see who else is there. Fresh tears spill down my cheeks when I see Sadra. She blinks rapidly to staunch her own tears and we don't talk at first, but hug each other tightly instead. I want to tell her how brave her husband was, and how no one else could have done what he did that day, but words fail me. Nothing seems enough.

"I'm sorry, Sadra," I say instead. "So terribly sorry. Malir should not be gone."

She smiles tremulously, and I notice how much she's aged in a few months. "I'm grateful for any time I got with my husband. You're not to blame; such is life. And with the passing of old life, comes new life." She winks at me.

I look past her at Kedir and know Sadra is right.

I kiss her weathered cheek, and she pats me, prodding me onward.

I keep one eye on the twins as I'm passed around Rhone, Roman, Sole, Macy, Shard, Blizzard, Avalanche, and Ice. Even Alzona and Crystal are there.

"Hello, sister." Adnan pulls me into a stiff hug.

"Brother," I say shyly. I look forward to knowing my reclusive Bruma brother more. I have a feeling we're going to help each other a lot in the coming months, while figuring out a relationship with our father.

"The king said we all had to be here, so you'd want to stay," Shard whispers in my ear. I untangle myself from Adnan.

"You should see all the presents in your room," Shard continues.

I bite my lip. "Like what?"

"Like everything you've ever shown interest in, ever. I saw a guitar there."

Laughter bubbles up in my throat, and I glance toward the throne platform. Jovan stands in the middle of it, in front of the table laden with food. Meat! My mouth waters at the thought. I've craved meat for months.

The others clear the way between Jovan and I. The twins trot up beside me, and I pull them forward as I reach the king.

"Chave, Beron, you remember the king of Glacium?"

They stare up at him. I'm fairly sure Jovan has replaced Olandon as the coolest fighter ever. I don't believe much debate goes into the selection process—whoever has the larger sword, wins.

Jovan bends down to their level and fixes them with a serious look. "I need to talk to your beautiful sister. Would you both go sit on my throne?"

They push past him without another word.

"You'll never get them off," I say with amusement.

The laughter dies on my lips as Jovan bends downward, on one knee. What on Solis is he doing?

"Did I drop something?" I ask. He smiles and realization dawns; this is another Bruma custom. I begin to kneel, too, but stop when the assembly laughs.

My confusion must be plain. I stay standing, however, and that appears to be the correct thing to do as Jovan begins to speak.

"The first time you stood in front of me, you had my respect." His voice wavers. "The moment I saw your eyes, you stole the floor from beneath me."

My eyes round. What's happening?

"I knew I loved you when I sat beside you when you heard music for the first time. And that is when I crafted my plan."

My eyebrows snap together. He's said that before and I've never known what he meant. Jovan swallows nervously.

"You are not aware of our customs, my Lina. But my people have known who their queen would be for quite some time."

I cannot speak. My mind races to think of what I might have done.

"A Bruma man must clothe his wife. He must feed her. And protect her. It is the old way of marriage for our people." He grips my hands tightly. "You wore my tunic at the ball."

My eyes narrow.

"I have protected you with my bare hands."

"I think we're pretty even there," I mutter.

"And before the army left to reclaim your throne, I fed you."

That's what that was about? That bit of roast meat was our wedding? My jaw drops open. "So. You. W-what are you saying?"

"We are not married yet, despite my best attempts." He starts to grin, then sees my face. "Marriage in the old way is sealed with a dance. And you would never dance with me."

A buzzing fills my ears. All those months I agonized over whether we would be together, and we were one dance away from marriage?

He hurries on. "I set out to capture your love, realizing early on that we were made for one another. I was determined to make you see it. And yet, after making these efforts, I found it was not enough to capture you for my wife. You had to come willingly, or I would never know if you chose me, and if your heart was truly mine."

I hear sniffing from the assembly. Seriously? They think their king is romantic because he's decided not to trick someone into marriage? I think I would have had something to say about this old tradition if Jovan hadn't fessed up before completing it!

But... did he say he's wanted to marry me right from the start?

Jovan grips my hands. His palms are sweating. "I kneel before you to ask if you can share my love, and be my partner in this life. I will walk with you anywhere, because I know a life without you has no meaning."

My eyes blur with tears as my throat burns. Maybe it is a little romantic.

"Lina, Frost, Willow…"

I half-sob, half-chuckle.

"Will you be my cherished queen?"

Tears threaten to overwhelm me, and I urge them back. I cannot speak; he has completely shocked me to silence.

He was willing to give up everything to be by my side. I cover my face. "Yes." It doesn't come out as "yes"; rather, as half of the word.

Jovan understands.

The assembly erupts into wild cheers as their king swings me high. I laugh and pull his face to my own.

We kiss with everything we have. Alone in the food hall for that moment. And his lips are just as soft and firm as they always are. They're mine now.

And I plan on kissing them every day.

"It's lucky you said yes," he whispers. "The ceremony is tonight."

I am too happy to pretend I'm offended by his high-handedness.

"And…" He hesitates.

I arch an eyebrow.

A flush rises on his handsome face. "Will you dance with me?"

I kiss him long and hard, melding my lips to his. "With all my heart."

EPILOGUE

"*J*UST BECAUSE IT'S never been done, doesn't mean it shouldn't be, my King," Roscoe says in disagreement.

Roscoe has developed the tendency to support everything I say.

I've forgiven my blood-father for hiding the truth from me all that time—though not verbally. I simply treat him with professional politeness. It's a step up from before. I had no other option, being queen, and I think this will make things easier for Adnan. Adnan hasn't spoken to Roscoe yet, and I see how much it affects my reclusive brother. I have taken the first step and I hope it will help father and son mend their bond.

Other than recovering my manners, I have no desire to explore a deeper relationship with my blood-father. I'm raw from Aquin's death. Growing closer to Roscoe would feel like a betrayal, like I'd be replacing my old trainer in some way. I might feel differently in time, but I'm content to put the matter to the side for as long as I need.

Jovan shakes his head. "No."

I place my hands on my hips. "Are you saying that the king can marry the ex-Tatum of his ex-enemy world, but I can't have a Dome battle for my wedding celebration?"

His blue eyes gleam as he puts down whatever paper he's pretending to read. "That's right."

My eyes narrow and his advisors back away. "When I agreed to this marriage thing, I didn't think you'd be telling me what to do all the time."

If anything, he's given me free rein—Shard wasn't joking about the room full of presents.

My exaggeration makes his smile grow. "Your mistake." He raises an eyebrow. "Want to try another angle?"

"The fight between us will send a great message to the women of Glacium."

"You *want* them to see me beat you? I would have thought that was counter-productive."

I toss my blue-black hair where it ripples down my fur-and-leather-clad back. "I don't see how, when they'll just see me handing the king's ass to him."

A booming laugh leaves Jovan's lips, and I grin.

"I'll set it up for tomorrow morning." I turn for the door.

"I won't fight against my queen, Olina. It's not how things are done. I took a vow to protect you."

"It's how we do things on Osolis. Would you deprive me of this one remnant of my culture?"

Drummond opens his mouth and Jovan glares him to silence.

"Funny thing, that," Jovan says quietly, standing from his chair. He holds up a note. "Your brother isn't aware of that particular custom."

I scowl. Damn the quick communication between worlds these days. And Olandon didn't lie for me! Even after I made him Tatum.

An idea occurs to me and I smooth my expression. "Okay."

He eyes me warily. "Okay, what?"

I bow low. "I respect you too much to go against your wishes."

Stepping around Drummond, I exit the lounge of our suite in the castle. It's more beautiful than any room I've ever stayed in. I love it. It's the only part of the castle I didn't redecorate.

My king is awfully thoughtful sometimes, and then other times… It's just a Dome fight. What's the harm in it? It provides the opportunity to reintroduce me to the people while reminding them I am, or was, Frost. And I'll be able to highlight our efforts in the Outer Rings with a pre-battle demonstration from Alzona's girls. It's my secret plan to reopen the pit fights in the Dome itself. But that will take time. Really, this fight between the king and future queen has a lot going for it. And Jovan will come to understand this.

"Wrath," I call. "Sorry," I say at his look. "Warren."

Wrath winks from where he stands post.

"Could you fetch Ice for me, please? And send him to the kennels." It won't take Jovan long to guess my plan.

"I've been waiting for him to be sent there for months."

I laugh as he jogs away.

I shiver in the kennels five minutes later, occupied with giving a demanding Kaura a hearty scratch. Ice slides through the door. He furtively checks the area, running his tongue over the front of his teeth.

"I've got a job for you," I say.

"Why not Shard?"

My eyes dart around the kennels. "You and I both know Shard has had a reshuffling of his priorities."

Ice gives me a confused look. "Eh? Speak plain, girly. Ain't got time for your fancy shit. The spy business is booming."

I sigh. "He ain't visiting the same whorehouse anymore. You get my snowdrift?" I could bend Shard on most things, but he wouldn't cross Jovan on this matter.

"Ah." His eyes widen. "Got it." He smirks. "You need something done the Outer Rings way."

"There's gonna be a fight in the Dome. Between me and the king. I need you to spread the news."

Ice rolls his eyes. "That's the easiest job I ever heard."

"I need you to visit Zona first. Tell her I want her to organize four demonstration fights with her girls. Negotiate a price."

The spy pales visibly. "Blizzard can't do that part?"

"He's in Sector Five and won't be back until morning."

Ice gulps. I don't judge him for it. Alzona is one scary business bitch.

"Just when is this fight?" he asks.

"Tomorrow."

Ice darts out a wiry arm and whacks me on the side of the head. "Well, hell, girly, why didn't you say so? I gotta get started!" He runs to the door, blithering over his shoulder. "Talk about a near-impossible task. You're damn lucky I have the network I do."

"Love you, Ice," I call, a smile on my lips.

He scratches at his stubble. "Yeah, okay."

I laugh when he's gone, giving him ample time to get away before I return to the castle.

The roar of the Dome vibrates the gritty cobblestones under my feet.

I spread my stance wide, grinning at a furious Jovan.

He's extra pissed off because I've dragged out the harness.

"Stop scowling. Your people are watching," I admonish.

His expression doesn't change. "Our people," he says. "And you're in trouble, my queen."

I shrug. "Did you think I'd be a pliable wife?"

The king of Glacium narrows his eyes and I shiver.

"You were pliable last night." His eyes linger on my frame.

We both look to the stage, where my twin brothers stand. They wave their arms up and down.

And the fight begins.

I watch the king's footing. After a handful of training sessions in the yard with the watchmen, I learned this is the surest place to guess Jovan's next move.

Honestly, this could go either way. I don't really care; in my eyes I've already won. Against all odds, I found acceptance and a place where I belong.

I'm content.

Jovan closes the gap in a blur, and I spin to the side so quickly my head spins. We circle a little closer.

"How did you like my female fighters?" I ask. Time to put him off.

He snorts. "I think the men of Glacium are cursing your name to the wind."

My face falls as I aim a punch at his throat. He jerks his head back and my other arm catches him in the kidney. "You really think so?"

He turns his eyes to the sky as he attempts to sweep my legs from under me. "No, not really. They were amazing. And will prove an asset."

I grin. "Are you saying I was right?"

He growls, catching me with a bruising punch to my right shoulder.

I glare at him. "Really? A punch to the shoulder? You're not even trying!" I attack him in a flurry that he has no option but to match.

We break away, both panting.

"Possibly because there is nothing in me that wishes to hurt you."

Unwillingly, my eyes flick over his handsome face. I love him more than anything in two worlds. *Three*, I correct myself.

I love him, but that doesn't mean I'll let him win.

"Wait!" a voice shouts. "Wait!"

We both turn in confusion to the sound. Sadra has flung one of the entrances to the Dome floor open and hurries toward us.

"Stop!" she cries.

Jovan and I flicker a look between us.

Sadra reaches us both, puffing and stretching her arms out between us. Jovan grips her arm to support her.

"What is the matter, Sadra? What has happened?" he asks.

She pants, raising her head slightly to look at me. "I thought you were keeping the news to yourself," she huffs. "I thought this was a ruse for the announcement. Not that you'd actually fight."

"What announcement?" I'm completely baffled.

Sadra straightens, holding her side. She looks between Jovan and I. "Can it be that you don't know?"

"Know what?" Jovan booms. His patience is running thin.

"Your queen is pregnant, my King."

My world screeches to a halt. My hand reaches to my stomach.

"I'm not?"

"You are," Sadra says stubbornly. "Several months down the line. You're showing." She studies my face. "You have honestly not noticed?"

I rub my lower abdomen. "I—"

"Have you been sick?"

I blink. "Yes, but the stress…"

"Been dizzy and exhausted? Had cravings?"

Tears prick my eyes. "Yes, but—" I look to Jovan, who hasn't said a word.

Sadra presses. "You haven't noticed the absence of your cycle?"

I shake my head in a daze. "That isn't unusual," I whisper. "I've been kicked many times." I look down at where my hands curl protectively. The harness is tight. I thought it was all the meat I'd been eating. *Cravings.* My breath comes sharply as I cover my mouth with both hands. "I'm pregnant."

And amazed. And... "How could I miss it?" I ask myself.

"You've been rather busy," Sadra says drily. "But you look about four months."

"Three months, three weeks, and three days." Jovan's voice is hoarse.

I turn to him. Isn't he happy? I cannot bear it if he's unhappy about a child.

He lifts his eyes from where the harness is tightest. "That's how long it has been since the cave."

I blush as he reveals this fact in front of Sadra. "You don't know that's where I fell pregnant."

His jaw sets. "You were sick a week later. And you started to... get a little emotional." He flicks me a nervous glance.

"That's why I've been reacting weird?" I ask, incredulous. Another thought occurs to me. "I went off apples, and they're my favorite!"

Jovan and I stare at each other.

"We're going to have a baby?" he asks.

A tremulous smile wobbles on my lips. I share a look with Sadra, who cries without shame. *This* is what she meant about new life to replace the old? I thought she was talking about Fiona's baby!

I whisper, "You're going to be a father, Jovan."

Sadra backs away as the king of Glacium staggers to me and drops to his knees. He stares at my stomach as though he can find the answers to the world there. "You're... ?"

A lump rises in my throat at his bewildered, endearing expression.

His own eyes are moist as he finally tears his piercing blue eyes away from my middle to gaze at me, wonder foremost in his expression. "We're going to have a baby," he repeats.

I nod, unable to speak.

A beaming expression fills his face, and it so transforms him, the memories of our first meeting are called to mind. We are both so changed, yet, as Jovan swings me in circles shouting to the crowds that I'm pregnant, I decide a few things will never change.

Not my vow that I'll never be controlled or cowed by another again.

Not my belief that I deserve freedom just as much as any other person.

I close my eyes, still spinning high. And I feel my hair fanning out in the cool, Glacium air. I will care for this child with my dying breath. I will be all the mother our baby ever needs. Jovan will be there as a father should.

And I smile.

Because in the wildest fantasies of my heart, until now, I never truly believed I would be free.

ACKNOWLEDGEMENTS

When I sat to write Fantasy of Freedom, the feeling was bittersweet. I didn't want to say goodbye! But Olina nagged at me, as she has from the start, and demanded her story be told. I will remember The Tainted Accords as one of the best experiences of my life. For the last two years, one month, and twenty-five days, I was lucky enough to have the banter of the barracks, the excitement of Olina's adventures, and—arguably the best of all—the hotness of Jovan for company. Writing Olina and Jovan's story has changed me forever, as I imagine all my stories will, though I'm sure The Tainted Accords will have special pride of place.

When I think back over the support I've received during my time as a writer, I am mind-blown. To my family, and new family (now I'm married), a million thank-yous for bouncing ideas with me and being cool.

To my friends. If you think I miss the little things you do—the likes, the shares, the comments, the word-of-mouth—you are mistaken. I watch you all the time. In fact, I'm outside your window right now. A particular mention to Ushy, Stacka, Nelcat, and Boris Bleaker for being ka mau te wehi—a Maori term that my four Australian friends will need to Google if they want to make sure I haven't insulted them. Mwahaha.

To my beta readers. Some of you have stuck around for the last TWO YEARS. You gave this series your very valuable time, and you had the balls to be honest, which is harder to do than most think. *Thank you*. And also, you should beta read my next series because you love me? *cute, irresistible face*

To my content editor, Melissa Scott, aka brain twin. You have become a great friend. We sometimes hold five conversations regarding five different topics on five different platforms, simultaneously. How the heck do we do that and still like each other? I value your criticism and comments, and the effort you put into my books.

I would like to thank Robin Schroffel for her eagle-eyed copyediting skills in the last few books I've written.

To the people I've met along the way—bloggers, designers, formatters, authors—you've made this journey so fun. My author friends in particular are uh-muh-zing. You guys have me laughing every day.

To readers of The Tainted Accords, you've run alongside Olina through four books and I know many of you love her as much as I do! The small details and messages you guys pick up from her story never cease to amaze me. To those who have emailed me and interacted with me on social media, I want you to know how much this spurs me on to keep writing. Who knows where this series would be without you. Thank you, thank you, thank you, thank you for loving the world(s), the story, and most of all, the characters.

Finally, to my husband, Scott. I think the dedication says it all. You stop the ground from shaking.

You are the most precious thing to me in three worlds.

– Kelly St. Clare

Books by Kelly St. Clare

The Tainted Accords
Fantasy of Frost
Fantasy of Flight
Fantasy of Fire
Fantasy of Freedom

The Tainted Accords Novellas
Sin (2017)
Olandon (2017)
Rhone (2018)
Shard (2018)

The After Trilogy
The Retreat
The Return (Mid-2017)

SIN

(The Tainted Accords: Novella One)

Sin is content to fight, fornicate, and drink his life away—in that order. He's got friends, he's got goldies, and he's blissfully free of females—during the day, anyway. If there's one thing his father taught him, it was to never to let a woman get too close. "Women weren't capable of loyalty." His father would say over a bottle of brew. "They'd leave you as soon as a better offer came along."

Just like Sin's mother.

Yet when Sin comes across, quite frankly, the ugliest woman he's ever seen, he finds himself offering her friendship, safe in the knowledge he'll never feel anything more.

Even if she's different to any female he's ever met.

Even when he can't stop thinking about her.

Olorna is still recovering from the effects of starvation after struggle to survive during the war. Now she feels horribly out of her depth as a new member in the solati court. Desperate to fit in for her mother's sake, who has been given the role of her dreams, Olorna's desperation soars when a royal change puts her mother's new position on tenuous ground.

When the sinister Satum Namas offers an easy way to make all her problems go away, Olorna is determined to accept his offer despite the consequences.

Even when a man incapable of love, steals a kiss from her lips.

Even if she is making the biggest mistake of her life.

Now Available

THE RETREAT

(The After Trilogy, #1)

Earth was ruined. Humankind destroyed. It's old news.

Romy's life is simple—for a genetically enhanced space soldier; pick up space junk with her four friends, and stave off the Critamal obsessed with stealing Earth from under their noses.

It isn't much of a life. But it's temporary—if you consider 850 or so more years, temporary.

Whatever it takes, Romy will stand on her home planet again.

After Knot 27's battler tangles with a gulp-worthy alien mothership, the friend's return to Earth is brought forward at hurtling pace.

Strength comes from the unlikeliest of quarters.

As does leadership…

… As does betrayal.

Now Available

Sign up to my newsletter to receive once-monthly emails with release information, giveaways, interviews, and more at:

www.kellystclare.com

In doing so, you will receive a chapter extra from The Tainted Accords titled *His Fantasy*, which offers a glimpse into Jovan's head, and the Tainted Accords mini coloring book!

For more regular updates, follow me on:

Facebook, Twitter, or Instagram

HAVE YOU ENJOYED THIS BOOK?

Thanks to your reviews and support, The Tainted Accords is a bestselling series!

A review takes a couple of minutes and means a huge amount to a self-published author like myself. They help my book reach a larger audience.

I would like to bring you the stories you want to read. Help me to do this by telling me what you liked and didn't like. (All kinds of reviews are welcome.)

Your time and effort is greatly appreciated.

SIN

SNEAK PEEK

CHAPTER ONE

"*I* DON'T UNDERSTAND," OLINA said. She fixed her piercing blue eyes on his face. "How hard is it to put on robes? I don't need a valet... Wait! I don't even *want* a valet." She shook herself. "You're a pit fighter, Sin. You can't expect me to believe you're here because you've 'found your true calling.'"

Sin flung out a set of royal blue robes with an expert flick of his wrist—at least in his not-so-humble opinion. The silken fabric came to rest over Olina's shoulders. He studied the color with a critical eye. It looked good, he guessed—he should know what looked good on a female. Did a valet put more thought in? Fashions and fabric... quality, or whatever. He couldn't believe there were people who did this for a living. Permanently. He'd rather sleep with the same woman twice.

"You need a valet, oh Tatum of vast wisdom." He drawled his reply. "You tend to pick clothing I wouldn't wish on my worst enemy. You have the greatest valet in three worlds in your employ. Just sit back and enjoy the *ride*." He added a suggestive wink.

Olina plucked the robes out of his grasp and disappeared behind a screen to change. "Could you be serious for once?"

Had it been anyone else, he might have followed. But Olina was exceptionally skilled with a knife, and he was exceptionally fond of what hung between his legs.

Choosing to believe the question was a rhetorical one, Sin stretched languidly over the new Tatum's bed. He ran a hand through his hair to tousle the short golden curls—despairing of the missing long locks that had been burnt and shorn off during a brush with death. He was putting a smolder into his expression when his well-formed chest muscles caught his attention. Sin tensed them both, watching as they leaped in response.

"Sin...." Olina had reappeared, dressed in the royal blue robes.

"Shh," he murmured. "Are you seeing this?" He admired the sculpted plains once more as they twitched at his command.

When he heard no reply from the young Tatum, he stopped his pectoral ministrations. She usually gave him an exasperated huff at the very least. Back on Glacium, she might've even laughed. Now, two months after the war, she spent as much time looking out that window as she did anything else, and when her eyes weren't fixed on Glacium, they were turned inward. He studied her despondent profile.

She missed that arrogant son of a bitch—the king of Glacium.

What's more, if Sin wasn't mistaken, and he rarely was in such matters, she'd been loyal to King Jovan the *whole* time. Not one illicit affair. Not a single stolen grope. A *woman* had been loyal for two months, a whole sixty days. It had to be some kind of record.

The object of his reflection had moved and now stood directly in front of him, hands on delectable hips. He worked to restore his confident, relaxed demeanor and cocked his head toward the empty space beside him. That was all it usually took for him to get a female into bed. Yet Olina rolled her eyes in response and spun for the door. "You're going back to Glacium tomorrow."

Sin's smirk slid from his face. "No!" He wrenched himself upright.

The Tatum slowly pivoted back to him, her face a mask. He swallowed, cursing himself. Delivery was *everything*, but the word had been out before he could control it.

"No?" she asked quietly. "You seem rather adamant about staying...." Olina circled toward the bed. He doubted she knew how predatory she looked doing it.

Sin pressed his lips together, struggling to settle his erratic heartbeat. He relaxed against the bedpost and gave her an unhurried smile.

She eyed the change with interest. *Damn woman didn't miss a trick.*

"I'll make you a deal, Sin," she said matter-of-factly. "Solis knows you're not here because of a sudden passion to dress people. I've got enough to deal with trying to control my asshole Satum of Regeneration without this on top."

"What's he doing?"

"What he's always done. Except I'm not my mother, and this is no longer her court." Olina sighed heavily. "A village boy was found yesterday, beaten half to death. A young girl said she saw Namas there. Anyway, I'm trying to get to the bottom of it, but the court isn't being incredibly forthcoming with information. *Yet....*" She unleashed a feral grin before eyeing him. "Stop trying to distract me. Tell me why you want to be here, and I might let you stay."

Tatum Olina was four years his junior, and damn scary when she wanted to be. She was unlike any woman—no, any *person* he'd ever met. He'd instinctively distrusted her at first. . . .

She cleared her throat loudly.

Sin stood in a powerful movement, boyish grin in place. "I stay for the brilliance of Osolis, oh merciful and just Tatum."

"Bullshit."

"To help your starving people."

"Bullshit."

"To protect you from harm."

"*Bullshit.*"

Sin sighed heavily and rubbed his forehead in frustration. *Time to draw out the cavalry.* He looked over to her, moistening his lips and only briefly meeting her eyes. *Her* lips were slightly curved. "You want to know the truth?" he whispered.

She snorted. "I do."

He gripped the sides of his robes in tight fists. "The sight of the female form in those robes you all wear does something to me. Something... *sinful.*"

"Ugh! Stop." Olina covered her ears with both hands.

He groaned loudly. "So much left to the imagination."

"Stop."

One more should do it. "You have no idea how many nights I've held my—"

"*Enough.*"

He bowed modestly and held his arrogant poise under her scrutiny.

"You're staying on Osolis to sleep your way through my court? Seriously?"

He shrugged one shoulder up. It couldn't be further from the truth, but it *was* an added perk.

Laughter pinched the sides of Olina's mouth. "You're despicable. What makes you think they'll fall for that?"

He cocked an eyebrow and smiled in what he knew to be a self-deprecating yet attractive kind of way.

"No!" she said incredulously. "How many?" Olina quickly shook her head. "Hold that thought! Forget I asked." She gave him another curious look and turned to the door.

Sin listened to her receding steps and let out his pent-up breath, sagging.

"If that is why you're here, then I shall let you stay," she called from the doorway. He jumped.

"Solis knows, some of the court members could use a little loosening up." She giggled at her own joke. An unwilling smile tugged at the corners of his mouth. "However, if I find out you are somehow part of this 'interworld spy network' Ice has been boasting about, you'll be out of Osolis faster than you can say—"

"Blizzard bathes batches of boil-ridden Bruma?"

Her nose scrunched. "Gross. But, yes. That."

Olina swept through the doorway, her ten elite—always lurking outside in the hall—leaping to attention to flank her sides.

Sin watched her disappear around the corner of the dark hallway before turning to collect her brown robes from behind the screen. He balled up the material and stared into the mirror hanging above the single empty sink, his joking expression from mere minutes ago long gone.

It came in handy on occasion, the whole 'man-whore' reputation.

He wasn't here to be a valet, or to sleep his way through the court. And he certainly wasn't part of Ice's interworld spy network. Sin was here for an entirely different reason.